I0672350

Journey's End

The mountain man's search
for purpose.

James Oliver Virmala

.

Edition 1

Cover Photo James Oliver Virmala

ISBN: 978-1-7340021-3-3

DEDICATION

In memory of Richard Russell, my friend and hunting
partner of over 40 years.

CONTENTS

Dedication   i

Chapter One   Pg 1

Chapter Two   Pg 17

Chapter Three   Pg 34

Chapter Four   Pg 47

Chapter Five   Pg 67

Chapter Six   Pg 87

Chapter Seven   Pg 100

Chapter Eight   Pg 119

Chapter Nine   Pg 138

Chapter Ten   Pg 161

Chapter Eleven   Pg 182

Chapter Twelve   Pg 210

Chapter Thirteen   Pg 224

Chapter Fourteen   Pg 244

Chapter Fifteen   Pg 268

Chapter Sixteen   Pg 286

Chapter Seventeen   Pg 312

Chapter Eighteen   Pg 327

BOOKS BY THE AUTHOR

Oli's Gold Book One
Search For Oli's Gold Book Two
Return To Oli's Gold Book Three
To Be A Mountain Man
Trouble On The Kansas Plains
Frontier Justice
Return Of The Mountain Man
The Tall Man
The Prospector
The Green Valley
Twilight Of The Mountain Man
The Mother Lode
Quest Of The Mountain Man
Journey's End
Rufus Pike
Rufus And The Pup
The Winding Trail Home
Rufus The Lost Years
The Kankakee Kid
Bogus Island
Tyler Tomas The Brothers' War
War of 1812 The Choice
Kyle Oliver The Next Horizon

JOURNEY'S END

CHAPTER ONE

A bitter, cold wind swept across the sea ice as the two men sat on a snow-covered cliff. Below, a drama was playing out between a polar bear and a seal. The bear lay near an opening in the ice that the seals used to come up for air.

One of the men watching was Beau Levesque. His gloved hands held a Sharps 1853 slant breech, often called the John Brown. His beard and moustache were covered with ice particles from his breath, which froze instantly when he exhaled. His wool shirt and pants were covered by a fur-lined caribou skin coat and britches. When he spat, the saliva would freeze before it landed on the snow.

Seated beside him was an Inuit who went by the name Noah, given to him by British missionaries. They had also taught him to speak English. The short, barrel-chested Eskimo carried the more traditional harpoon with a whale bone tip and a line fastened to it. When hunting seals, the animal would dive back into the opening on the ice and attempt to escape with the harpoon embedded in its flesh. Noah would haul it back out with the attached line once the seal quit struggling.

Noah had thin whiskers on his broad face and strands of black hair protruding from his hooded caribou skin coat. Beau heard him snort and say, "The bear ruins our hunt. You should shoot it and we will take its meat back to the village."

Beau sat, remaining quiet as he listened to his hunting partner complain. Noah was probably right. He should try and shoot the bear, but he had spent a year traveling thousands of miles to see the "ghost bears". Finally, on this seal hunt, he had seen one. Beau was fascinated watching the polar bear hunt the seal. Several times the seal had stuck its nose out of the water, taking a quick breath and then disappearing before the bear could react.

"The seal knows the bear is there," the mountain man said. "Shooting the bear would spoil the game."

Less than a mile away the two men had their camp. They'd already had success hunting and their sleds were packed with seal meat and blubber. This was to be their last day of hunting before heading back to Noah's village.

The mountain man had wintered at the Inuit village. He had been surprised at the two months of darkness beginning in December. The sun had begun to show toward the end of January, giving a short period of semi-daylight. It was now the end of March. The longer days were beginning to melt the snow and would soon break up the sea ice. The polar bears were hunting the seals to put on fat to help them survive the lean times of summer hunting.

Beau had met Noah in the coastal village of Otkiawik, known for the hunting of bowhead whales. The whales could be found offshore during the summer, starting around May. Noah and others from the village would be out on the sea hunting, some in small groups using kayaks. Others would go to work on the whaling ships.

When successful, the whale would be butchered for it meat, bones and blubber. The skin and blubber would be cut into short, square strips called maktak and eaten raw. The whale was shared with the other Inuit families in the village and the surrounding area.

Finally, Noah said, "We will leave the hunting to the white bear. It is time to start back to Otkiawik."

The two men were upwind of the hunting bear, and as they slowly got up to leave, the polar bear gave them no notice. It was only a matter of time: The crafty seal would hesitate a bit too long on the surface and the bear would lunge after it, disappearing into the hole with the fleeing seal. Chances were good that the patient hunter would resurface, dragging its next meal out onto the ice.

The men's camp was simple. Several blocks of snow had been cut and stacked, making a crude igloo. A skin hung over a narrow opening on one side, and a second small opening at the top allowed smoke from their soapstone oil lamp, or kudlik, to escape. The kudlik was fueled with blubber that was pounded with a hammer made from an antler. Then Artic cotton, or moss, was saturated with oil from the blubber, moved around with an antler prong and pressed along the near edge. Using a flint and steel, the cotton was lit. The lamp provided light, some heat, and a means to melt snow for water. The cotton grass, or moss, used for a wick required frequent tending to prevent the burning oil from smoking.

Their meals consisted of raw blubber, dried meat, or fish. Beau had gotten used to the bland taste and the slow process of chewing the maktak. When he and Noah managed to kill a seal, the animal was slit open and, using their tea cups, the blood would be scooped out and drank first. Then the organ meat would be eaten raw. His Inuit friend would also eat the intestines, but Beau drew the line there.

Their chores were few when they arrived back at the camp. They fed the dogs blubber, lit the oil lamp to melt snow for tea, and then methodically chewed their raw meal. They continue to melt snow and mix it with grain, bone meal, or blubber for the dogs' morning meal. The dogs needed to stay hydrated and they couldn't get enough water from the snow. Beau also learned that they didn't like cold water, so a tepid gruel or blubber mixture was most satisfying to the dogs.

The two sleds were each pulled by six huskies. The dogs were bred for strength rather than speed and would average six miles per hour. Beau and Noah would both be carrying packs and would step off the runners when the dogs were pulling up a long or steep grade.

"We have hunted for two weeks and have six seals," Noah said with satisfaction.

"You spoke of the caribou moving north soon," Beau said. "If we see some, I can shoot a couple to bring back to the village."

"This far north it is still early," Noah said. "After we bring the seals to Otkiawik, we can go inland and hunt the caribou. The time will be right then."

The mountain man knew that they were almost two weeks from the village. He had seen the impressive caribou horns on the front of some of the Inuit lodges and looked forward to bringing down one of the animals and displaying the antlers as a trophy. He was also looking forward to steak fried in a blackened frying pan.

After feeding the dogs and packing their gear, the ganglines were stretched in front of the sleds. The huskies were impatient to start and danced around, yelping and barking as the harness and tuglines were put on. Beau buried his gloveless hands into their thick fur as he worked to share their warmth. The lead dogs were the most important. The men depended on them to keep the gangline taut and respond to the musher's commands.

Haste was made as the teams were readied. If left waiting the anxious huskies would tend to start nipping at each other in their excitement to be off. The mountain man went to the back of his sled and ran his hand along the work-worn handles before pulling on his fur-lined gloves. Then he stomped to break the frozen sled runners loose, which started some of the dogs pulling.

In unison the two men shouted, "Hike!" The lead dogs took control, tightening up the gangline, and with the help of the men pushing the sleds were off.

Beau let Noah take the lead breaking trail through the crusted snow. They let the dogs run for a short while, getting the excess energy expended, before slowing them for the day's travel. The commands used to drive the dogs were similar to those used with oxen. "Gee" and "haw" would turn them, and "whoa" would stop them.

After an hour of travel, Beau shouted, "On by!" and his team passed to break trail for Noah's. The mountain man shoved with one foot, pedaling, to assist the dogs getting by the other sled. The wind picked up, blowing biting bits of snow into Beau's face. They were pulling in a straight line across the tundra, so he pulled his hood down in the front to protect his cheeks and eyes.

This time of year they had 14 hours of daylight. When traveling after the sun went down, the men would use the stars to navigate across the white expanse. Having taken only a few breathers this first day, the two men finally stopped shortly before dark. Beau cut blocks of snow for a wind barrier, while Noah took care of the dogs. They had traveled about 10 hours and had made almost 50 miles.

Beau knew that the dogs could keep up the pace day after day if properly fed and cared for. A horse could only make about 30 miles a day. Grinning, Beau had to admit that the horse was only one animal. There were six dogs pulling the one sled.

Later that evening, using the soapstone oil lamp for light, the two men checked the dogs' paws and gave them personal attention, treating them to pieces of fat. In the bitter cold of winter, the dogs would be brought into the shelter to provide warmth for the inhabitants. With everyone sleeping outdoors, the men brought the dogs close to give them some protection behind the wind break.

The dominant lead dog pulling Beau's sled was named Kip. While all of the dogs were the property of Noah, the mountain man had developed a bond with the lead husky. When sleeping under the stars, Kip would curl up next to Beau and growl a warning if anything moved past the camp. It would also warn off any of the other dogs that tried to lie too close.

* * *

After a week of traveling south, Beau was noticing the longer length of daylight and the rise in the day's temperature. The nights were still frigid, but the snow on some of the rock outcroppings was beginning to drip when the sun was up. The men made camp near one of the outcrops and took advantage of the newly formed icicles to make their water.

They were beginning to see some scrubby bushes and even a few bare patches exposing moss and short, brown grass. That night, as they slept, Noah was woken by a sound in the distance that he recognized as caribou. The tundra was bathed in an eerie light of the dancing northern lights. He lay thinking, *Tomorrow I will let Beau shoot one caribou. Between the two sleds we can carry it.*

It was just getting light when the two men woke up. They had hardly moved before the dogs became active, stretching and yawning. Other than Kip, the rest of Beau's dogs were tied to the sled to prevent them from wandering. As the mountain man dug into the packs to get frozen blubber for the dogs, Kip growled and bared his teeth, warning the others to stay clear until he was fed.

Using a small hatchet, the mountain man chopped chunks off and tossed them to the dogs in turn. Noah had the oil lamp lit and was warming water to mix with fat and meal to finish feeding the animals.

"I heard the sound of caribou passing last night," Noah told his friend. "We could use extra meat and should stalk and shoot one."

"Maybe we can shoot a couple," Beau suggested.

"The sleds carry much weight already," the Inuit told him. "The caribou will add over 100 pounds to each of them."

Although he was disappointed, Beau knew his friend was right. The heavier the load, the slower the dogs would travel. They wanted to make good time getting to Otkiawik, because the longer days were melting the snow. Some of the southern hillsides were already showing last year's grass. Opening up his possible bag, the mountain man checked the long, narrow tin containing paper cartridges for his Sharps rifle. He also had an 1851, .36 caliber Colt Navy Revolver in the bag.

"There are two ridges to the east," Noah pointed out. "They can't be any farther away than that."

"Are we taking the sleds?" Beau asked.

"We will be crossing a stream that might be breaking up," the Inuit replied. "We will let the dogs rest today while we hunt and bring back the caribou."

Leaving the dogs on their leashes, the two men headed to the east. Beau carried his Sharps, while Noah took his 1853 Enfield. The Enfield was a muzzle-loading, percussion cap rifle. It had the shorter 33-inch barrel, making it easier to carry when used to hunt on the water.

The thick, frozen crust supported the men as they walked. Noah told Beau that the caribou were called reindeer in other parts of the world. Beau was half listening to his friend while he looked ahead, anxious to cross the next ridge, hoping to sight the animals.

They reached a frozen stream with some open spots near springs or rapids. They stepped carefully on the rotting ice, trying to avoid breaking through. The watertight, knee-high mukluks would keep the water out should they break through. As they crested the second rise, the men stopped in mid-step. Below them was a small herd of caribou. Most were lying down, enjoying the warmth of the sunshine and chewing their cuds. Only a couple of animals had antlers.

"They must be mostly females," Beau whispered.

"Many of the males have already shed their antlers," Noah said. "By the time the summer is over, they will have grown replacements."

Embarrassed, Beau felt a blush grow under his beard. He knew that, but in his excitement of seeing the caribou, he had spoken without thinking. Quickly regaining his composure, Beau said, "I will shoot the one grazing above the herd."

While Noah would have preferred to have the mountain man pick one of the smaller animals, he nodded his consent. The men had moved back below the crest and Beau opened the breech of his lever-action Sharps. Taking a paper cartridge, he slid it down into the opening. When closing the breech, the end of the cartridge is sheared off, exposing the black powder to the spark of the percussion cap. Beau's Sharps rifle had an automatic percussion system that would insert one as the rifle was fired, but he had long ago run out of the disk-shaped caps that fit the system and he was using the same caps that fit the nipple of his Colt Navy Revolver.

With the rifle ready, Beau crawled back to the ridge and looked for the big male. It had turned and was slowly working its way up the far side, pawing away snow while grazing. "Damn," the mountain man muttered under his breath.

"Get ready," Noah told him. The Inuit then gave a shrill whistle.

The herd began to stand up and the large male turned to look, ready to flee. Without hesitating, Beau lined up the sights and fired. Smoke and fire belched out of the barrel as well as from around the breech as the .52 caliber bullet was sent at the caribou bull.

Dropping its head, the large male leaped forward, intent on fleeing. The herd below the male departed at a full run. Stumbling, the male fell headfirst and rolled to its side, sliding a short distance down the hill, leaving a bloody streak on the snow.

"Good shot!" Noah shouted as he took off across the ravine.

Gathering up his possible bag and clinging to the still smoking rifle, Beau hurried along, following his friend. Reaching the caribou, Noah knelt down and slit the animal's throat, catching the blood in a tin cup.

Gasping for breath, the mountain man came up to the downed animal. Suddenly, disappointment showed on his weather-worn, lined face. One of the antlers had broken when the caribou had hit the frozen ground.

"Damn horn is broken," Beau exclaimed.

Looking up, the Inuit replied, "We didn't shoot the animal for the horns."

"Well, . . . no," Beau said, feeling foolish for the second time. "Although I was kind of hoping to have a set to bring back to the village," he explained.

Laughing at his friend, Noah extended the blood-filled cup to Beau. "Have a drink to a successful hunt."

Taking a mouthful of the rich salty liquid, the mountain man handed it back and then pulled his knife to start gutting the caribou. Suddenly they heard a gunshot. Busy with the animal, they weren't sure where the shot came from.

"Must be another hunter saw the rest of the herd," Beau suggested.

"Wrong direction," Noah replied. "Could be shooting at a wolf or even a bear."

The men made a meal out of the raw liver once the carcass was opened up. Noah scooped up any remaining blood in the caribou and drank it with the meat. The sun was high and the men shed their caribou skin coats before finishing with the animal.

With all the edible and useful parts stored inside the caribou carcass, they tied the front legs to the remaining horn and then two lines for dragging. With a loop on the ends of the lines to sling over their shoulders, they headed back for camp pulling the animal, leaving a large, bloody patch on the snow as evidence of their successful kill.

The crust had weakened and with the extra load in tow, the men began to break through the crust, sinking into the knee-deep snow. It was almost a mile back to camp and they were thankful when they went over the final rise and could see their sleds in the distance.

Exhausted by the burden they had been pulling, the men sank down in the snow to catch their breath. Beau had his wool shirt unbuttoned and only continued to keep the caribou britches on to prevent the wool pants from getting wet. Both men were sweating, which is a danger in the frigid north, but they knew there would be time to dry the damp clothing before sunset.

Beau could see Kip standing next to the sleds, watching their progress. The dog must have chewed its leach. Beau had expected the dog to run and meet them. "Looks like Kip is guarding the camp," the mountain man chuckled.

"We better keep going," Noah warned him. "We'll start shivering pretty fast just sitting here."

As they approached the camp, Noah swore. "Looks like some of the damn dogs got into the packs on the sled."

The mountain man could see that the packed sleds had been torn open. The seal skin covers were lying half on the snow and one or more seals were missing from the near sled. He called to the dog. "Did you buggers get hungry and get into the . . ."

He stopped in mid-sentence. Kip was snarling at them as they approached. He then saw the blood on the dog's fur. "What the hell!" he exclaimed. "Were you fighting over the damn seals?"

The men stopped short of the camp. Kip was not on a leash and a glazed, killing look was in his eyes. Beau took off his gloves and pulled the Colt from the possible bag. Holding it at the ready, he spoke to the dog.

"Kip, it's me," he said softly as he moved slowly closer to the dog. At any second he expected to be attacked.

"You best keep back," Noah cautioned his friend.

Kneeling down, 20 feet away from the animal, he continued speaking, hoping that the dog would realize that Beau was a friend. Suddenly, Kip began to whine and limped toward the mountain man. The look in the dog's eyes was gone.

Reaching out toward the injured animal, he asked, "What happened to you, Kip? Come here and let me help you."

A cold wave washed over Beau as the dog reached him. The blood was not from the dog's fighting. Kip had been shot! Noah was checking the other dogs when the mountain man heard him say, "We are missing four dogs."

"Damnit!" the Inuit shouted, "We've been robbed! Someone has taken some of the seal meat!"

While Noah went through the camp ranting in a language Beau did not understand, the mountain man checked the severity of the dog's wound. The bullet had creased the side of the Kip's neck and a front leg. With the loss of blood, it looked worse than it was.

The leash had been cut and what remained dragged on the snow. Noah came over to see how the dog was. "He'll be okay," Beau said stroking the dog's head. "Kip won't be able to pull a sled until the wounds heal."

"Whoever was here went though our packs," Noah said. "The oil lamp is gone, two of the seals, four dogs, some powder and lead. I'm sure we'll find other things gone."

While his friend sat looking every bit a victim, Beau slowly moved around the camp. Kip stayed by his side and would growl every time they passed the tracks of the thieves. The four dogs that had been taken were from his sled. The leashes had been cut at the knot and the dogs had been retied to the robber's sled.

There had been two men. One had been taking the dogs and the other had removed the seal-skin covers from both sleds and had strung the gangline out on Noah's sled, intending to take it with them. It was only a guess, but Beau believed that the robbery had been interrupted when Kip's leash had been cut. He believed that the dog had attacked the thieves and, in a panic, they had shot at Kip, then grabbed the seal meat and other items as they attempted to flee.

There were drops of blood on their trail as they'd departed and Kip had continued to chase them. One of the running men also left a blood trail, which was probably from an injury inflicted by the dog. Walking back toward the camp, Beau saw that the robbers had come in from the northwest. One had been driving the dogs and the other had been traveling on snowshoes. In their haste to get away, these had been left behind along with a possible bag.

The mountain man grabbed up the bag and went to sit with Noah. He told his friend what he thought had happened and about the snowshoes and possible bag. "Not a very even exchange for the dogs, seals and my lamp," Noah muttered.

Beau opened the bag and went through its contents. A knife, a flint, some caps, a bullet mold, and a few other items were spilled out onto the snow. The bone handle knife had the initials, H.G. scratched on it. The mountain man went to look at the snowshoes. They also had the initials.

Coming back to his friend, Beau said, "The initials are little to go on, but it will be a start. I want to take one of the sleds and go after Mr. H.G."

Looking up at the mountain man with sad brown eyes, Noah shook his head. "They are gone, my friend. Two hours south they will hit the main trail toward the coast. Their tracks will be lost. It will take them to any one of several small villages."

While still half in shock, the two men knew they had things that needed to be done before the sun went down. Their sweaty clothing had to be taken care of, the caribou skinned, the packs secured, dogs fed, and Kip's wounds tended to.

Once the most of the urgent tasks were finished, Beau built a fire using some brush and fried up caribou steaks in his frying pan. It should have been a special meal to celebrate a successful hunt, but the men ate in silence. They gave the dogs some extra meat from the caribou. They were the only ones that seemed to enjoy the evening.

CHAPTER TWO

The next morning, using the snowshoes, Beau followed the thieves' trail. Noah remained behind to set the sleds up with three dogs on one, and four on the other. The robbers had headed south and kept their dogs at a full run for the two miles that the mountain man followed them.

The injured man who had been running had jumped onto the sled shortly after leaving the camp and had knocked one of the seal carcasses off. They had lost one of the four stolen dogs during the escape. It had headed to the west and was nowhere to be seen.

Beau returned to the camp carrying the snowshoes on his shoulder. He found it easier to walk without them. He also had the seal, which Noah was happy to see. The mountain man was pleased to find out that the dog that had escaped had come back to the camp. Now they would have four healthy dogs on each sled. The caribou was divided to balance the loads on the two sleds.

While tying the seal skin covers on the sleds, Noah told his friend, "The two men that stole from us were white men. The bag was the type used by soldiers as well as the bullet mold."

"After we bring the meat back to your village, I will go and find the bastards and they will regret shooting our dog and stopping at our camp," Beau said as he tied the last dog to the ganglines.

It was a week before the two men mushed the sleds into the Inuit village. Their dwellings were comprised of igloos and some tents and a few sod structures. The men were greeted with shouts of joy. Several of the villagers dropped what they were doing and ran to meet them. Kip had ridden in a bag on top of Beau's sled to prevent him from jumping off. The mountain man loosened the ties and let the impatient dog free.

Turning, he looked into the broad smile of an Inuit woman he called Tomi. Putting his arms around her, he held her as she pressed herself close to him. Feeling awkward at the show of affection, Beau stepped back and held her at arm's length. Smiling, he told her, "It's great to see you again."

Tomi spoke to him in rapid Inuit, which the mountain man knew very little of. He just kept smiling and agreeing with her. Noah stepped in and told her something and she nodded. Reaching up and placing her hand on his bearded cheek, she laughed and hurried away.

Looking at his friend, Beau said, "I only wish I understood what she was saying."

Noah shrugged. "Something about cold blankets, long nights, loneliness. I don't think you will get much sleep tonight."

To the sound of his friend's laughter, Beau began to help unload the sleds. "Who needs sleep?" he mumbled.

The seals and caribou would be shared by the 200 residents of the village. It was taken to the village center to be cut up. With the dogs taken care of and short visits with those who came to greet them, the two men went to see the village council. They sat in an open area with caribou skins stretched on frames to reflect the sun onto the occupants.

Noah told them about the success of the hunt and the robbery. He told them he suspected it was white hunters. He also let them know that the caribou had started coming north. The news of the robbery was quickly forgotten when they learned of the caribou. Plans were made to move their village closer to the migration.

As the two men left the council, Noah said, "The thieves will quickly be forgotten. We can not live on what is gone. The village will be moving in a week to hunt the caribou. In another month the ice will be gone and then the ships will come. Some of us will return here to go after the whales."

After walking together in silence for a few minutes, Noah added, "You are welcome to join us on the hunt so you can bring down a caribou with big horns."

"I am going to visit some villages to the south and look for those who took from us," Beau replied. "If I find them, I will return with your dogs. They will pay for what they did to Kip. If I do not find them . . . it's time for me to continue south, back to the mountains where I hunt and live. You have taken me to see the white bear and I will be forever grateful to you."

"You should stay and hunt the caribou and then the whales with us," Noah encouraged him.

The mountain man grinned, shaking his head. "I kind of miss my meat burned over a nice wood fire." While it went unsaid, he also missed whiskey, which was scarce this far north.

"If you find the ones that robbed us, you will know what to do," Noah said. "What they did should not be paid for with their lives, but you must make sure they understand it was wrong. If you find the dogs, they are yours to keep or sell. Send the kudlik back to me if you can. You will know it by the three crosses on the bottom."

Beau left his friend thinking he was being too generous with the thieves. Then his thoughts changed to pleasanter things. He was near the igloo shared by Tomi's family. The Inuit igloos were built on top of the firm, drifted snow. Blocks to construct it were taken from the inner circles of the wall, giving additional height on the inside. The mountain man ducked through the skin-covered opening and stepped down into the dwelling. He saw Tomi lying on the bed made of ice and covered with caribou furs.

The dwelling was shared by her parents and two siblings. It appeared that they were all sleeping. Their soapstone lamp gave the room a soft glow of light as well as some warmth. Crossing the igloo, he sat on the ice bed next to the Inuit woman. Soon his clothing was in a heap on the packed snow floor. He turned to Tomi as she raised the caribou blanket, revealing her soft body.

* * *

The sound of movement in the igloo woke Beau. With his eyes still closed, he felt for Tomi. He knew she had gotten up just moments before due to the warmth of the blanket next to him. He lay quietly in his long johns as he listened to the morning sounds. He sensed someone coming near him. Then he felt her face against his.

"Good morning," the soft voice said. They were some of the few English words Tomi knew.

Opening his eyes and smiling at her, he replied, "It is a good morning."

Reaching down, he felt for his clothes. "Mother put them on the rack to dry," Tomi told him.

The normal chatter during the morning meal was subdued by the knowledge that Beau would be leaving. There was a shout from outside and the outer opening was lifted, giving a flash of sunlight and gust of cold air as Noah entered.

"It is time to load the sled," he told them.

Beau knew that within the hour the whole village would be on the move. His pack was near the opening and it was time for him to go. Tomi gave him a hug before he stood up and then her mother began to give them instructions of what she wanted packed on the sled first.

The mountain man felt a twinge of regret as he stepped up out of the igloo. It seemed like he was always leaving those he had become close to. The desire to see over new horizons was strong within him, always pulling him away.

Realizing that he would only get in the way if he stayed longer, Beau hoisted the heavy pack onto his back. The snowshoes that had been abandoned by the robbers and a bed roll were tied to the pack. He was dressed in the caribou britches and coat. Tomi came out of the igloo and placed folded blankets onto the sled, waved to Beau, then quickly turned her head and went back to get more items.

Noah walked with Beau to the edge of the village. "She will miss you."

"Her kindness will stay with me forever," Beau replied.

"If you come back this way, you can always find us in this area during the time of the whales," his friend told him.

"I want to wish you good hunting," Beau said, "and I will let you know if I find the ones who robbed us."

With little else to be said the two men parted, the mountain man walking south and the Inuit moving east to hunt the caribou.

Adjusting his pack for more comfort, he faced the cold wind. The snow-covered ground was firm, making walking easy for Beau. The fur-lined hood on his coat was pulled tight around his face, protecting him from the cold and cutting the glare from the snow. He cradled the Sharps rifle in the crook of his arm, and a canteen of water hung under his parka. The endless white, rolling tundra stretched out ahead of him.

He was headed for a location called Wainwright Lagoon. It was a three-day walk from the Inuit village. There he hoped to catch a ship going south and work his way down the coast. He had a desire to see a friend, Jocko, and his family before heading back to the Yellowstone area.

The first night, Beau dug down into the packed snow using an ice knife, creating a hole and removing blocks of snow to build a wind break. Then, sitting in his temporary camp, he pounded blubber in the small, soapstone lamp Noah had given him. Then, soaking moss with oil and arranging it along one edge, he poured a thin line of black powder. Striking a flint, there was a flash and the lamp was lit. It was much faster than the method used by the Inuit.

While the snow-filled tin cup heated over the lamp he took out some maktak, or cubed blubber, and chewed on it, washing the chewy fat down with water from his canteen. The wind blew waves of snow over his crude shelter and he waited for the tea water to heat. After the meal and warm liquid, Beau packed snow in his four-by-four shelter to make sleeping more comfortable.

The night air was filled with the sound of wolves hunting. It was a chilling sound and though rare, he knew they'd been known to attack people. As a precaution, he placed the loaded .36 caliber Colt on top of his stomach. Beau then spread his ground cloth over himself, the rifle, and the other gear as protection from drifting snow. As the northern lights put on a show above him, he dozed off.

* * *

The area around Wainwright Lagoon was abandoned for much of the winter months, only to come alive again with the appearance of the whales. Beau walked along a river that emptied into the lagoon. The surface churned as the ice broke up, tumbling and splashing. The favorable sea breezes had taken out the sea ice and a few of the whaling ships were already at anchor. They carried firewood on the main deck to start the fires in their try-works, where the blubber was boiled to get the oil. Once the first pots were boiled the remaining scraps were used to fire the pots, creating dark, sooty smoke.

When the whaling started, cargo ships would carry the laden oil casks south and then return with empty casks and additional wood for starting the try-works fires. On the shore there was a narrow, wood-framed trading post that included a blacksmith shop for making and repairing harpoons, and a crude tavern to satisfy the men's thirst.

Shelves lined both sides of the building, containing bags of dried peas, beans, rice, hard-tack, coffee beans, tea, and tins of molasses. There were also barrels of salt pork, salt beef, coils of rope, and other items needed by whalers. Along the center of the long room there were three tables for card playing or dining.

After three days of walking south, Beau stood with his elbows on the plank bar, hugging a bottle of rye and a half-filled glass. The whiskey was watered down, but after months without any, it tasted just fine to the mountain man. A stocky man named Otto owned the place. It was said he'd been a ship's captain at one time, but he'd run his vessel aground. Rather than abandoning it, he'd decided to dismantle it and build the trading post.

The mountain man intended to catch the next ship going south. He could trade many of the items that were needed to survive in the frigid north to help cover the cost of fare. Otto came over, his thinning hair plastered to his scalp.

"So, did you see the white bears?" he asked.

Beau had stopped here on his way north and Otto had sent him to Noah's village. "Yes, I did," the mountain man replied. "I even got me a caribou."

"Why, hell. Stick around," the stocky man replied. "A month from now the hills around here will be lousy with them."

"A month from now, I hope to be where it is one hell of a lot warmer," Beau said, already feeling the glow of the rye.

Suddenly, the mountain man sniffed the air. "Is that cooking I smell?"

"I'm warming yesterday's stew," the owner replied.

"Hot food. Damn!" Beau declared. "What would it cost to get a helping of that?"

"Two bits, and I got some bread to go with it," Otto said as he headed for the steaming pot.

The mountain man had eaten two bowls of the tasty stew and a half-loaf of bread before he was satisfied. Burping in satisfaction, he pushed the empty bowl away and began to make a serious dent on the rye.

The bar filled up with French, English, and some American whalers as the evening went on. Some were off the ships at anchor, while a few had wintered in the north. The ones that had wintered, Beau would check out when his head became clearer the next day.

That night, Otto let the tipsy mountain man sleep on some furs toward the back of the trading post. He had gotten a promise that some wood would be split in return. A potbelly stove glowed in the middle of the building, providing warmth that Beau hadn't enjoyed for months.

The smell of coffee woke the mountain man the next morning. After months of being away from meals made on a hot stove, his senses seemed to amplify the aromas. Sitting up too quickly, Beau's head spun and the all too familiar ache of his hangover stopped him. He could hear Otto talking with someone beyond the stove.

Whoever the customer was had left by the time the mountain man got to his feet. "Damn, I feel lousy," he groaned.

"You should," the owner called to him. "You put away two bottles of my best whiskey."

Coughing to clear his dry throat, Beau replied, "I am damn fortunate that you cut the stuff with so much water. I might have killed myself otherwise."

He could hear Otto chuckling as the owner came around the stove. "Seeing how you'll be splitting wood for me today, I'll get you started with some strong coffee and a slab of bread smeared with bacon fat."

While his stomach was tending to rebel, Beau ate down the bread anyway and slowly sipped the hot coffee, enjoying the strong brew. With the heat of the stove last night, and the furs to pull over himself, the mountain man had removed his fur lined britches and the parka. These he planned to trade with Otto. With his stomach somewhat settled, the mountain man headed outside to pay his debt for the night's boarding.

Touching up the heavy, single-bit ax with a whetstone, he began to work on the pile of logs. Throughout the morning he swung the ax. An impressive stack of wood showed his appreciation for the nights lodging. Next to the woodpile, he collected the chips, not wanting to waste any fuel this far north.

Sticking the ax into one of the uncut logs, he headed back into the trading post carrying his coat and wool shirt. "That stack should get me another couple of nights," he called to the owner as he ducked under the low doorway.

"Dip yourself a bowl of beans and have a seat," the owner said, ignoring the claim of a couple more nights. "Last night you were mumbling something about a robbery and an oil lamp with three crosses carved on the bottom."

Beau placed the steaming bowl of beans on the table and slowly sat, his eyes on Otto. "It must have been after I was working on the second bottle, 'cause I don't quite remember talking of it." Blowing on a spoonful of beans, the mountain man winced as he put them into his mouth. Chewing on the mouthful, he continued, "I was robbed and I am looking for a lamp with three crosses."

The owner got up and went to a shelf. Returning to the table he placed a soapstone lamp face down on the table. "I took this one in a few days ago from a Cree. He goes by Big Joe. I believe his father was Russian and his ma was Cree."

The mountain man stared at it as he ate the beans. "That's the one. Did he have dogs to sell?"

"He was selling his dogs and sled. Had a few spares he was leading behind the sled." Otto said. "He come in with a story of his partner dying from a bear attack."

"Did you know his partner's name?" Beau asked.

"I knew him as Hube Green," the owner said. "I think he was put ashore from a British ship for doing something wrong. He and Big Joe kind of took care of each other."

Beau had stopped eating and the bowl of beans had gotten cold. "This Big Joe. Did he sell his dogs?"

"No market around here for a dog team in the spring," the owner replied. "He stopped in here this morning and picked up a few supplies. He's heading south about a day's travel to sell the works to some Chipewyan."

Pushing the bowl away, Beau suddenly stood up. "I have to go after him."

Motioning the mountain man to sit back down, Otto said, "Let me warm up your beans. He will be back in a couple days and you can ask him about having the oil lamp."

Feeling edgy, Beau took his seat. "He better have a good reason for having the lamp."

Beau continued to do odd jobs for his keep at the trading post. He got word that a ship bringing casks and wood for the whaling ships would make

Wainwright in a few days. After offloading the cargo and taking on oil, if it was available, it would be returning south for more.

Otto had told him that Noah would be stopping at the trading post before returning to fish and hunt whales at Otkiawik. He would give the oil lamp back to the Inuit. Beau offered to pay him for the kudlik, but the owner refused. "It is not your responsibility. When Big Joe returns, I will get back what I paid him."

While Otto kept the mountain man busy, time seemed to drag for Beau. As far as he knew, the only thing he would be able to do was get some money back for the three dogs, and give the Cree a good scolding. Just maybe Big Joe would take a swing and open the opportunity to give the man the thrashing he deserved.

The mountain man drank sparingly while waiting for the Cree's return. He did not want to be drunk when facing the man. Beau began to carry the Colt in its holster positioned in the front. He hoped that it would not be needed, but Otto had told him stories about the Cree's meanness.

After finishing a meal of caribou stew, Beau sipped on a shot of rye. There was a shout of recognition as a big man with shaggy black hair and narrow, mean eyes entered the room. He leaned his rifle against the wall and tossed his pack near the door. Three acquaintances were calling him over to their table to play cards.

Otto went past Beau behind the bar. "That's him."

Big Joe called to his friends, "Let me get a bottle first."

He stopped beside Beau and, slapping a coin onto the bar, called for a bottle.

"Be right there," Otto called to the man.

"Too bad about your partner," the mountain man said.

"Ain't got no partner," the Cree snapped.

"You know it weren't the dog's fault," Beau continued. "He was just protecting our stuff."

As if stung by a bee, Big Joe stepped back. "I don't know what the hell you're talking about!"

Still leaning on the bar, Beau turned to face him. "I believe you do. It looked like your little party was broken up when my lead dog was cut loose."

The mountain man straightened up, facing Big Joe. "It must have been Hube that done it. I figure the dog tore him up pretty good. Probably tore his arm wide open. That was when Hube took to running and I figure the dog went after you and you tried shooting it. With your rifle empty and a damn mad dog after you, you jumped on the sled and ran, leaving your partner. I saw that he did get on the sled. Did you even slow down when he struggled to climb on?"

"You are one dead son-of-a-bitch," the Cree growled.

With unexpected speed, Big Joe drew and threw his knife at the mountain man. Beau felt the breeze as the knife passed by his neck. The mountain man stood watching as the Cree sunk down to his knees holding his stomach. In Beau's hand was his 1851 Colt, the smoke still curling up from the barrel. He suddenly realized that he hadn't even heard the shot. Beau had just reacted, and now the man in front of him was shot in the stomach and would no doubt die from the wound.

There was the sound of chairs being knocked over by Big Joe's friends. Beau shifted the Colt in their direction. "Any of you want to get in on this?" he threatened.

The men were standing near the table with their hands showing. "Don't shoot at us. We just wanted to take some of his money."

Otto came around the bar. "Put that damn gun away. You damn near scared the piss out of me when you fired the thing."

Big Joe lay moaning on the floor as the owner knelt down near him. "Is it true what he said about Hube, that it was a dog, not a bear?"

"What the hell difference does it make?" Big Joe said, coughing as blood spread on his shirt. "He gut shot me. I am going to die."

In a surprisingly gentle voice, Otto said, "We'll get you to the *Alfred* anchored in the lagoon. I hear they got some kind of a doctor onboard."

The mountain man stood feeling helpless as he watched the three men carry the Cree outside. Noah had asked him not to kill the man. His intention was to provoke Big Joe and give him a good beating.

"You were mighty nice to the man," Beau told the owner.

Shrugging his shoulder Otto replied, "What the hell. He's gonna die and I figure that was punishment enough." Then, looking Beau in the eye, he added, "You done the world a favor. I wouldn't be surprised if he left Hube Green to bleed to death or freeze so as to lighten his sled."

Word came back the next day that the Cree had died. His pack still lay where he had left it as he entered the room. Otto brought it over to a table and dumped out the contents. It contained little of value, but the owner did find six scalps that Big Joe probably intended to sell to some of the whalers.

"No doubt some unfortunate Inuits that crossed his path," Otto muttered.

Whatever money that had gone with the injured man was probably now in the pockets of the men who carried him out or the doctor on the ship. It was decided that the Cree's rifle would be kept for Noah, along with the oil lamp.

Little was said about the killing of the Cree in the days that followed. The mountain man traded his caribou clothing, the mukluks, his small oil lamp and anything else he had that was required for living in the frigid north. He got a pair of low-cut boots, another knife, extra socks and a pair of wool britches. Beau would be glad when it was time to climb into the whale boat and head for the schooner that would be taking him south.

CHAPTER THREE

The three-mast schooner was American and named the *Phillip*. For the past three days, it had been loading its cargo hold full of whale oil, and some baleen also known as whalebone from a ship named *Pettibone*. The oil would be used for lamps and lubricating machines. The baleen were plates that ran along the roof of the whale's mouth and were used for strong, thin supports in corsets, collar-stiffeners, and even umbrellas.

The *Phillip* would sail down to Astoria, Oregon and offload the cargo. It would then return with supplies needed for whaling in the Artic. The round trip would take six to eight weeks. Beau had arranged a working berth on the ship.

The mountain man had been sent to the whaling ship *Pettibone*. He stood on the deck, pulling on the handles of the windlass that was connected to the block and tackle system that lifted the oil-filled casks out of the ship's hold. The 250-pound cask required 40 pounds of pull on the windlass handles. A rachet was engaged to prevent the cask from falling in case Beau's hands should slip off the handles. A leather-lined brake was fitted to the windlass to slow the descent of a load being lowered.

While waiting for the next cask to be secured to the lift the mountain man would look around the deck of the whaling ship. A brick try-works was positioned between the foremast and mainmast. There the blubber would be boiled in large bronze try-pots. The smell of rotting blubber and blood was strong on the ship. Care had to be taken on the deck to prevent slipping on the oil-impregnated planks.

Smaller whales would be hoisted onto the deck for removal of the blubber. Larger whales would be secured alongside the ship and the blubber stripped by men hanging over the side of the ship using long-handled, sharpened spades. Evidence of the gruesome process was visible throughout the ship.

After the last cask was lifted and the whalebone transferred, Beau put a loop over a windlass handle and climbed down the rope ladder with his pack to the whale boat below. The whale boats had what appeared to be a bow on both ends, allowing them to be maneuvered in either direction without having to be turned around. One end had a platform for the man throwing the harpoon, or using the killing lance or spear. Six men would man it while stalking and killing a whale.

The mountain man's eyes were on the schooner now holding the cargo of oil. The *Phillip* would be setting sail tomorrow, taking him south. For the past few nights he had berthed in the *Pettibone* crew quarters, which were filthy. His berth on the *Phillip* lacked comfort, but should be somewhat cleaner. The smell of whaling was on both ships.

The wind had picked up and the waves hitting the bow sent a spray over the whaleboat. Beau tucked his Sharps under his pack to protect it from the salt water. It was the 3rd of May in 1862. The mountain man was 45 years-old and was surrounded by all his worldly goods: The clothes on his back, a spare set in his pack, a buckskin coat, a wool skull cap which some called a Monmouth, a Sharps rifle, a Colt revolver, molds, powder, and lead, blankets, and a few other odds and ends that made life in the wilds a bit more comfortable.

At the age of 45 he carried a wealth of knowledge about hunting and trapping and could guide a man to about any part of the mountains or plains that he wanted to go. He had a horse and saddle at his friend's farm in Oregon. In a small leather sack in his possible bag, he carried enough money to buy supplies to get him through the coming summer, and a little left over for whiskey and tobacco.

Beau had never thought about being rich someday, or even planned too far ahead. As long as he was able to move quietly and shoot straight, he would never go hungry or lose his scalp. Over the years he had loved and lost, finally giving up on love.

The whaleboat bumped against the side of the schooner. Hefting his pack over his shoulder, the mountain man climbed the rope ladder. Before he went over the bulwark, he reached down for his rifle. After assisting the rest of the sailors, the whaleboat was hoisted into the davits. Beau saw that the hatch had been closed on the cargo hold and everything was ready to set sail with the tide.

Captain Sterling was watching from the quarterdeck. He shouted down, "Get yourselves some chow and a bit of rest. We sail in five hours."

Beau followed the others to the galley. The cook had a pot of lobscouse, which was considered a special meal. It consisted of a stew made with salt pork, onions, some type of root vegetable, and plenty of pepper. There was hot tea and hard tack to go with the meal.

The men carried their steaming bowls back toward the crew quarters. Most put the hard bread into the broth to start it softening. The mountain man had seen a few of the faces of the crew before, but couldn't place them. None gave notice that they recognized Beau.

Care was taken while eating the stew, to pick out any roaches or other bugs that were floating in their bowls. There were no complaints when something was found. It was just the way of life on the whaling ships.

Beau was in a deep sleep in his hammock as the rolling of the ship gently rocked him back and forth. The bosun whistle blasted "take your stations" and the men rolled out of the hammock and hit the deck running. The mountain man woke, confused for a minute about where he was. "Damn," he muttered as he pulled on his boots and wool skull cap, then ran for the forecastle.

Knowing little of rigging sails, he was assigned to watches at the wheel. He would also be assigned to hauling in lines, manning the capstan or windlass, and the pumps. When getting underway he was one of the crew members that manned the capstan for the anchor.

The others had already started to raise the anchor when he got there. He grabbed hold of the remaining bar and started pushing. He glanced up, saw the bosun and realized that his tardiness had been noticed. For the rest of the time hauling the anchor, he pushed harder than anyone else.

With the anchor up, Beau pulled the bars and stowed them in the rope locker. Many of the crew had climbed the shrouds and were letting out the sails. Beau's next job was to man lines connected with block and tackle to the sails as they were let out and set. Once the ship was underway the deck had to be cleared of all lines and unneeded gear.

As they left the lagoon, waves broke over the bow, sending saltwater rushing across the decks. The mountain man tended to stagger as he headed for the quarterdeck to man the wheel. He slipped on the ladder between the main and quarterdeck, barking his shin. Gritting his teeth against the pain, the mountain man pulled himself up and reported to the helm.

Relieving the man, he took hold of the spokes and called to the captain, "I've got the wheel."

"Set a course at 270," the captain barked.

Beau had been a helmsman when coming north the year before and learned the fundamentals of steering the ship. A compass near the wheel showed him the direction that the ship was sailing. Often two men were needed to handle the wheel when in rough seas, but Beau's rugged life and strength made it possible for him to handle it alone most of the time.

It was still dark with a star-studded sky as the ship cut through the water. The crew depended on the captain's knowledge of the route to keep them off rocky shoals and islands. The man in the crow's nest kept an eye out for floating ice or other vessels.

Twice during the first week, the ship spotted whales heading north. "They'll be going back south as oil," the bosun remarked.

The ship stopped over in the Aleutian Islands and took on water and a few supplies. This would be the last stop before they reached Astoria.

It was a sunny day with a brisk wind. Beau was thinking that it was a perfect day to be at sea as he came out of the galley with some kind of excuse for stew. As he passed the mainmast something hit the deck next to him. Startled, he jumped to the side as the trailing line landed. It was a block from the rigging that had fallen.

"Heads up below," came a call from above. Looking up he saw a sailor named Tod Jenson grinning at him. Beau glared at the man and continued to the crew's quarter to eat his meal.

Another seaman who had followed him said, "That weren't no accident."

"Maybe so," Beau replied. "I can't think of anything I've done to the man."

"You best watch your back," the man advised. "If Jenson got a grudge against you, he's the type that would put a knife in it on a stormy night."

The mountain man knew that many a sailor had disappeared overboard during rough seas, cause unknown. Beau carried his knife at all times and would keep his eye on the rigging and on Jenson in the future.

The fair wind that had propelled them south died as they sailed along the coast. The sails hung limp and the vessel slowly drifted back north on the current. The *Phillip* was several miles offshore in water that was too deep to drop anchor.

The captain had the men lower the whale boats. With lines secured to them, the men rowed, towing the ship toward land. Beau pulled on the oar, happy to be doing something. Within two miles of land, they reached a shelf that allowed dropping the anchor. The sky continued to be clear and the ocean flat.

That night the crew turned in early, with little to do until the wind picked up. Several of the sails had been taken in, in the event that the wind came up quickly. Beau stood the midnight watch on the quarterdeck. The night had an eerie silence due to lack of movement. The normal snapping of sails and creaking of lines taking the strain of the wind filled-sails was gone.

The still night air was cold, and Beau turned up the collar of his peacoat provided by the ship. Anxious to reach port, he prayed for a breeze and then wondered if it was selfish and God would begrudge his impatience. At 4 a.m. he went to the crew quarters and woke Jenson to take the watch.

The man glared at him as he headed for the quarterdeck. The mountain man was too tired to care and climbed into his hammock, still wearing the peacoat for warmth. It was just getting light when the bosun shouted, "All hands on deck!"

Beau rolled out of his hammock, realizing that he had only gotten a couple hours of sleep. The men gathered around the bosun, hoping that the wind had started to pick up. As it turned out, it had not.

"We got boats watching us on the port side," the bosun told them. Everyone turned to look. Four whaleboats manned with a half-dozen men each were sitting about a quarter-mile off the port side. "They might just be curious, or up to no good. We've got some rifles and those that can shoot are to take one and report back for your station assignment."

Beau went back to the crew's quarters and got his slant-breech Sharps rifle, his Colt, and possible bag. Returning to the deck, the bosun asked him, "Can you hit anything with that?"

"I generally hit what I aim at," Beau replied.

The bosun then noticed the Colt in the mountain man's holster. "Good, the revolver will be handy if they try and board us." Then he added, "Stay near me for orders."

The crew was scattered about the ship at the ready, most keeping out of sight. One of the whaleboats began to row toward the *Phillip*. It stopped within shouting distance. The captain called to them. "What is it that you want?"

"We will be taking over your ship," the man at the bow shouted, his French accent evident. "You have two hours to run up a white flag. We'll then let you and your crew take your whale boats to shore and spare your lives."

Without waiting for a reply, the boat headed back to join the others. Speaking more to himself than the others, Beau mumbled, "We should have shot the bastards."

The captain was standing next to him. "Look through this, Levesque."

Taking the spyglass, Beau looked at the boats. Inwardly he gasped. Two of the whaleboats had swivel guns mounted on the bow. "They are out too far to be effective," the mountain man said.

"They can harass us at that range shooting balls," the captain said. "If they come to board us, they will be loaded with grapeshot and spray our defenders."

As they watched, there was a puff of smoke from one of the swivel guns followed with a loud thunk just below the bulwark. The sound of the shot was heard seconds later. One of the crew looked over the edge. "She put a dent in the side, but no real damage."

"They didn't wait the two hours," Beau pointed out.

"I imagine they are trying to help us make up our mind," the captain replied.

For the next hour the small cannons were fired every few minutes, the projectiles doing little damage to the ship's structure but serious damage to the crew's nerves. Then one of the men was struck by a ball, breaking his arm.

Beau could see the strain on the captain's face. "I can hit them from here," he told him.

"If we injure one of theirs, any protection they have offered will be gone," the captain said.

The mountain man gripped the barrel of the 1853. "I do not believe they intend to let us live. Their offer was to get us into the whaleboats and finish us off with grapeshot."

Anger showed on the captain's face having his actions questioned. "So, you can read their minds?"

"We are dealing with French pirates," Beau replied. "Our lives are worth nothing to them. They want the ship and cargo. And they want us silent."

The mountain man could see the indecision in the captain. Frustrated, he thought, *A man like the captain leading men against the Indians would get his men killed.*

For the next half-hour, the bombardment continued, with the captain remaining silent. Beau had decided that when the order was given to abandon ship, he would stay and take his chances on the *Phillip*. At the very least he'd have a chance to take some of the pirates with him.

He almost didn't hear the words when the captain finally decided. "Return fire, Levesque."

Relief flooded over the mountain man. "Thank you, captain."

Beau had about 100 rounds for the Sharps in his pack. 20 were in the tin he had in the possible bag. He sent one of the crewmen to get additional paper cartridges from his pack. He then took a position at the bulwark. With the rifle loaded, he adjusted the open ladder and took aim at one of the boats that had floated broadside to them. Three men sat together, using a spyglass. "You are my target."

The Sharps fired, sending a plume of smoke into the air. The bullet clipped the boat rail and then struck the man in the center. "You got a hit!" the captain shouted. "Next one a bit higher."

His next targets were the men on the swivel guns. After firing four rounds at them, he had two hits and the pirate whale boats began to put distance between themselves and the *Phillip*. Beau continued to score hits until they were over a half-mile away.

The swivel guns were of no use at that distance and it appeared they were at a temporary standoff. Without wind, the *Phillip* remained a sitting duck. With the range of the Sharps, Beau could keep them away. The pirates would now wait for darkness. All hands on the ship knew there would be no survivors if the pirates, boarding was successful.

Just before dusk, two additional whaleboats joined the other four. The strain was plain on the captain's face. "Where the hell is the wind?" he whispered.

The bosun came up with a last-ditch strategy. "After dark we will fill two whaleboats with oil and powder. We'll put them a safe distance from the ship. When we hear the sound of their oarlocks, we light the powder and oil, giving us plenty of light to see our targets."

The captain agreed and assigned four crew members to ready the whaleboats. Then, everything changed. An audible gasp was heard on the ship. A breeze fluttered the sails.

"Weigh the anchor! Ready the sails for light wind! Let's get the hell out of here," the bosun shouted.

"The whaleboats are pulling hard towards us!" the captain shouted. "Levesque, stay at the bulwark and harass the bastards!"

As the anchor lifted from the sea floor, one of the men on the capstan yelled, "Anchors aweigh!"

Beau continued to fire in the direction of the whaleboats as he heard the sound of the sails snapping tight, filling with air. Slowly, the ship leaned with the wind and began to put distance between them and the whaleboats. Beau thought, *My prayer was answered. Thank you, lord.*

* * *

Safely away from the pirates, the mood on the Phillip was jovial. The cook made a simple cake to go with the stew. It was made with lard, flour, and molasses. The captain provided measures of rum for each of the crew. One of the crew members commented, "It must be Christmas."

They had less than a week before they'd reach Astoria. Soon the ordeal with the pirates was put behind them and the day-to-day routine brought down the crew's mood. Boredom and bad food had a way of doing that.

The captain, on the other hand, remained in high spirits and would remain on the quarterdeck whenever Beau was standing watch. There was a lot of encouragement to stay on the *Phillip* after Astoria.

Beau was feeling pretty good about himself as he got up for his midwatch. He was enjoying the attention of the captain, even though he knew he would not be staying on the ship. The night was clear and the stars bright as he crossed the main deck.

There was a flash of light and he felt himself falling. He was being pulled at and his head was swimming. Beau came up hard against something. His eyes seemed to flutter as he saw someone standing in front of him. The man hissed, "This is for Big Joe," as he grabbed under Beau's arms and was attempting to lift him.

He was at the bulwark! The man was trying to put him over the side! In a desperate move, Beau reached out and brought his arms up. They were between the man's legs. The mountain man heaved for all he was worth and the man went over Beau's head screaming as he plunged over the bulwark and into the water.

Then all was quiet. Beau felt the blood running down the back of his head. Someone from the quarterdeck came down the ladder carrying a lantern. "What's happening down here?"

Again, Beau's head began to spin and he began to vomit. Then there was blessed darkness.

CHAPTER FOUR

The sun was shining as the *Phillip* entered the Columbia River outlet and sailed toward Astoria. Beau was at the wheel, still supporting a large bandage on his head. As it turned out, Tod Jenson had made a final attempt to avenge Big Joe. He had hit the mountain man with a belaying pin and then had tried to put him over the side, only to end up overboard himself.

The ship spent a half-day looking for the man, with the full intention of hanging him if they found him alive. He was not found. Beau was happy to be back in Oregon and was looking forward to visiting his old friend Jocko.

The *Phillip* dropped anchor near the port of Astoria. As soon as space was available for offloading, the ship would be brought to one of the docks. The bosun was busy barking out orders as the sails were furled and lines stowed. The captain sent out a request that Beau see him in his cabin.

The mountain man had his pack on the deck and was anxious to help lower the whaleboats and set foot on land. Beau asked one of the deck hands to watch his gear and then headed for Captain Sterling's cabin. This would be the first time he'd been invited to the captain's quarters.

Knocking on the door, he heard, "Enter."

Stepping into the room was like entering another world. It was clean, with cushioned chairs, a bed with curtains, a large dining table and windows which were open letting in a soft breeze. Captain Sterling was seated at a cherry wood, roll top desk. Without looking up, he said, "I've something for you."

Feeling quite uncomfortable the mountain man walked over and waited for the man to look up. Leaning back in his chair, the captain looked up and smiled. "You saved our bacon when the pirates tried to take us over. As a thank you, I want you to have this bonus."

He held out a thin packet tied with string. Taking the packet, Beau replied, "Thank you, but it is not necessary." At this point, all he wanted to do was get into the whaleboat and off the ship.

"Please have a seat," Captain Sterling said, motioning to a chair.

Damn, Beau thought. Taking the seat, he watched as the captain poured two glasses of sherry. "I wanted to have a drink with you before you left and give you some advice."

The mountain man tasted the sherry and decided it was something he did not care for. Smiling, he lied, "This is very good. You said something about advice."

Rising, the captain paced around the cabin for a moment, as though he was searching for the right words. "I asked you if you'd be interested in staying aboard the *Phillip*. I understand your desire to go back to your home. I feel it is my duty to caution you about Astoria."

Confused over where this was going, Beau finished his sherry and set down the glass. Captain Sterling continued, "When you get ashore, make haste getting as far as you can from Astoria. The hotels will try and get you into debt and once you're broke they will sell you for what they can get."

"The streets are thick with crimps looking for ways to get blood money offered by shorthanded ships' captains. They'll buy your debt from the hotel and then put knockout drops in your drink. The next day you will wake up with a headache and be on your way to the Orient working off the debt."

Beau couldn't help but glance at the glass he'd just emptied. Then he said to the captain, "I appreciate you letting me know this."

Nodding, the captain continued, "I know you don't want to live the life of a sailor and I felt it important to warn you about being shanghaied." Then, smiling and picking up the bottle of sherry, he said, "Now. Can I pour you one more before you go?"

Standing quickly and shaking his head no, Beau replied, "You have been very good to me, but I must be going. As you recommended, I will make haste leaving Astoria."

Without giving the man the opportunity to say any more, the mountain man nodded and left the quarters. Rushing to the bulwark, we saw that he'd missed the first boat to the docks. "Damn," he muttered, "I hope what's in this packet makes it worth having to wait."

Beau smiled broadly as he looked into the packet. He would not have to worry about the cost of supplies this coming winter. Two crewmen he'd gotten to know quite well came by. The one with bright red hair was named Kelly said, "Hey, Levesque. Will you join us for some drinks in Astoria? I know a place that has good whiskey and pretty women."

"I got some things I've got to do first," Beau replied, "but if you give me the name of the place, I will meet you later."

Topper was a towhead. He piped up, "It's Carrie's Tavern."

It was almost an hour before the whaleboat returned and Beau was the first one at the rope ladder with pack and rifle in hand. The mountain man wanted to find a local doctor to take a look at the split on his head, then pick up some supplies for the trip to Jocko's farm. Once these were done, he'd find a room and stow his pack for the night. Carrie's Tavern was near the docks and could be a dangerous place to drink. He promised himself that he'd only have one or two and then retire for the night.

Astoria had a dentist who took care of most doctoring things. He unwrapped the bandage and did some hemming and hawing before wiping the wound down with carbolic. The stinging almost brought tears to the mountain man's eyes.

"The ship did a fine job of sewing up the scalp," the old dentist said. "You got a little redness around the stitches. I'll cut the hair back a bit and give you some salve that works on both men and beasts. You can let the air to it and the salve will keep off the flies."

Beau sat there wincing as the man cut at the hair with dull scissors, pulling as much out as cutting. Then the salve was smeared on, which had the smell of witch hazel. It caused a tingling sensation as it was applied. Then a last bit of instruction was given. "In about a week, have someone cut out those stitches."

With the small, round tin of salve in his possible bag, the mountain man settled up with the dentist. Beau carefully put on his wool skull cap, taking care to keep it off the wound, and headed out to purchase needed supplies.

The man at the mercantile took his list and began filling the order. "If you need a place to stay tonight, you best get off the docks. About a mile upriver there's the Beam Inn. It ain't fancy, but it's clean. He's my brother-in-law."

Placing down a sack containing the supplies, the man said, "That will be $4 even. I got the latest newspaper from San Francisco just this morning. Only four bits if you want one."

Beau realized it had been over a year since he'd looked at a newspaper. "I'll take one."

Reaching under the counter, the store owner folded a paper and placed it into the sack. Leaving with his supplies, the mountain man sat on the porch of the mercantile and opened a can of peaches with his knife. Spearing the fruit, he shook open the newspaper. His brow furled. The headline read, "Fighting Continues Between The North And South."

"What the hell?" he muttered. Setting the peaches down, he began to read about the Civil War raging in the east. "Thousands killed? Damn," he said.

The merchant came out of the store with a broom. "You reading about the war? The damn fools are fighting over owning slaves. It ain't our fight. We got no slaves in Oregon."

Beau moved his peaches when the man started to sweep off the road dust. Drinking the last of the juice, he tossed the can into the alley and left with his pack over his shoulder, cradling the Sharps in his left arm. The mountain man decided that the Beam Inn was too far, so he looked for a room closer. Finally, he saw a place with a sign: "Rooms $2."

In the lobby was a tall, slim man with thinning hair and a hawk nose. When Beau walked in, the man smiled quickly, revealing several rotting teeth. "You off the ships?"

"I just got in," Beau replied.

"We got a fine room for you," the man said, turning the register toward the mountain man.

"$2 for the night?" Beau asked.

"You don't have to worry about that right now," the man said. "We'll keep it on the books for you in case you decide to stay longer."

"I'll pay the $2 right now," the mountain man replied.

The clerk frowned. "You don't want the $2 room. They're kind of small and the beds are awful. There's just a curtain for a door. If you are a man of means I recommend our $4 room."

"That's a lot to pay for a night's sleep," Beau complained.

"You ain't got to pay it up front. Go out and have a good time and we'll settle up when you leave," the man urged.

The captain's warning went through Beau's mind. Shaking his head, he replied, "I think I'll be on my way."

"You won't find a better price in this town!" the man shouted after him.

Beau saw a man leading two horses into a side street. The mountain man followed him for three blocks before he arrived at the livery. A young, red-headed man got up from a weather-beaten chair.

"You finished with the horses, Mr. Anderson?"

"Yes I am, Alvin," the man said, handing some coins to the young man. "I'll need them again next week. The same ones, if you can."

Taking the reins, Alvin replied, "I'll have them for you."

Beau walked over to the bay doors while the young man led the horses to their stalls. Coming back, he saw the mountain man. "Can I help you?"

"What would it cost me to spend the night in your barn?" Beau asked.

"Can't do that," the young man replied. "Mr. Hooper don't allow no drifters to sleep in the barn."

"Is Mr. Hooper around so I can talk to him?" the mountain man asked.

"He don't live in Astoria," Alvin said.

Beau noticed a coffee pot on the potbelly stove inside the livery. "I sure could go for a cup of coffee. What say I trade you a can of peaches for some coffee?"

"Peaches?" the young man replied, his eyes getting larger. "The coffee is a little old."

"So am I," the mountain man told the young man. Leaning the rifle against the barn wall, he fished out the can and handed it to Alvin. The young man quickly went and got another chair and a tin mug of coffee. Soon the two men were seated in front of the livery, enjoying the rewards of their barter.

The mountain man talked of the white bears in the north, the pirates attacking the ship and then the Rocky Mountains. The young man began to ask questions and for the next hour Beau told him about a life Alvin could only dream of.

Tossing the dregs out of his cup, Beau started to collect his gear. "Well, I best find someplace to sleep tonight."

"I got a room off the barn. You can stay with me if you want," the young man offered.

"Mr. Hooper won't mind?" Beau asked.

"If it comes up, I'll tell him you are an uncle or something."

The lean-to on the side of the livery was also the tack room. It had a single cot and a couple of shelves with Alvin's meager belongings. There was an area that the mountain man could roll out his blankets.

"It ain't much," the young man apologized, "but you are welcome to stay as long as you need to."

"I only need one night," Beau replied. "I got to meet some folks in town. If I pay you, will you watch my pack and rifle?"

"You don't need to pay me," Alvin said. "Just tell me some more stories."

Smiling, Beau replied, "I'll tell you about hunting grizz over coffee in the morning."

The evening air was cooling off, so the mountain man dug out his buckskin coat and put it on. He took the loaded Colt Navy Revolver and put it into his waistband under the coat. His hunting knife was in its sheath on his side.

Alvin watched him get ready and asked, "You planning to kill someone? They'll hang you right quick if you do."

"They're just to make the bad guys think twice before coming at me," Beau assured him.

Walking back out to the street along the water, Beau looked out at the *Phillip*. Lights had been hung on the bow and stern. The whaleboat was in the water near the rope ladder, bumping against the ship with the waves.

Adjusting his knife and revolver, he turned up the street to find Carrie's Tavern. Several of the drinking establishments had ladies out front who called to the passerby, trying to get them to come in and sample their favors. The mountain man stayed to the center of the street and just smiled and waved to them.

Three young boys suddenly surrounded him, all talking at once and bumping him. Without hesitating, Beau grabbed two of them and shoved them

into the third. The boys went tumbling into the street.
Then like a flash they were up and running away.

Feeling around, the mountain man found that
his knife was gone! "Damn little buggers," he
muttered. A quick check told him that the rest of his
valuables were still there. Shaking his head, he thought,
Another minute and I'd have been standing here naked.

Carrie's Tavern was a weathered, clapboard
building with a full-length porch. A narrow alley went
down both sides, with one blocked by a picket gate.
There were benches on the front porch with several
ladies dressed to attract. It was evident that they didn't
have to hawk the customers to get them into the
tavern. Beau could hear music coming from the open
double doors.

Several customers were playing cards or at the
faro tables. Beau was immediately joined by a sweet-
smelling brunette as he stepped onto the porch. "My
name's Honey. Let's find us a table and you can buy
me a drink."

Most of the mountain man's money was in a
leather sack that hung around his neck under his
clothes. His spending money for the night was in an
inside pocket of the coat. He let the lady lead him to a
table. "What are we drinking tonight?" she asked.

"A bottle of rye and two glasses," he told her.

"I'll need $2," she said, smiling sweetly.

Giving her the coins, he watched as she hurried
to the bar. The bartender had slicked-back dark hair, a
thin handlebar moustache and a pot belly. Returning,
Honey sat close to him and placed the bottle and
glasses onto the table. Beau could feel her warmth

against him. She poured a measure into each glass and then held hers up to toast him.

Beau barely let the rye touch his tongue on his first taste. He had heard that the knockout drops, which were opium, would numb the lips and tongue. While watered down, the rye just burned as it should.

Suddenly he felt Honey's hand moving along his leg and onto his lap. Taking her hand gently, he put it back onto the table. "While your attention was very pleasant, it is a bit early in the evening," he told the lady.

"Maybe you are just shy," she cooed. "Have a couple drinks and then we can go into the back and get to know each other a little better."

As her hand started to move off the table, he put his over hers. "I am supposed to meet some friends here tonight. A couple of young men. You couldn't miss them. Kelly has red hair and Topper is almost white-blond."

He felt Honey stiffen just a bit. "That would describe several men that come in here."

Looking around at the crowd, Beau didn't see a single customer with red or white-blond hair. "Too bad," the mountain man said. "I figured with your keen eye they'd be easy to spot."

Honey, suddenly quiet, stared at her drink, playing with it. Beau continued, "The young men haven't had too much experience in places like this. They're crewmembers on the *Phillip,* trying to save up enough money to bring family west."

What he said was mostly true, but to tell her they were young and foolish would not have made any sense.

Suddenly, Honey smiled and breathed softly into Beau's ear. "Stay still," she whispered. "In a minute I want you to say no to me. Say it loud. I am going to slap your face and then knock the bottle over. After I leave, Ed will come over with a replacement bottle. Don't drink it. Make him tell you where the two boys are."

Realizing that it was her way to stay out of trouble, Beau played along. Pushing her away, he snapped, "No!" Then he received a ringing slap and his bottle went smashing to the floor. With real surprise on his face, he watched her stomp back out to the porch, thinking, *She is one hell of an actress.*

As promised, the bartender came up with another bottle, gushing with apologies about her behavior.

Accepting the bottle, Beau asked Ed to sit for a minute. Pouring a glass of the amber brew, he slid it in front of the bartender. "I want you to drink this."

Starting to get up, Ed replied, "I can't drink on the job. Just enjoy this on the house."

There was a loud click of the Colt being cocked. "You best stay seated. There's a Colt Navy Revolver aimed at your fat belly and you either drink this whiskey or tell me about two boys that was in here. One a red-head and one a tow-head."

"I'm just trying to make it right because Honey smashed your bottle," Ed hissed.

Beau poked the gun barrel into Ed's ribs. "One more chance and I pull the trigger. You'll have two or three days of a slow death to think about not answering me."

"Honey didn't say anything?" he asked.

"That was the one," Beau snarled.

"No! No! Please don't," the bartender pleaded. "I know where the boys are."

"I'm listening."

Ed's hand was shaking on the table. "Two alleys over, down at the end of it is a small barn. They were taken there."

"You go back to work, Ed. If anyone follows me out of here, I won't even ask questions before I shoot," Beau instructed him.

The bartender reached for the bottle as he got up. "Leave it," the mountain man said, "and when you get behind the bar, I want to see your hands."

Beau glanced around the tavern. Evidently the rest of the customers weren't interested in anything but the cards they had in front of them. When Ed got behind the bar, he stayed at the end with his hands spread out on top.

Taking the bottle that the bartender had brought, Beau moved to the back door and quickly slipped out. He was in the alley without the gate. He moved to the street, keeping in the shadows. It was empty except for an old man pushing a hand cart.

He let him go by before trotting up the street to the second alley. Staying in the shadows, Beau moved slowly along the narrow opening. In the feeble light from the crescent moon, he could make out a building at the end.

With the Colt ready and his heart pounding, Beau reached the small barn. The doors in the front hung open. Moving as quiet as a mist, the mountain man entered the barn. Within moments it was obvious that it was empty. "The damn bartender lied," he muttered.

From within the dark barn, the area in front appeared much lighter. He was able to make out two tracks leaving the barn. "That old man had them in the cart," he growled.

Beau heard running footsteps. Throwing caution to the wind, he cut behind several buildings managing to avoid the men sent by Ed before taking an alley to the street.

There was no sign of the cart. "The bastard was headed for the docks," Beau hissed.

He ran toward the docks, taking advantage of the shadows when possible. He passed two ships tied to the dock that had been loaded or unloaded that day. Stopping at the second ship he listened. There were voices. He could see the cart ahead.

Remembering some of the songs that the crew had sung while underway, Beau put on his best stagger and began to sing, waving the bottle of tainted rye he'd taken. As he passed the cart, he grabbed ahold of the wheel.

Looking down at the men who were getting into the whaleboat, he slurred, "Any chance of getting a ride to the *Phillip?*"

The old man hurried up from the whaleboat. "Get the hell away from my cart, you damn drunk."

The man pushed Beau and the mountain man staggered back, almost falling. Holding up the bottle, he offered the old man a drink. Ignoring him, the man grabbed the cart and started pushing it back up the street.

Suddenly, the two men in the whaleboat stepped back onto the shore. Beau could see the blond head of Topper laying on the bottom of the boat. One of the men called to him and they got closer. "We'd be happy to row you over to your ship. What did you say the name was?"

Beau noticed that they were separating to come at him from both sides. The mountain man began to laugh and stomp his foot. "What's so funny?" one of the men asked, pretending to laugh with him.

As the men got closer, Beau raised the Colt. "I was just wondering which one of you I was going to shoot first."

The moon light reflected off the threatening barrel of the revolver. The men stopped, one of them holding up both hands. "We were just going to help you into the boat and take you to the *Phillip*."

"Now you remember the name of the ship," Beau snapped. "I suppose you were taking my friends back to the *Phillip*."

The man who had remained quiet started to move around Beau's blind side. Stepping back, the mountain man fired a bullet into the man's foot. The sound of the Colt was deafening in the stillness of the dock.

The wounded man cried out, falling to the ground and grabbing his foot. At the same time the other man charged at Beau with a raised club. Ducking the club, the mountain man swung the Colt, striking the man just above the ear. Like a poleaxed steer, the man went down into the dirt.

Beau stood on the dock, his heart pounding, adrenalin racing through his veins. It was all he could do to avoid putting a bullet into the man he had just hit. Looking at the wounded man, he said, "If you have any weapons, you best toss them towards me."

The groaning man tossed a short club and a clasp knife in the dirt near Beau's feet. "We was just doing our job. Bert decided to take you along as a bonus."

The mountain man checked Bert over and found brass knuckles and a knife. What's your name?" he asked the wounded man.

"Warren, it is Warren," the man said.

"What ship were you taking the boys to?" the mountain man asked.

"The one anchored by itself on the left," Warren said. "It'll be going out tonight with the tide."

"Well, Warren, I want you to help me get Bert into the boat and we'll bring the boys you have below back to the *Phillip.*"

Still carrying the bottle and Colt, Beau followed the wounded man down to the whaleboat. Suddenly Bert's arms began to flail as he swore. The mountain man reached out with the Colt and gave the man a gentler knock on the head. "Behave there, Bert. I don't want to have to put you out again."

With a look of hatred, the man settled down. "Now, help Warren into the boat and row us over to the *Phillip*."

Setting the bottle against a rib of the boat to stop it from rolling, he took a seat on the spearing platform. As instructed, the two men started rowing toward the ship. At first Beau feared that the two boys were dead, but then he finally saw some movement from their breathing.

Once alongside the *Phillip*, Beau called for assistance to get the two boys aboard. No explanation was needed when the men on the ship saw Kelly and Topper. The bosun stood by while the boys were hauled aboard. Once done, he called down to, Beau, "I appreciate you watching over these young'un's."

As they pulled away, Beau reached down for the bottle. "I hold no grudge against you two," he told Bert and Warren. "You can share my bottle. It will help with the pain in your foot, Warren."

The two crimps both took a long swig. "Save some for me," Beau told them.

"You ain't going to turn us in?" Bert asked.

"Would it do any good?" the mountain man replied.

"No, it wouldn't," Bert boasted. "We pay off the law in Astoria."

"Have another drink and then give the bottle back here," Beau said, smiling.

Halfway back to the dock, the two crimps slumped down into the bottom of the boat. Beau took the oars and rowed out to the ship anchored alone to the west. There were four crewmembers at the bulwark waiting for the shanghaied boys.

Beau called to them, "I got your new crew here."

"It took you damn long enough," one of the men on the ship said. "Damn tide's just about to go out."

"One is a bit injured," the mountain man advised them. "He tried to get away and I had to stop him. He'll be limping for a while."

Beau tied the line that was tossed down around each man in turn and watched as they were hoisted onto the ship. There was a quick discussion as they looked over their new crew. Then a small sack with money was tossed down to the boat. "Tell Ed that the injured one was only worth half."

"That's his problem," Beau replied as he pulled on the oars, heading back to the dock.

The mountain man couldn't believe that he'd been able to pull off the switch. Evidently all the ship was concerned about was a head count. Whose head it was did not matter. Once the whaleboat slid up against the shore, Beau tossed the bottle into the river.

Clouds had covered the crescent moon and a gloomy darkness shrouded the dock. He walked up the street, watching for the narrow street to the livery. Hefting the bag that had been tossed into the boat, he did some figuring. He had planned to pay fare on a boat to Oregon City and then walk down to Jocko's farm which was located in a town now named, Silverton. With the unexpected windfall, he decided to find out if the livery had a horse for sale. He had a buckskin at the farm and could use another as a pack horse.

The mountain man felt no remorse for taking money for the two men. They had no doubt shanghaied many men in the past and it was only fair that they took their turn. Ed the bartender was a crook and would have to do without these ill-gotten gains.

The young man was asleep when Beau entered the tack room. Making as little noise as possible, he spread out his blankets and lay awake for a long time. The night's events continued to race through his mind.

CHAPTER FIVE

The ride from Astoria to Silverton would be four days' steady travel. Beau had made a deal on a palomino and a saddle with a scabbard for his rifle. The mountain man was impressed with the young man. He was a first-class horse trader and didn't miss a lick to maximize the deal. Little did Alvin know Beau didn't really care what the horse cost. He was happy to let the young man make some extra money.

After finishing the deal, Beau began getting the horse ready for the trip. Alvin ran over to main street to get them a meal from a local restaurant. The mountain man heard running footsteps as Alvin burst into the livery.

"You ain't going to believe what I got to tell you," he said, gasping for breath.

Beau was just tying the horse to a metal ring fastened on the stall post. Turning to the young man, he asked, "What won't I believe?"

Alvin's face was flushed and his eyes large. "Folks are looking for you. Twice I was asked if I seen a man of your description. They was offering money if I did."

"Did you take any money?" Beau asked.

"It was Ed that had them looking for you," the young man told him. "He ain't a good man and I wouldn't tell them nothing." Then Alvin smiled. "Would you tell me why they're looking for you?"

"Let's have some of the food you brought, and I'll tell you all about it," Beau replied.

After one more story about danger and intrigue, the mountain man tightened the cinch and led the horse out of the barn. "You best go around back of the livery and continue until you come to a creek. Follow it until you reach a road crossing it. Take that south and you will be far enough from Astoria and should be safe."

Beau left the livery leading the palomino. His wool cap was in his possible bag, allowing air to get to his injury. There had been $10 left in the sack after he paid for the horse and saddle. This he gave to Alvin for his hospitality.

The creek was about 10 feet-wide and had brush on both sides. A narrow trail ran along the north side and Beau continued to lead the horse. Twice he heard riders in the direction of Astoria and stopped to wait in some of the thicker brush. Once he was startled by crashing in the brush ahead and it turned out to be a black tail deer that was using the same path and had been coming towards him.

Finally, a road appeared in the distance. There was a log bridge across the creek that had been covered with a layer of dirt to make a roadway. The brush thinned to almost nothing 100 paces before the bridge.

There was a steep bank on the south side of the creek. His only options were to go back down the creek until he found a location which the banks would allow him to cross, or go out into the open to cross the bridge and hope nobody was watching.

The impatient palomino stomped and snorted, wanting to go and get away from the flies harassing it. Beau rubbed the side of its neck. "Easy, girl, we'll be moving in a minute."

The mountain man decided to use the bridge. Checking the cinch on the horse, he climbed into the saddle. Suddenly he felt very exposed sitting above the brush. He looked up and down the road for anyplace watchers could be positioned. Toward the town there was a large chestnut tree with a thick trunk that would offer cover for an observer. To the south it was about a half-mile before the road entered the woods. Between the creek and the woods, there were several clumps of brush that concerned Beau.

"Hell with it," he muttered. "Sitting here, I'm only giving them more time to get ready."

Tapping the horse's flanks, he left the creek at a trot and crossed the bridge. His back felt tight, expecting the impact of a bullet at any time. With what seemed to take forever, he finally entered the trees and slowed the horse to a walk.

The narrow road wound through the trees, avoiding the need to cut several large maples and firs. The late morning sun filtered through the trees, bringing out the bright green in the new foliage. Beau liked the seclusion of the forest. He was daydreaming about Jocko's farm when the sound of riders got his attention.

"Damn," he said. As he rounded a bend he saw two men. Both wore light-colored canvas dusters. One had a rifle across his front and the other's rifle was in a scabbard. Beau was sure that they also wore revolvers on their hips.

As they approached him, Beau called out, "Been hunting?"

The two men pulled up, taking a long look at the mountain man. One of the men spat a stream of tobacco juice. Wiping his mouth with the back of his hand, he replied, "Just coming to Astoria to help a friend find a sailor." The man was carrying his rifle and shifted it a little forward.

"Your friend ain't looking for more help by chance?" the mountain man inquired, trying to keep things casual and thankful he wasn't wearing the wool skull cap.

"His telegram just said us," the man replied. "Ed might be willing to pay you, but I can't say. Sounded like a small job."

"Well, I'm headed down the coast to do some hunting," the mountain man said, smiling. "I should be back in a week, maybe two. I'll look up your boss Ed and see if he still needs men."

The men pushed ahead, riding close on each side of the mountain man. Beau smiled and nodded as he tapped the flanks of the palomino. "They are a couple of tough characters," he said to his horse. "They'll be some upset when Ed describes the man he's looking for."

Beau decided that it was time to get a shave and haircut at the next town he stopped at. He would also get a proper hat, not the wool cap generally worn by those on ships. While he could change his own appearance, there wasn't much he could do about the palomino and he liked the filly.

Late in the afternoon he stopped in a small community called Elk Creek. After leaving his palomino with his gear and rifle at the livery, he headed for a building with a weathered sign advertising haircuts, baths, and a laundry. He was carrying his extra set of clothes, which needed washing. The mountain man had only had cold water bathing since before heading to see the white bears. And he'd had little of that.

The tin tub was filled with warm, soothing water and Beau remained in it until most of the heat had gone. In a room nearby his clothing was being washed. The owner provided him something that resembled a night shirt while he got his shave and haircut. His moustache with streaks of gray remained. For no additional cost, the barber removed the stitches.

"Will you be staying in our town long?" the man asked Beau, making conversation.

"Nope. Someone told me about some mighty big trees south of here. Thought I might go that way and see if the game is as big as the trees," the mountain man replied.

"I come up from that way once the gold played out in California," the barber said. "Them trees are damn big and tall. It would take five men to circle some of them."

Beau had decided to use the big tree story with folks he met just in case anyone came looking for him. It was dark when he left the shop. The clothing Beau was wearing could have stood a little longer drying, but it was either wear them damp or wait until morning to be able to dress.

He noticed that the light was still on at the mercantile. Stepping in, the store owner looked over. "I'm already late for my supper, but if you need something in a hurry, I can help you."

"A hat and a good cigar," Beau replied. "I got a new haircut and need a hat to keep my head warm."

Within minutes, the mountain man was the proud owner of a flat-brimmed leather hat. It had a leather strap to pulled down the brim in the cold, or to wear under his chin in a wind storm. The rounded top would shed the rain. The owner hurried him out and locked the door.

Nightlife in the saloon sounded lively, so the mountain man adjusted the new hat and headed in to test the rye. The men folk of Elk Creek appeared to prefer it to staying home. The tables were filled with cardplayers. The long bar was crowded with those trying to get drunk. A half-dozen ladies were working the room, looking to fleece those they could.

Squeezing in at the end of the bar, Beau ordered a rye. While waiting for the drink, he looked around the room. Lanterns mounted to the walls around the room provided muted light in the smoke-filled building. The plank floor was covered with sawdust. A husky man in a sweaty white shirt played the piano.

Receiving the drink from the red-faced bartender, the mountain man leaned against the wall and sipped the amber liquid. *They serve good whiskey*, he thought. He wiped the drops of whiskey from his moustache. Men continued to come in through the batwing doors next to him. Pulling the cigar from his shirt pocket, Beau used the lamp next to him to light it. Even the cigar tasted good.

Barely audible over the raucous crowd, Beau heard horses galloping along the street. Glancing out the batwing doors, he saw two riders wearing light-colored dusters go by. "I guess they found out who I was," he said to nobody in particular.

Confident that his appearance had changed a lot since he'd passed the two men, Beau ordered another rye and stayed against the wall. The buckskin coat he'd been wearing was with his gear in the livery. The longer hair and beard were gone and he had on a new hat. He realized they'd know he was in town. They would see the palomino at the livery. The mountain man had hoped that they wouldn't figure things out until tomorrow and he'd be gone from this town.

Adjusting the holster with the Colt Navy Revolver on his hip, Beau waited, still enjoying the cigar and the burn of the rye. He carried five loaded cylinders with .36 caliber balls in the revolver and he generally hit what he was aiming at.

The mountain man was sipping his third rye when the batwing doors were knocked open using the barrel of a rifle. The two men wearing dusters swept into the room with their revolvers in one hand and rifles in the other. One of the rifles had a long scope mounted on it for long range shooting. They looked somewhat upset from the long day of riding.

The mountain man continued to drink his rye, his head tilted slightly down, as the two men's eyes searched the room, looking for the man they'd passed on the road. Beau felt his stomach tighten as he anticipated the possible chance of being recognized.

As the man nearest him looked his way, Beau stared back with an unsmiling face and cold eyes. He hoped the smoky lanterns didn't show off his freshly shaven face too well. No sign of recognition came and the two men went into the room and to the other end of the bar, where some customers who wanted no trouble vacated.

Placing their rifles on the bar, they ordered some drinks, all the time watching the room. Both men spread the dusters open and put the revolvers into their waist bands. A hush had fallen over the room.

Tossing down his drink, one of the men addressed the room. "We are looking for a man that killed some people in Astoria. He's a tall man, beard, long hair, wearing a leather coat, and rides a palomino that was put up in your livery."

A murmur when across the room. "There is a reward for anyone that can give us information on this man."

Beau's heart was pounding. *Here it comes*, he thought. There had to be someone in the saloon that saw him. It was possible that the barber might even be here.

An old man with stooped shoulders got up from one of the tables and went over to the men. Whatever he said, Beau couldn't hear him. He pointed down the street, in the direction of the barber. The two men picked up their rifles and, pushing the man in front of them, went out of the saloon. Beau could hear the man saying as they went by, "I seen him. He went into Harry's."

Harry would be the barber, Beau figured. Already they might be thinking the beard was gone. To the back of the room there was a door that led to the outhouse. The mountain man had seen men come and go through it.

He ordered another rye and place a coin on the bar. "I'll be right back," he told the bartender.

Stepping out into the cluttered area behind the saloon, the stench of urine greeted him. There was a small building with a lantern hanging on a peg, driven into the wall. "Not too damn many men made it to the little house" he muttered.

Most of the buildings on each side of the saloon had low fences to protect their kitchen gardens from wandering chickens. It would be difficult to make his way back toward the livery without alerting local residents. The livery was out on the far edge of town and couldn't be reached without crossing the street.

Beau's plan was to get back to the livery and ride away from this town. The other clothes at the barber would have to be left behind. After snagging and tearing his pants several times and receiving scratches on his arms and legs, from everything from barbed wire to bramble bushes, he was finally alongside the building across from the livery.

The barber shop was just four structures down from the livery, and Beau could hear loud voices. Harry was shouting, "How the hell should I know where he went! You disturb a man's sleep with damn fool questions."

The discussion was going on somewhere inside the shop, so Beau took advantage of the empty street and went across to the livery. Inside the dark barn he tried to calm his breathing. He was sure the hostler had already been asked about him and might be willing to turn him in for the reward.

He could hear the horses in the back. The half moon came out from behind the clouds and cast a pale light through the open bay doors. In the meager light Beau saddled the palomino. Tying on his blanket roll with his buckskin coat, and settling the saddle bags in place, he picked up the rifle and thought a moment of carrying it before deciding to slip it into the scabbard.

He then put his possible bag over his shoulder and took the reins of the horse. He had taken only a step toward the bay doors when a voice almost stopped his heart. Grabbing the Colt, he searched for the source.

"Don't shoot," the man whispered. "You'll want to go out the back door. It's for cleaning the stalls, but your horse will fit through it."

Finally, Beau was able to make out the hostler. "I got men hunting for me," he whispered.

"I know," the hostler replied. "I figured you'd be back tonight, so I put out the lantern. I didn't think you'd want to be seen."

"I appreciate it," Beau told him.

"I've seen these man hunters before," the man told him. "With them there is no trial. They'd haul you back to Astoria tied over a saddle."

Before going out the back door, Beau reached into his pocket and placed a coin into the man's hand.

"I want to thank you, old timer. I hope you don't get in trouble helping me get away."

"Why hell," the hostler replied. "I'm going to take this money and drink myself blind at the saloon. I won't know when you might have come and skipped out on me."

Once outside, the mountain man led the horse away from the building. The moon cast enough light to see where he was going. A small stream ran across the back of the building and he let his horse take a quick drink. Then, swinging into the saddle, he rode south and then took the first road to the east.

Cautious of the horse tripping on the rutted road, Beau kept it at a walk. The gentle swaying in the saddle soon had the dampness of his clothing chafing him. Struggling to stay awake, he began to talk to the horse.

"You know that I lost my extra set of clothes. That means I'll have to buy new clothes or grain for you. Which do you think I should do?" Chuckling at his own dry humor, he patted the horse's neck. "Don't you worry. You'll get your oats."

A half-hour later, as Beau rode, his head began hanging as he half-dozed. The palomino continued to plod along the dark road. A mist started to fall. The sleepy mountain man's slicker was wrapped up in his blanket roll. When the larger drops started to pelt the rider and horse, Beau came wide awake.

"For crying out loud! As though I'm not wet enough already!"

Pulling the horse off the road, he stopped under a cottonwood tree. Swinging out of the saddle, Beau slowly moved around, stiff and sore from the ride. He tied the horse to some low brush and pulled the gear off.

Soaked from the rain and without a change of clothing, he sat against the tree surrounded by his gear and spread the ground cloth to protect himself and it from drops making their way through the leaves. While the new hat drooped a bit from the rain, it did keep his new haircut nice and dry.

Beau woke to a gray, dreary morning. The rain was lighter, but still falling. He shivered from the cold in his damp clothing. He could see the road from under the tree. He realized that the first thing he had to do was move farther off so anyone passing by wouldn't see him.

He unrolled his blankets and pulled out the slicker. Slipping it on, he figured it would prevent him from getting wetter. He led the horse well off the road and stopped under some evergreens. As he went back for the additional gear, the horse pulled hungrily at the wet shoots of grass.

After two trips, Beau had all the gear moved. He heard a wagon go by on the road, the wheels splashing though the water and oozing mud. He was please that he was unable to see it from the new camp. The mountain man was sweating under the slicker from the effort of moving his gear.

His breath came out in clouds in the cool morning, so he knew he'd soon be shivering under the damp slicker. Beau's fingers were stiff in the cold morning air. He searched around for dry tinder and wood for a fire. Once he got the flames going, the pine branches would burn hot whether dry or rain covered.

He thought about the newspaper in his saddle bags. Shaking his head, he continued looking elsewhere. He hadn't finished reading about the war. Finally, he found material for his fire. The effort of searching had helped to warm him up a bit. Striking the flint, Beau was rewarded with smoldering, crushed pine bark.

Feeding broken pine branches and pine cones to the flames, he soon had a crackling fire. He put the coffee pot on, using the remaining water in his canteen. Beau moved the palomino to another area, allowing it fresh grazing. After adding grounds to the coffee, he sliced a generous portion of side meat into his blackened frying pan.

Removing the slicker, he sat close to the fire. Beau's stomach ached with hunger. He realized that he hadn't eaten since noon the prior day. The smell of the frying meat made his mouth water as he huddled close, absorbing the wonderful heat. His wool shirt and pants began to cast off steam in the morning air.

The morning remained gray with waves of misty rain moving through. Beau drank the coffee and ate the side meat from his frying pan. As he poured the grease over his fire, he regretted not having biscuits to sop it up. While safe for the moment, the mountain man knew he had to continue away from the coastal area. With luck the two men looking for him would give up the search. Just maybe the miserable weather was a good thing.

Taking his time, Beau wiped the rain from the horse's back and saddled the palomino. He put his gear on and noticed that everything had a damp feeling. Putting the rain slicker back on, the mountain man climbed into the saddle. Guiding the horse through the trees, he headed back towards the road.

The road was a river of thick, dark mud. The only advantage was it would prevent anyone from following his track. He felt sure he was ahead of the two men. Even if they discovered that the palomino was gone, they wouldn't have been able to find tracks leaving the livery until morning.

Unsure of how far he'd gone the night before, he kept the horse at a fast walk. The only sound was the sucking sound of the horse's hooves in the muck on the road. A light rain began to fall again, causing water to drip from the ends of his moustache. Beau pulled the brim of his hat down to protect his newly exposed cheeks.

There was the repeated crack of thunder, promising a more severe storm. Water was rushing in a stream that ran just off the road. It was just a miserable day for man or beast. Squinting against the driving rain the mountain man began to look for a place that would offer protection from the storm. The rain slacked enough for him to see down the road.

All of a sudden, the palomino reared back, catching the low-spirited man off guard. Beau struggled to stay in the saddle as he fought to control the horse. "Damn you!" he shouted. "It is just thunder!"

Then the horse went down onto its side, sending the mountain man sprawling into the mud. Something smacked the kicking animal and then there was the crack of a rifle. The screams of the horse stopped and it lay still. Then there was another shot that clipped the saddle and whined away, barely missing Beau.

"Son-of-a-bitch! I'm being shot at!" he exclaimed as he rolled into the flooded stream.

Clinging to the bank, he searched for the source of the rifle fire. It was coming from somewhere up the road. He reached for his Colt and grabbed a hand full of mud. The weapon would be useless. He looked at the butt of the Sharps sticking out from under the palomino. It would be suicide to try and get to it.

Then the heavens opened up and a blinding rain came down. "I can't see the damn bastards, and they can't see me," Beau growled.

Crawling on his belly to the horse, he pulled at the Sharps trapped under the animal. Almost in a panic, expecting to be hit by the shooters, Beau pulled for all he was worth, bracing his foot against the dead palomino.

As the rifle came free, he scrambled back off the road. The chilling water flowed over his lower body and he tried to see through the rain. His hat had come off and was somewhere on the muddy road. Drops pelleted the top of his head and water ran down his face and neck.

The rain slackened, and Beau realized that he would again become a target. He pulled his possible bag up near his shoulder for easy access. He heard the mud splat as another bullet hit somewhere near him. There was a rocky ridge about an eighth of a mile down the road. It was the only cover in that direction. It had to be the source of the gunfire.

For a moment the rain stopped. Beau saw the puff of smoke from the shot as another bullet hit the mud just short of his position. "All right, you damn horse killers," he growled. "I know where you are."

Sliding back down the bank to give himself a bit more cover, Beau attempted to clean the mud from his hands in the stream. The Sharps rifle stock was covered with the dark muck. He plunged it in the water, rinsing off whatever mud he could. Then, reaching into his possible bag, he pulled out the wool cap. Keeping his eyes on the ridge, he wiped the water and remaining mud from the rifle as best he could.

He had seen movement on the ridge a couple of times. The ambushers were trying to move and get a better view of him. "I hope the hell the breech opens," Beau whispered as he wiped his hand on the inside of the cap and reached into the possible bag for a paper cartridge.

Working the lever, the slant breech slid opened. He could feel dirt in the action. Beau pushed the cartridge into the rifle and close the lever. The hammer had protected the nipple, so he was confident that it wasn't plugged with mud. Placing a cap, he lay with the loaded Sharps aimed at the ridge and watched for a target to appear.

There was the glimpse of the light duster as one of the men moved up the ridge, trying to keep low. Beau squeezed the trigger and the Sharps bucked, sending a bullet at the ridge. The man spun and disappeared. "I may have only hit close, but I got their damn attention," he told the lifeless horse.

Again, the rain came down. Beau had seen some brambles along the stream, a short run down the road. Without hesitation, he climbed up the stream bank, slipping and sliding in the mud. Gaining the road, he sprinted toward the brambles. He heard a rifle shot, but had no idea how close the bullet might have come.

Sliding to the ground near the brambles, he hoped they'd offer enough cover to prevent the ambushers from seeing a clear target. The flash of the duster had confirmed that the shooters were the two men. Somehow, they had gotten ahead of him. "Damn determined hunters," he acknowledged.

A bullet tore through the brambles as Beau reloaded the rifle. He found a narrow opening at the base of the brush that gave him a view of the ridge. He lay with the rifle ready. For a half-hour the mountain man waited with the Sharps loaded, watching for movement on the ridge. Just a quick show of a head was all he would need.

Then it came, someone was looking out near the base of the ridge. In one smooth motion, Beau put his sights on the target and fired. Fire and smoke belched from the Sharps. The mountain man had only a second to watch as the man fell forward before he moved, expecting return fire.

His heart was pounding, wondering if he had hit the second man. He had seen the one at the top go down with the shot . . .

There were running horses! Looking back through the bushes, he saw a man with a duster riding away, leading the second horse. "What the hell," Beau swore. His Sharps was empty and a target was in plain view.

Scrambling to his knees, Beau retrieved another cartridge and put it into the rifle. His cold, stiff hands fumbled with the cap for a second. He was bringing up the rifle when the man disappeared around the corner. Beau's brow furled. The second horse had come to a stop beside the road. Its wet reins must have slid loose from the ambusher's hand.

Standing, Beau could see the man he'd shot was partly exposed near the base. "One down," he said, "one to go."

Crouching, the mountain man ran up the road to the base of the ridge. He held the rifle at the ready, watching the loose horse and the bend in the road. Stopping next to the downed ambusher, there was no doubt that the man was dead. A good part of his forehead was blown away.

Beau needed the loose horse. Quickly he pulled the dead man's duster back to see if he had a revolver. The mountain man's was useless, being plastered with mud. The revolver was gone. Beau gasped. His first shot had been through the man's body. His partner had used the wounded or dead man to draw Beau's fire, allowing his escape.

"What a cold bastard," the mountain man snapped.

The mountain man's first impulse was to head for the horse. Then he paused. It could be bait to draw him into the open. He could see brushy Sitka alder all along the road beyond the ridge. If not completely giving him cover, it would make him a damn poor target.

Crouching at a run, Beau quickly entered the scattered alder. Doing his best to minimize the breaking of branches, he moved opposite the loose horse. There was a shot that cut through the alder brush near the mountain man. He dropped to the damp ground, keeping the rifle clear of the mud.

Crawling on his elbows and knees, Beau worked his way behind a fir tree. Looking out through the brush, he could see that the loose horse had run a short distance, startled by the shot. It was looking back in the direction of the shooter.

Using the fir tree as cover, Beau got up on one knee and lay the rifle barrel alongside the trunk. He watched for movement in the direction the horse was looking. There was a cluster of white birch. He saw something tan between two of the trees.

"What the hell, it just might be . . .," Beau breathed as he lined up the sights and squeezed the trigger. Black powder smoke obscured his view and he pulled back behind the fir tree. Beau reloaded the rifle and then, keeping low, he looked back around the trunk. There was movement near the birch trees. The man in the duster was crawling along the ground, away from the white birch.

Beau took aim at the man. He no longer moved and was in plain view. "The bastard is making himself the bait this time," he muttered.

"You're trying to make me come out in the open, aren't you?" he shouted. "I got my rifle on you and will shoot at the count of three!"

"One! Two! . . ." The man in the duster hadn't moved. "You are going to make me come out," Beau said, as he slowly moved through the alders toward the road.

The man in the duster lay about 50 paces beyond the other side of the road. He could be playing possum, holding his revolver out of sight. As Beau got close, a quick move and a shot would be all it would take to put a bullet into the mountain man.

Using the scattered trees as cover, Beau moved closer, the Sharps leveled and ready. "Let's see how still you can stay," he said as he picked up a piece of broken branch and threw it at the man. It bounced along the ground and came to rest against the ambusher's side. There was no movement.

"Well, maybe you're dead," Beau concluded, and he moved near the man's legs and prodded them with the outstretched rifle barrel. That was when the mountain man saw the blood trail from the man. He had been hit somewhere in the front.

Both of the man's hands were in view, so Beau rolled him onto his back with a shove of his boot. His chest and stomach were covered with blood. The man's sightless eyes stared back at Beau. The mountain man felt cold inside. He had no remorse for the man he'd just killed. As he went to collect the two horses, Beau wondered if he was becoming indifferent to killing men. It was not the kind of man he wanted to be.

It took most of the day to collect his gear, drag the palomino off the road, sort through the dead men's gear, and make camp for the night. His saddle had been in poor condition and he left it with the horse. Waves of rain continued to move through until late afternoon and then the sky cleared, allowing the sun to shine onto the dripping trees.

There was a town, about a half-day's ride to the east. Beau planned to bring the two ambushers there and let whatever law they had take care of the dead men. He'd found enough money on them to make it worth the town's while to do the burying.

He discovered clean and dry clothing in the men's saddlebags and, after taking a cold bath in the stream to wash all the mud off, Beau huddled near his fire and put on the warm clothes. He'd found his new hat in the mud near the palomino. He had washed it and had it drying near his fire.

Beau sat eating his evening meal of side meat and biscuits, which he'd found in the men's saddlebags. A half bottle of rye stood near the gear for later. He stared at the two bodies wrapped in their ground cloths. The men had been well-equipped, which was evidence that being a hired killer paid well. Smiling, Beau thought, *It had its risks too.*

CHAPTER SIX

The rutted road was filled with puddles as Beau guided the chestnut into the small town. He led the bay with their bodies tied over the saddle. The town was called Kuder Creek and was basking in the early afternoon sun. It was comprised of several private dwellings, a mercantile, a saloon with rooms, a livery with a smithy, and one clapboard building that housed town offices.

The town was a zig zag of planks that had been laid down to keep the residents out of the mud. At one end of the clapboard building a sign read: Jail. A man sat on a bench in front of it enjoying a chew and whittling.

Beau stopped at the hitching rail and asked, "Are you the law in this town?"

The man leaned over to get a better look at the bodies on the bay, then spitting into a puddle he replied, "That would be me." Then, standing and tipping his hat back, he continued. "Would those be the Brodie brothers you got there? I noticed you're riding their horse."

The sheriff was medium height, with a few extra pounds on him. His hair was salt and pepper and he had a thin moustache on his upper lip. There was a well-worn Colt on his hip that his hand remained close to.

"All I know is they are back shooters, and did their best to kill me a half-day west of here," the mountain man told him.

With doubt on his lined face, the sheriff replied, "You tell me you got in a shooting match with the Brodies and took them down?"

"Both shot in the front," Beau said. "They shot my horse out from under me and then did their damnedest to finish me off. They hadn't counted on the rain being on my side. A good part of the time, it was my only cover."

The sheriff walked over to the bay and pulled one of the ground cloths back to identify the body. It was the one with the head shot. Wrinkling his nose, he dropped the cloth and went back to the small porch at the front of his office.

"Why the hell did you bring them here?" the sheriff asked. "We can't arrest them for attacking you, and we sure as hell can't hang them. You should have left them where they fell."

"I didn't have a shovel, and I didn't want them stinking up the road," Beau replied. "There's money on them that will pay for a burial."

"Take the bodies around back of the building before they attract a crowd," the sheriff told him.

The mountain man rode around the building, leading the bay. Swinging out of the saddle, he tied the horse to a small tree. Coming out of the back door of the office, the sheriff pointed to a small shed. "We'll put them in there."

After setting the bodies on the dirt floor in the shed, the sheriff went through their pockets, retrieving the money. "Any more in their shooting bag or saddle bags?"

"That's the only money I found," Beau replied. He then pulled the saddle off the bay and put it into the shed along with the rest of the Brodie brothers' gear, which included their rifles and revolvers.

Looking the sheriff in the eye, the mountain man said, "They shot my horse, which was a damn fine animal. I figure they owe me these two horses they were riding and one saddle. You can do what you want with the rest."

The sheriff rubbed his chin for a second and replied, "Sounds fair to me. Come into the office and I'll give you something in writing to make it legal."

The office was small, with one cell that was barely bigger than the two bunks fastened to the wall. The sheriff asked Beau's name and then scribbled something onto a piece of paper and handed it to him. The mountain man noticed that the sheriff's name was Abe Sylvan.

"So, this here piece of paper will prevent anyone saying I stole the horses?" Beau confirmed.

"That it will," Sheriff Sylvan replied, "but it won't prevent their cousins from trying to even the score. The Brodies come from Westport way. I can give you a few days before I send word that these two were killed."

"How will I know them?" Beau asked.

"Well, they pretty much look like these two. Kind of take a fancy to wearing the dusters," the sheriff replied. "Albert and William here have been around this area a might, but the others only come through once looking for a man that killed one of theirs."

"Thanks for the warning," Beau said. "I imagine you'll keep my name from them."

Smiling, Sheriff Sylvan replied, "They will pay good money to get it."

Leaving the office, the mountain man brought the two horses to the livery. The hostler was also the smithy and had massive arms that were well scarred from the sparks of his forge. The man looked over the animals and asked, "Are Albert and William with you?"

A shiver ran down Beau's spine as he heard the question. Ignoring what the man asked, the mountain man said, "I'll need the horses brushed and fed some grain before I take them south."

"Will it be on account?" the hostler asked.

"No. I'll pay," Beau replied. "I'll need the horses first thing in the morning."

Before leaving, the mountain man asked, "Is there anyone that works on guns?"

"Cliff, the owner of the store, is a pretty good hand at fixing firearms," the hostler replied.

Leaving the livery, Beau went straight to the mercantile. Both his Sharps and Colt had dirt in areas that he didn't have the tools to get at. Cliff was reading a newspaper when Beau entered. The man loved to talk and told the mountain man that he'd get right on tearing down the weapons. While Beau listened, the owner talked about the war going on in the east, about Indian trouble in the west, and bragged about wheat production in the Willamette Valley.

Beau was able to buy some cheese and bread to make a meal while watching the owner strip down the guns. Cliff shared a pot of coffee and told everything one could want to know about the little town.

When the man stopped talking for a second, Beau was able to say, "I hear the Brodies come to your town."

Smiling, Cliff replied, "They sure do. They spend money too. Can't say that I like the way they get it, but they like to live high."

Becoming concerned about sticking around Kuder Creek, Beau asked, "How much longer on my guns?"

"Just about done," the owner said. "You know them boys keep a room at the saloon and don't even spend more that a few days a month there." Laughing, he continued, "They say it's their home away from home."

The mountain man was beginning to wish he'd left the Brodies where they'd fallen. He realized it would have made little difference. Everyone in this town knew their horses. Before leaving the mercantile with his cleaned Sharps and Colt, Beau picked up a few supplies he'd need. He replaced items that had been ruined in his possible bag and got enough powder to fill the powder horn and some extra to carry in his saddle bags.

His original plan was to have a few drinks in the saloon and get a room for the night, but he decided that there was no safe place for him in Kuder Creek. Hell, one of the townspeople might kill him for blood money if they found out he'd shot Albert and William.

The hostler was sitting on a stool near the big doors when Beau walked toward the livery. "You get your rifle and revolver fixed?" he called out.

Beau took a few more steps before answering, the mud sucking at his boots. "I did," he replied. "Cliff is a good man with tools."

"I imagine you'll be leaving now," the hostler said. "I brushed the horses and gave them a bait of grain."

"You got the chestnut saddled?" Beau asked.

"When the sheriff come by and told me who you brought in, I thought about it," he said laughing.

"How far are these horses known?" the mountain man asked.

"The Brodies worked out of Westport, up on the Columbia River, and didn't go too much farther south," the hostler replied. "If I was the owner of their horses, I wouldn't keep them long."

"I will be leaving tonight," Beau told him. "You can tell anyone that comes looking that I am traveling south."

"The road from here don't go south," the hostler replied. "I'll tell them you talked of California."

An hour later, Beau rode out of Kuder Creek in the dark. It was hard to believe a couple of killers like the Brodies could have such a positive impression on a town. Unfortunately, folks will overlook most anything if money is involved.

He left the bay at the livery, figuring that that would be one less thing to identify him as the man who'd shot the Brodies. The chestnut was a strong horse and could cover a lot of territory in a day. Four hours out of Kuder Creek, Beau camped near a small stream just off the road. He went to sleep thinking about Jocko's farm.

* * *

It was early June when Beau saw the white two-story house that Jocko and his family lived in. There were wheat fields on both sides of the road that would be harvested in a couple of months. Jocko also raised horses and had some dairy cows. His eldest son, Jon, helped him on the farm and he and Lisa had two additional children, a boy of 17 and a girl of 14.

Jocko was just coming out of the barn when he saw Beau. "Did you see the white bears!" he called to his friend.

Beau swung out of the saddle and tied the chestnut to an apple tree in the yard. "I did see the white bear," he replied, shaking his friend's hand.

"You got a new horse," Jocko said, looking over the chestnut.

"It comes with a story," Beau replied. "I'll tell you about it over a drink."

Lisa came hurrying out of the house. "I thought I heard you out here," she said, giving the mountain man a big hug. "I got a venison roast in the oven and pie cooling on the window sill."

Flushed and smiling, she headed back into the house, calling to their son Beauford to get more wood for the stove.

The front of the two-story house had a full-length porch. The two men sat on the handmade rockers with glasses of a lemon-flavored drink laced with tequila. "Tell me about the chestnut," Jocko said.

Sipping his drink, Beau replied, "This drink brings me back to the small Mexican town I met Ana in."

"The chestnut," his friend repeated.

Taking a deep breath, the mountain man said, "I killed the owner and his brother on the way down from Astoria. They were hired by a man named Ed who took offence to me hampering with his shanghai business."

"You killed these guys and then took their horses?" Jocko asked. "Sounds like horse stealing to me."

Smiling, Beau replied, "No, not stealing. It was done legal by a sheriff in Kuder Creek. The Brodie brothers shot my horse and then I got theirs."

"Brodie brothers!" Jocko exclaimed. "There's a whole damn clan of Brodies. They'll all be after you."

"That's what I've been told," the mountain man agreed, "and that's why my visit here will have to be short."

'Maybe you can swap it for one of mine and I'll send it south with a few I just sold," he friend suggested.

"I don't want to get you involved with this horse," Beau said. "It will only bring you trouble if it is ever traced back here. I'm taking it over the mountains and if the bastards want to chase me that far, they'll be buried a long way from home."

"You talked like there was another horse," Jocko said.

"I left the other one at the livery in Kuder Creek. I got my buckskin here and three would have been too many to travel with."

Lisa called the men in to eat. Gulping down the rest of his drink, Beau followed his friend into the pleasant-smelling kitchen.

After a hardy meal of roast venison, new potatoes, and greens, the men returned to the porch with mugs of coffee. Lisa put their pie on the small stand between the rockers. "There is more pie in the kitchen if you want seconds," she told them.

After thanking her, Jocko boasted, "The apples in this pie was from the tree near the road and stored in our root cellar. We made cider out of some of the apples, but that was drunk by Christmas."

The small talk continued until the last crumb of pie crust was eaten. Then, after a refill of coffee and a couple of cigars, the men stared out at the setting sun. Suddenly, Beau turned to his friend and asked, "What are your thoughts on the war in the east?"

"If it was closer, I could get more money from my horses," Jocko kidded.

"That you could," Beau said, and then there was a pause in the conversation. Finally, the mountain man said, "I am thinking about going east and join up."

"Why would you do that?" Jocko asked. "We aren't at war out here. It is their war, the easterners."

"Well, my home was in Arkansas," Beau said, "so I kinda feel akin to it."

Shaking his head, his friend replied, "You plan to go east and fight for the South?"

"I have been pondering that very thing," the mountain man said. "Most of my young life I lived in the South and that's the closest thing to roots that I've got."

"You are willing to die for slavery?" Jocko asked him.

"Now there is my problem," Beau said. "If I had never met Elijah and become his partner and friend, I wouldn't have ever thought what the war was about. I would have just chosen the side I grew up in."

"Sort of like the Brodie clan," his friend replied. "It don't matter that the brothers were man hunters and killers as long as they were family."

"Well, I don't want to think of it quite that way," Beau said, a little frustrated. "I'm not sure I could look through a sight and line it up on a possible neighbor."

"That's a better reason why you should stay out west and let them fight it out amongst themselves," Jocko pointed out. "That way you don't have to choose who you're going to shoot at."

The two men sat in silence for a while and then Jocko stood up. "It ain't something we can solve sitting here, but I got a bottle of rye and I'd like you to tell me about the white bear."

For two days the mountain man visited the farm. After several tough years starting out, the farm was doing well. The chestnut had been put into a back pasture to keep it out of sight and Beau rode his buckskin when going into town. He learned that Jocko's eldest son was engaged to be married in the fall. The men had talked of the emigrants they'd met on the wagon train. Jocko had lost touch with most of them.

Concerned that some of the Brodie clan might show up in the area, Beau readied the horses for travel on the third day. The chestnut was a better riding horse, so he saddled it and put packs of supplies onto the buckskin. During the trip east, he would rotate the horse he rode on to make better time and keep the animals in better shape.

Lisa came out with a gift for him to take along. Reaching into her apron pocket, she pulled out a book. "I thought you might like to read this on the lonely nights on the trail."

Taking the book, the mountain man looked at the title, *The Long Road West*. "I thank you," he said, "but I don't tend to read much during the summer. I save that for the long winter days when I'm snowed in."

In an almost scolding voice she replied, "Then save it for next winter. Reading it is like reading the story of your life."

Realizing she was speaking a bit harshly and it was probably due to his leaving again, Lisa spoke a bit gentler. "This book's about taking a wagon train west and it reminds me of things you and Jocko talked of. The author also wrote some other books about hunting in the mountains and trapping beaver."

"Where did you come by this book?" Beau asked.

"A newcomer that was short of money traded books and some other things at the mercantile for a few supplies. Our eldest son saw it and got it for Jocko last Christmas," she said.

"If it was a gift, I can't take it," the mountain man replied.

"Sakes alive," Lisa said, "we read it a dozen times over the winter and Jocko filled in some parts of the trail that were left out. He was the one that suggested I give it to you."

"I've never owned a book before," Beau admitted. "I want to thank you again."

Suddenly, she stepped close and gave him a hug. Burying her face against his shoulder, Lisa whispered, "You best come back this way, Beauford Levesque."

With tears streaming down her face, Lisa pulled away and hurried into the house. Jocko was watching them from the porch. He had a bottle of whiskey in his hand. "People are giving gifts today and I want you to have this to keep you warm in the mountains."

He walked down the step and handed the bottle to Beau. "The book she gave you was written by Walter Johnston. It pretty much matched our trip. I figure someone from our wagon train met this man and told him the story. Liking what he heard, he put it in a book."

The mountain man put the book and bottle into his saddle bag. Smiling at his friend, he said, "I will enjoy both of the gifts on my way east. Now I best be going."

Climbing into the saddle, he nodded at his friend and rode away, and like the times before he did not look back. Beau worried that he had stayed too long, and if trouble was coming from the Brodies it could be somewhere ahead of him. As soon as the farm was out of sight, Beau decided he would cut across and come out near the Dalles. He rode east into the Cascades.

The Cascades were beautiful, with wild flowers in bloom and grass-covered meadows nestled in between mountains. Beau decided he wouldn't think about the war in the east. Instead, he would enjoy the scenery that surrounded him. He was heading for Fort Laramie, and once he got there he could ask around what some of the soldiers thought. Maybe it would be over by that time.

CHAPTER SEVEN

It was late morning on a sunny June day when Beau reached the ruins of Fort Boise. With each thaw the spring floods would tear at the structure and wash more away. There was smoke coming from the stone chimney located in a portion of the fort that was on higher ground. It was either a squatter or a fellow traveler.

There was no sign of a wagon or any horses. Tying his horses to some low brush, Beau took his Sharps rifle and then put some caps onto the Colt cylinder nipples. Moving quietly, he walked the 100 paces to the fort. He edged up to the near corner of the building. There were the sounds of someone making a meal.

Slipping the Colt out of the holster, he leaned the rifle against the back wall. Looking around the corner, he called out, "Hello in the building."

There was a clatter of pots and dishes, and then silence. "Sounds like you got a meal going. I could use a might of food," he said.

There was the snap of a twig behind him and Beau wheeled around with the Colt leveled. "Don't shoot!" the young girl said. She dropped the short stick she was carrying and put her hands up.

"Where is your friend?" the mountain man asked.

"He's inside," the girl said. "I told him to stay put."

Lowering the Colt, Beau told her, "Call him out here."

"Toby," she called, "he wants you to come out."

Then, looking at the mountain man she begged, "You ain't going to hurt us, are you? We didn't know this was your place."

"I ain't going to hurt you," Beau assured her. "How old are you and where are your folks?"

He watched as a young boy came around from behind the wall. The girl moved between them, protecting the boy from the mountain man.

Gaining a little confidence, she replied, "I am ten and my brother is eight. Our pa was killed . . ." Her voice broke for a second. "He was killed when the mules were startled by a bear and went over into a ravine. Me and Toby were walking behind the wagon when it happened."

"What happened to the bear?" Beau asked.

He could see her tear-filled eyes as she fought to be brave. "It just come out on the narrow trail and then kept going up it. It weren't even after the mules or wagon."

"I'm going to get my horses," he told her. "You stay here and I'll be right back."

Beau felt prickly all over. Were the kids bait? Was the pa somewhere around, just waiting for a chance to take him down? The story sounded believable, but he had heard about kids being used to distract a traveler and then their folks would club or shoot the unsuspecting traveler and take everything he had.

The children didn't stay put. They followed Beau as he headed for the horses. Walking kind of sideways, the mountain man got to the horses. Suddenly, the young boy spoke up. "You ain't going to leave us, are you?"

The mountain man turned the horses to cover his back and faced the two children. "I got nowhere to take you." Expressions of fear crossed the children's faces. He added, "Don't worry, I won't leave you here in the mountains."

"How far back did the wagon go off the trail?" he asked.

The girl scrunched her face as she thought. "We just stopped to eat before it happened. We climbed down and saw that pa was dead. Two of the mules were still alive and I took pa's skinning knife and cut them loose. They run off before we could catch them. I was afraid the bear would come back, so Toby and I grabbed a few things and climbed back to the road and walked until dark. We spent the night here and I was making something to eat when you come."

The mountain man's heart softened as he looked at the two stranded youngsters. "Your brother is Toby. What's your name?"

"My pa called me Sis, but my real name is Mary, like Jesus' mother," she told him.

He looked at the two blond tykes and wondered where he could take them. Where would he find someone who would take them in? Deciding that was a worry for another day, he asked, "Well, Mary, do you have a meal ready?"

"We were going to have some hard bread and honey," she told him. "I forgot to bring something to cook on the fire."

"I was the one that made sure we took the honey," Toby piped up.

"That was good thinking," Beau told him. "Come here and I'll lift you on the horse."

The young boy's eyes were shining as he clutched the saddle horn. Mary walked beside the mountain man and asked, "Are you going to take us to Oregon?"

"Do you have family in Oregon?" he replied.

"Pa had a brother," she said, "but we never met him."

It turned out that all the girl had taken from the wrecked wagon was their hats, the clothes on their backs, a sack containing a pot, a couple tin plates, hard bread, honey, and some jerky. They also had two blankets still lying on the dirt floor of the dilapidated building.

Beau added wood to the fire and then sliced side meat into his frying pan. He sent Toby to fill the coffee pot at the river. Soon they were eating a satisfactory meal. Though he said nothing, the mountain man couldn't help but ponder the fate of the two children.

There was no way he was going to bring them back to Oregon to search for their pa's brother, because of the Brodies. If he brought them to Fort Hall someone could bring them to Oregon. With the war going on in the east, there were fewer wagons coming west on the trail. That meant whoever had the children could be charged with taking care of them for some time. With less business at the forts, nobody was looking for another couple of mouths to feed.

With the meal finished, Beau said, "I want you to show me where the wagon went off." It would only take a couple of hours to backtrack riding the horses.

He arranged the packs on the buckskin so Mary could ride on it, and he put Toby sitting on the bedroll behind him. Two hours down the trail, the girl called out, "Ahead near the bend is where it went off."

The drop had been about 30 feet. The wagon was on its side and contents were spread at the bottom. The body of their pa was trapped under the wagon. He saw that a cloth had been placed over his face. The slope was a combination of ridges and jutting rocks.

"I am going down," he told the kids. "You stay with the horses."

Retrieving rope from one of the packs, he tied it to a tree root and tossed it down the wall. Bouncing from ridge to ridge, Beau worked his way to the bottom. The smell of death near the wagon was strong. He noticed that something had been feeding on the mules. So far, their pa was untouched.

"I am going to bury your pa," he called up to the children. "I want you to pray for him after I'm done."

Prying the wagon box up, Beau kicked a crate under the edge and then pulled their pa clear. He could hear crying from up on the road. He quickly checked the man's pockets and found a folding knife and a few coins. Still tied to the wagon side, he found a shovel. Digging in the rocky soil was difficult, but he was determined to bury him deep. Despite the dry mountain air, Beau's shirt was wet with sweat by the time the chore was finished. Then, removing his hat, he prayed over the grave, making sure it was loud enough for the children to hear. As he finished he heard "Amen" from above.

Beau then looked through the wagon. Most of the contents would be impossible to carry with them. He found the children's clothing, a few personal items, a small wooden box with a clasp, some beans, and a bag of rice. He also found an older Hawken rifle and their pa's possible bag and powder horn. Putting all the smaller items into sacks, he brought them to the edge of the cliff.

"I am going to tie the sacks and bigger things to the rope and I want you two to haul them up," Beau called to them.

The children took instruction well and soon had everything on the trail above. "Is there anything special you want me to look for?" he asked.

"No," Mary said.

"What about mama's picture?" Toby demanded.

"Where was it?" Beau called to him.

"It was hanging on the inside of the wagon," the young boy said.

After removing most of the contents of the wagon, he found a small picture of an attractive woman fastened to one of the bows. It reminded him of Mary. "I've got it," he called to the kids, and he stuck it into his possible bag.

As he took one last look at the area, he caught a glimpse of something brown in the trees. "It could be the damn bear," he swore, "and me without a rifle."

Grabbing the rope, he started up, slipping on the rocky wall as some of the fragile ridges gave way. He looked back and was unable to see whatever it was. Gasping for breath, his hands torn by the rope, he gained the top.

Toby was pointing to something below. "It's one of our mules."

Frustrated at the scare, Beau looked where he was pointing and saw the animal. Then he shook his head as he looked at all the items he'd sent up. "I don't exactly know where I planned to put all this stuff," Beau muttered.

"We can help carry it," Mary offered.

A breeze from the valley brought the smell of decay to the group. Beau now had another worry. If the bear was still in the area, it could return at anytime to feast on the carcasses below. He had to get the children out of there.

"We need the mule below," the mountain man said. "I am going to pack the stuff here on the two horses. I want you two to lead them down the trail."

Then he looked at Mary's tear-stained face, "Did your pa ever let you shoot the rifle?"

"He showed me how to load it, but he said I was too small to fire it," she told him.

"Well, you just might have to be old enough now," Beau told her. "I will load the rifle and I want you to carry it while you lead a horse. If anything, that could hurt you shows up, I want you to aim and shoot at it."

"Like the bear?" she asked.

"A bear, a cat, even a mean dog," he replied.

She laughed, "A mean dog. I'd just hit it with a stick."

Without repeating himself, Beau had meant the bear, but he had thrown in the dog hoping it would prevent her from thinking too much about a bear attack. He showed her how the two triggers worked, and then the best way to hold the heavy rifle when firing. It would knock her off her feet, but it would also alert him that they were in trouble. Before he left, he also decided to show her how the revolver fired and how to hang it and the holster on the packs so she would have a backup.

"When I get back down, untie the rope and toss it to me. Then start leading the horses," he said.

Picking up the Sharps, he started down the wall. Carrying the rifle made the task much harder. Finally reaching the bottom, he saw the mule grazing about an eighth of a mile down the valley.

Coiling the rope and slinging it over his shoulder, Beau walked slowly toward the animal. He took off his hat and held it out toward the mule.

Looking up, it suddenly ran several steps away from him. The mountain man started talking softly to the animal. That was when he saw the second mule standing in the trees, favoring one of its front legs.

"This just might be good," Beau said softly.

After a couple of jumps away, the skittish mule finally stopped and then slowly came toward the mountain man, its head outstretched, expecting something good in the hat. It was trailing the reins and Beau slowly knelt and picked them up. "One caught and one to go," he said.

Leading the captured mule, he walked toward the one in the woods. His hopes of a second animal were dashed. The mule had a broken front leg. Tying the skittish mule to a balsam tree, the mountain man walked up to the second animal.

"You poor bugger," he said softly. "There is nothing I can do to help with the leg. It would be cruel to leave you here to be brought down by wolves."

Normally he would have just shot the mule, providing it a quick death. Doing so would only scare the children above. Beau slipped his knife out of its sheath. Taking ahold of its bridle, he continued to speak to the animal. In a quick movement, he severed the artery in the throat. Blood sprayed over the knife and his hand as he moved away. The mule brayed and went to the ground, kicking for a moment and then it was still.

Wiping the knife and his hand on the grass, Beau went back to the first mule and he rode it away, looking for some kind of access back up to the road. He finally found an area that had had a rock slide. Getting off the mule, he took the reins and led it toward the slide. While steep, the sure-footed mule followed him up. He was about a half-mile ahead of the children when he came out on the road.

The children hurried toward him, leading the horses. "You got it! You got it!" Mary shouted, while she struggled to hang on to the heavy rifle. As the girl approached him she said, "I heard a mule bray and thought it might have gotten hurt, but here you are with it."

Toby pulled on his sleeve. "Can I see mama's picture?"

* * *

Using what harness was left on the mule, Beau was able to load some of the packs. With the weight of the packs shared between the buckskin and mule, he then put one child on each. With a lead rope tied to each of the pack animals, the mountain man put distance between them and the tragedy of the accident.

The horses and mule were in good shape and they would be able to make more than 25 miles a day. Once, when Beau looked back, he saw that both of the children had managed to curl up on the packs and were fast asleep. He stopped near a small stream that cut across the trail about an hour before dark. Lifting the children off the pack animals, they both hurried into the brush to relieve themselves.

Normally, Beau would sleep under the stars, but with the youngsters he decided to put up a fly tarp. Pulling the packs off the animals, he placed them so they'd be partly protected at one edge of the tarp. The children gathered up kindling to start a fire. Soon they had a cook pot and coffee pot heating water.

The meal that night would be coffee and rice. Toby reminded Beau that they had honey to sweeten the rice. The mountain man would weaken the coffee and add a little honey for the children. While they waited for the meal to get ready, Beau got out the small wooden box. The children watched as he removed the pin from the hasp.

Opening the box, it revealed some money, a few papers, and a single-shot .45 caliber derringer and a bullet mold. Using the light of their fire, Beau looked at a letter. It was from Charles Allan to his brother Daniel Allan. It had been mailed from Portland.

"Daniel was our pa," Mary told him. "People called him Dan."

"So, your last name is Allan."

"Allan!" Toby said, nodding.

The other papers were receipts for the mules and some lists of items needed for the trip. Beau estimated that the box contained several hundred dollars in bills and coins. That he would count later. At least the children wouldn't be a burden for someone to take care of.

Once the meal was done and the bedrolls spread out, the two children said their prayers and got under the blankets. Beau sat near the fire, drinking the last of the coffee. He looked over the derringer, or pocket pistol. It would be the perfect size for Mary to carry. Soon he'd show her how to fire it.

The first real challenge came at the Three Rivers Crossing. Beau feared that the floundering horses' swimming from island to island could easily dump the children into the water. The youngsters remembered it from the crossing with their pa and their faces showed the fear.

"Crossing on horseback is much easier than with a wagon," he assured the children.

"Pa had trouble here," Mary told him. "One of our wheels was broken and the wagon almost tipped over."

She pointed to a cluster of boulders, "We camped there while pa changed the wheel."

The mountain man could see the damaged wheel that had been left behind. "I am going to bring one of the pack animals over first," he told them. "Then I will take each of you across on my horse."

Leaving the children with the mule, Beau led the buckskin into the river. While he didn't tell the children his purpose, he wanted to make sure there were supplies on both sides of the river in case he didn't make it across with one of the children.

In another month, the bellies of the horses would hardly get wet, but right now the water was halfway up the horse's flanks, with the current swirling around them. With the buckskin safely on the south side of the Snake River, Beau came back for Toby.

An hour later they were all safely across the river. It was the dry season and the lack of rain provided scant foraging for the animals. Game was scarce, so getting any fresh meat was out of the question. Despite the lack of resources, Beau decided to stop early to allow the children to rest. When they reached Salmon Falls there would be fish to eat and they could spend a couple of nights.

After wandering the nearby hills and collecting enough droppings for their cook fire, Mary asked him if he had anything she could read. Beau was surprised at the request and hadn't thought about the ten year-old reading. "I do have something, but tonight I want to show you how to fire the derringer."

Beau got the fire going and put on a pot of beans and coffee water. The beans would be their meal for that evening and the next morning. He then got the small pocket gun from the wooden box. With Toby looking on, he showed her how to load the derringer and he then fired the gun.

"Now you load it," he told her. "When you fire the gun, hold it with both hands. You don't have to aim it, just point it in the direction of what you want to shoot at."

While the bean pot bubbled on the fire, he had her load and fire the pocket gun twice. They then cleaned the derringer, put a measure of powder in and then pushed a .45 caliber ball wrapped in an oil patch into the barrel.

He would have the girl keep the gun within reach along with some caps. Should she need it, Mary could place a cap on the nipple and shoot, scaring whatever was coming at her, if not hitting it.

Two days later, they reached Salmon Falls. The Paiute were netting the salmon and had racks of fish drying. Beau made camp downstream on the river. Both children needed a bath and a change of clothing. He asked Mary to bathe her brother and get a change of clothes while he went and got some fish for their meal.

Moments later the children had their clothing off and were squealing and laughing in the shallow water near their camp. Beau tested some of the smoked fish while bargaining with the Paiute brave.

The sound of the children had caught the brave's attention. "You have the young ones now," the Paiute said.

Glancing in the direction of there camp, Beau replied, "Yes. I do have the children."

"Did you kill the old man that had them?" the brave asked.

Not expecting the question, the mountain man hesitated a moment before answering. "He was killed when his wagon went off the trail."

"You sell?" the brave asked. "I will trade you much fish. They would make good Paiutes."

"I cannot sell," Beau replied. Wanting to change the subject, he told the brave, "The wagon is three days' ride toward the setting sun. You will find many useful items there."

Beau couldn't tell whether or not the brave was interested in the wagon, but he figured he'd best finish the deal before the brave got to insisting he sell the children. He used the coins he'd gotten from the pockets of the youngsters' pa to pay for the dried, smoked, and fresh fish.

When he got back to the camp, Mary was finishing dressing her brother. Her hair hung in wet ringlets after a good washing. "Our meal tonight will be fresh salmon," he told the children.

The mountain man had planned to spend at least two days giving the young ones a break and resting the animals before heading for Fort Hall. Uncomfortable with the brave's offer to buy the children, he decided they would leave at first light. Once at the fort they could rest and with luck, he'd find a family to take the youngsters. It turned out there was $328 in the wooden box, more than enough to tempt someone to take the children.

After a meal of salmon and hard bread, Beau got out the book that Lisa had given him. "I will read to you until it is time to go to sleep."

"We haven't put up the tarp," Mary informed him.

"That's because we have to leave really early," he told her.

The children's bed was made up of a ground tarp underneath and one on top of them. As soon as they were settled down, it was time to start. Opening the book by Walter Johnston, the mountain man began to read to the children. It was about a married couple with two children that joined a wagon train bound for Oregon. The children squealed with excitement every time something was mentioned that they had seen.

It wasn't long before the tired youngsters were sleeping. Regretting having to stop reading, Beau put a piece of grass into the book as a marker and put it back into his possible bag. He looked toward the Paiute camp. They had all gone to their lodges. As the mountain man settled down, he kept the Colt close at hand, just in case the were visited by the brave.

Toby was a little cranky when he was woken up. The long day of riding on the pack horses was wearing on the children. The prospect of spending a couple of days resting and having the water to play in had been taken away and the youngster couldn't understand why.

After a quick meal of cold salmon from the night before and water from the stream, Beau got the horses ready and it was time to go. In an attempt to improve the boy's mood, the mountain man let him ride behind him on the chestnut. Pulling the brim of his hat down to shade his eyes, Beau led them east toward the rising sun.

Each night when they stopped, he and Mary took turns reading from the book. When she found words that were too hard to sound out she'd ask him for help. It was midday when they reached a plateau and stopped for the day.

Looking around, Mary said, "There isn't water close by and not much for the animals to eat. Why are we stopping so early?"

Beau pointed to the marker, "A friend is buried here," he told her. "I like to spend a little time talking to him."

"You can't talk to someone in a grave," Toby told him.

Chuckling, Beau replied, "You are right there, son, but I can pray and he can hear them in heaven."

"Like we did for pa," Mary pointed out to her brother.

"How did he die?" the young boy asked. Beau thought for a minute before deciding to give them a version of the attack that wouldn't give them nightmares.

"Are there any Shoshone's watching us now?" Mary asked.

"I don't think we have to worry about being attacked," Beau assured them with more confidence than he had, "but if they do, you have the small gun to protect you and your brother."

She patted the small bag at her side, "I'll be ready if they come."

With the memories of the attack haunting him, Beau spent only one night on the plateau. The next day they reached the Raft River and the parting of the ways. He pointed out the trail that wagon trains followed going to California. While he was smiling, his stomach felt tight. They were getting close to the narrowing of the valley called the Gate Of Death, where granite walls towered above the trail and any attacking tribes could fire down on those going through.

Fatigue was showing on the children as they spent the long days riding on the pack animals. Despite the hats they wore, their faces were burnt and peeling. While Mary hid her feelings better, Toby was becoming moodier. While he tried to hide it, he would often start crying as he clung on to the packs.

Beau had been watching for any sign of pony tracks prior to getting to the granite narrows, and had seen none. With game being scarce and wagon trains fewer, the Shoshone and Bannock were hunting in the mountain meadows or out on the plains.

They passed through the granite walls at midday. The mountain man told the children about some great water fall that they would be spending the night at. He told them they could build a large fire and read from the book as late as they wanted.

At that point they would be a long day's ride from Fort Hall and Beau was determined to get there. The children were tired. He was exhausted from worrying about them and taking care of them. They needed a good, structured home life so they could go back to being children and not additional baggage on the pack animals.

Just short of the American Falls, Beau held up his hand and shushed the youngsters. A small group of pronghorn were chewing on sage brush on a hillside. Beau pulled his Sharps from the scabbard. He always kept it loaded less the cap. Placing one on the nipple, he swung off the chestnut and took a stance, aiming at one of the lone pronghorns.

Smoke belched from the rifle as he fired. All but one of the animals sprang away at the sound of the rifle. Looking back at the children he said, "We'll have steaks for our supper."

CHAPTER EIGHT

The small party reached Fort Hall the last week of June 1862. The once great supplier to the fur trade, and then the emigrants on the Oregon Trail, had fallen to ruins. The army had abandoned it in 1856 and moved any valuable items to Montana. What was left of the fort was run by men trying to eke a living out of whatever fur trading was available and the few emigrants going west to get away from the War between the States.

Beau had witnessed its rise during the 1840s to its current condition. The fort would still satisfy his needs. They had basic supplies, whiskey, and possibly someone who could take over the children. The mountain man set up camp a short walk from the open gate.

There were several teepees occupied by Shoshone, Bannock, or Lemhi. A half-dozen covered wagons were camped just to the east of the fort, heading for California or Oregon. Spread around the area were small farms of local residents who had decided that this was as far west as they were going.

Stripping the gear off the animals, Beau set up a proper camp with a fly tarp and a fire pit surrounded with two logs he dragged over from an abandoned camp. Most of the trees had been cut by emigrants over the past twenty years, so he'd have to ride into the hills and drag some to the camp.

His plan was to spend about a week at the fort. They had grain that the tired animals needed and rye whiskey that he'd been without. With luck, one of the local farms would be willing to take the children. He had promised himself that it wouldn't be just any farm. It had to be a decent home for the youngsters.

Mary sat reading the book to Toby for the second time when Beau finished setting everything up. "I'll be going for firewood. I won't be gone long," he promised.

"Would you like us to help?" Toby asked. His mood had improved greatly, just getting to the fort and setting up a proper camp. It gave promise that they wouldn't be on the horses tomorrow.

"You just stay close to camp and don't be talking to anyone if you can help it," he warned them.

"Don't worry," Mary said. "I've got my gun."

Walking away, leading the mule, Beau shook his head. He may have created a monster. Within a quarter-mile, the mountain man found two decent trees. One was dead but still standing, and the other was a windfall. He returned to the camp with the trees and set to chopping them up.

Both of the children got up quickly and collected the wood and broken branches, stacking them by the firepit. Shortly after the chore was done Beau got a cook fire going to make some coffee. He also fashioned a spit and put the last of the pronghorn on to roast.

From the fort he could hear the sound of men making merry. While he was tempted to go and get himself a bottle, he chose to stay with the youngsters. Today had been a long day on the trail and he wanted to make sure they got to bed early and had a good rest.

While he was adding coffee grounds to the pot, Mary talked of being at the fort with their pa. There had been some men he had argued with and their pa had decided to leave sooner than he'd planned. Evidently talking about her pa brought other things to mind and she began to tell him about their mother and how she had taken sick. Her father had stayed in Iowa because their mother didn't want to go west when the rest of his family went. Mary let him know that this all happened when she was young and she couldn't remember too much about it.

With the meal finished, Beau walked the children down to a small stream so they could wash up. While they splashed in the water, he cleaned their supper dishes. He looked toward the fort. One side had been damaged by the spring floods. This now small stream had no doubt been a raging torrent.

He sat and watched the youngsters for a while and suddenly realized how tattered their clothing was. In the packs were a change of clothes that were in no better shape. Beau decided that he would get some proper clothes for the children before he talked to anyone about taking them.

It was dark when they got back to their camp. The mountain man moved a few packs around to make more room for the children to sleep. He tossed a few more pieces of wood onto the coals to give a little bit of light in the camp area.

"How long will we be staying here?" Toby asked

"I can't be sure," he told the young boy, "but it will be at least a few days."

Beau figured it made no sense in worrying them about being left until it was necessary. While he had began to get attached to the two youngsters, it would be nice to ride away and not have to worry about their well-being. And, he was convinced that it would be far better for them.

After sitting near the fire for a while holding his empty cup, Beau finally gave in. "I have to go to the fort and see if I can't get some grain for the animals," he told the sleepy youngsters. "I won't only be gone a bit."

They didn't answer him and might even be asleep, but he promised himself that he would make the trip quick. Checking the coins in his pocket, Beau headed for the fort. Just outside the gate, he looked back at the camp. It was peaceful.

The grounds inside the fort were cluttered with broken furniture and equipment. He remembered how neat it had been when the soldiers occupied it. The tavern door stood open and was dimly lit by a couple of lanterns. Men were playing cards at one of the tables, others leaned against a rough plank bar.

Beau stood to one side and ordered a bottle of rye. The bartender brought the whiskey over and looked the mountain man up and down with his one good eye. "Is that you, Beau?"

"It is, Shorty," the mountain man replied. "Remind me to bring some grain back to camp."

"Did you see the white bear?" Shorty asked.

"Yes, I did," Beau replied, "and I ate raw blubber all winter."

"I'd like to have seen the bear, but danged if I'd have eaten the blubber," the bartender replied.

The mountain man swallowed two quick drinks and then sipped on the third one. It warmed his stomach just right. For the next hour, Beau enjoyed the atmosphere of the small tavern. Shorty came over and set a sack down in front of him.

"What's that?" Beau said with just a bit of a slur.

"Your grain," Shorty replied.

"Damn!" the mountain man swore. "That's right. I come after grain."

Settling up for the grain and an extra bottle to go, Beau headed back for his camp, scolding himself all the way.

Mary was sitting up in her blankets. She had the small gun in her lap. "I've been guarding the camp for you," she told him. "Is that grain in the sack?"

* * *

The next morning Beau woke with a pounding head and a sick stomach. He pulled the blanket off his face and saw Mary building the fire. Noticing he was awake, she asked, "Can we have side meat and biscuits for breakfast?"

A feeling of guilt washed over him, adding to his misery. "Yes, I'll make some as soon as I take care of the horses."

"I got the bucket and the grain ready for you," she said.

"I'll need just a minute before I do that," Beau replied. "Slowly pulling one boot on at a time, he stood up and headed for the stream. Kneeling down, he scooped several handfuls of water and gulped them down. He then splashed water on his face, trying to clear the cobwebs.

Taking a quick detour to relieve himself, he headed back for the camp. Mary was patiently waiting with the bucket and grain. "I'm kind of moving slow. I had a bit of rye last night."

"That's okay," she said. "My pa used to come back from town late some times and he was always moving slow the next morning."

It was late morning before the morning chores and breakfast was finished. With his head feeling a bit better, Beau sat next to the fire drinking coffee. Mary had made up their beds under the fly tarp while Toby had found a stick that made a fine revolver and he was running around the camp shooting bad guys.

The men from the wagon train were California bound and hitching their oxen and getting ready to leave. It brought back memories of the wagon train he had led. Fort Hall had been much better equipped back then, but the competition for grass on the trail was much more severe.

Tossing the dregs out of his cup, Beau placed it onto a firepit rock. "Mary," he called. "Get Toby and we'll go into the fort and see if they have any clothing for sale."

She squealed with delight as she got her brother. As they walked toward the gate, Mary asked, "Do we have money for clothes? If we do, I want a dress."

"Your father had some money and it was enough to buy a dress," Beau replied as he walked into the fort, holding a child's hand on each side.

While the condition of the fort would be disappointing to any traveler, the store exceeded that. It carried some pants and shirts for men, some low heel boots, socks and long johns. The shelves had bags of beans, coffee, and rice. Most of the other items were dust-covered. They did have tobacco and peppermint sticks on the counter.

There were a couple of loafers poking through the goods, trying to find something they needed. The owner looked like he'd seen better days with his worn, stained clothes. His short beard was stained with tobacco juice and his greasy hair was in need of a trim.

Seeing the disappointment on the children's faces, Beau got them two peppermint sticks and sent the children out to sit on the porch. The owner watched them walk out. "The young'uns look like a couple of squirts that came through about a month ago."

"They would be the ones," Beau told him. "Their pa got killed in an accident and I was hoping to find them a home here around the fort."

"Hell, there won't even be a fort here in a couple years," the owner said as he spat toward a spittoon and missed. "There is talk of a stagecoach coming this way, but any new building will be done on higher ground."

"Maybe someone with a farm would be willing to take them in," the mountain man suggested.

"We got Indian trouble coming," the man said. "The army pulled out and folks are scared. You won't find anybody that would be willing to take on them children."

Picking up some tobacco, a bag of beans, and coffee, Beau left the store worrying about what he would do with the youngsters. The candy seemed to have done the trick. Both children were happy, their hands and faces sticky. It was evident that he would be taking the children further east and he wondered if he'd be able to find a wagon to make traveling easier on them.

Once back at their camp, Beau took the animals to the stream for water and the two children played at the water's edge while they washed. The mountain man marveled at how little it took for them to be happy. He gave them security, and the whole world was their playground.

Their supper was fish soup, using the last of the dried salmon gotten from the Paiutes. He and Mary collected greens to add to the pot. While they ate, two freight wagons with six mule teams pulled up to the fort. Shouts of excitement were heard from inside the walls.

Long awaited winter supplies had arrived. There were shouts far and wide beyond the fort as the good news was spread. "Looks like we'll be able to stock up on some of the things we'll need," he told the children.

"Will they have dresses?" Mary asked, her eyes shining.

"I don't think so," Beau told her. "Maybe some gingham to make dresses, but we'll be gone before that happens."

The mountain man watched the men climb down from the wagons. There was concern on his face as he noticed that two of the men had to be helped down and had bloody bandages. He saw people hurrying across the fields toward the fort. The wagons would not only have supplies, but also news from the east.

Once the meal was finished and dishes taken care of, Mary took out the book and began to read to Toby. Beau kept glancing toward the fort, wondering if he should go and find out what had happened to the men on the wagon. He didn't want the children to hear about an attack. It would only scare them.

He looked at the two children sitting under the fly tarp. "I am going over to the fort to see what the wagons brought in."

"I'll make sure Toby doesn't wander off," Mary promised him.

She sure was a little mother to the boy, Beau thought. The sun was low in the west as he hurried to the fort. The crusty store owner was trying to convince the anxious customers that they'd have to wait until tomorrow before he'd have the supplies in his store. Beau stopped near the tavern.

Shorty handed him a tin cup with rye. "The Bannocks attacked the wagons right after the soldiers left them. It was a run for the fort to save their skins. The teamsters had the Spencer repeater. It made it too hot for the Bannocks."

"The Spencer repeater?" Beau asked.

"The damn things hold seven shots before you have to load it," the one-eyed bartender said.

Beau was able to get an eastern newspaper. Its headline was about the battle of Chattanooga, which was a Union victory. It also spoke of the battle of Cross Keys, which Stonewall Jackson won for the South.

After a couple of drinks with Shorty, Beau headed back to the camp. He would come back to the store tomorrow once the rest of the goods were unloaded. He was thinking about the Spencer rifle that shot seven times before having to be reloaded. Then there was a shot. It was from their camp!

Breaking into a run, and pulling his Colt, Beau saw a man running toward him shouting, "She shot me! The damn brat shot me!"

The mountain man swung with the Colt as the wounded man went by, catching him on the side of the head and dropping him. Ignoring the downed man, Beau hurried to the fly tarp and knelt near the edge. Mary sat on her blankets with the small gun in her lap. Behind her, Toby sat holding his ears.

"I think I killed him," Mary said, a quiver in her voice.

"You didn't kill him," Beau assured her. "Tell me, what happened?"

"That man came after pa's money box," she said. "He said he recognized us and he'd seen the money box when we were here before."

Toby crawled to the edge and threw his arms around Beau. "Tell her not to shoot again," the boy begged. "My ears are ringing."

"Mary was just protecting you, Toby," the mountain man told him. "I'll make sure the man doesn't come back so she won't have to shoot again."

Taking a moment to reload the small pistol for her, Beau handed it back. "Make sure you see what you're shooting at," he cautioned her. "I'll be coming back in a little while."

In the moonlight, he could see her tear-filled eyes. "He scared me."

"I know he did," Beau said, trying to comfort her. "I won't be far away."

The man was groaning and crawling away when the mountain man got back to him. Grabbing him by the shirt collar, Beau dragged him to Shorty's tavern. "Do you know this bastard?"

The one-eyed bartender held a lantern up to look at the man. The front of his shirt was blood-covered and one eye was swollen shut. "They call him Tooley. He tends to hang around doing small jobs and hoping folks will buy him a drink."

"He tried to rob the children's money tonight," Beau told him. "He hadn't figured on the pistol the girl carries."

Crouching near the bleeding man, the bartender opened his shirt. "She hit him pretty good."

"If he dies," Beau said, "don't let the girl find out."

"I don't think we got to worry about the bullet killing him," Shorty said, "but it looks like he got a knock on the head. It might have broken the eye socket. He may end up one-eyed like me, only his brains might be scrambled."

"Well, I did that to him," the mountain man admitted. "You got some kind of sawbones around here?"

"Mrs. Yeager is about as close as we got," the bartender replied. "She can fix broken bones, deliver babies if needed, and has pulled a tooth or two. She was just working on the wounded teamsters."

Shorty called to one of the men at the bar to go and get the woman. He then helped Beau lay the man on a couple of sacks that were left on the porch.

Mrs. Yeager was a robust woman. Her husband had been killed by Shoshone a couple of years back and she got by now doctoring and sewing clothes for those who needed it. The .45 caliber bullet had broken Tooley's rib and lodged just below the right shoulder blade.

She was a rather coarse woman with a loud laugh. Dipping a rag into some hot water to wipe the wound, she said, "Should have aimed a couple inches to the left and I wouldn't have to work on this piece of trash at all."

"He is going to live, though," Beau said.

"More than likely," she said, "but I'm working for free here. The loafer ain't got no money."

Leaving her to do the doctoring, the mountain man went back to the camp to check on the youngsters. Mary was still sitting up, holding the loaded pistol. "I couldn't find another cap in the dark," she said.

Beau reached into his possible bag and got out a couple of caps. Sitting on the edge of the blanket, he handed them to her. Then he said, "You done good tonight. The bullet hit him hard enough to get his attention, but not where it would kill him."

"I just pointed and closed my eyes," Mary said. "He was so close that I couldn't miss."

"They got a woman that can fix shot up men," he told her. "She is working on him right now."

"The man told me that you were trying to get someone to take us," she said, her voice sounding weak. "Don't you want us? I been trying really hard to help you."

The mountain man's mind raced as he searched for the right answer. Suddenly, things became clear. There were very few choices, and only one made sense.

"I did ask if there was any place you and your brother could stay," Beau admitted. "It was mostly because I worried that the trip was being too hard on you and your brother. I now realize that there is no place out here that would be safe for you. And I would kind of miss having you two around."

She moved over and leaned against, Beau. He said, "I have to go east and help fight the war. The army wouldn't let me keep the two of you with me, because you might get hurt. So here is our plan. When we get to Fort Laramie, I have a good friend that could use some help running his boarding house. There is also a school where you can read lots of books. I am going to ask him to watch the two of you until I get back from the war. When I do, I'll build us a proper house to live in."

"What if you get hurt in the war?" Mary asked.

"If that happens, and I want you to know I don't think it will, my friend and his sister will keep you there until you are old enough to marry and start a home and family with some nice young man," Beau replied.

"Toby too?" she asked.

"Yes, both of you. Now I have to go back and check on the man." Beau walked away, realizing that he had just made a lifelong commitment to the children. Being as old as he was, he hadn't ever considered the possibility of having young'uns.

When he got back, Tooley had been moved to a small bed in one of the rooms off the tavern. Mrs. Yeager was washing her hands in a bucket of water. "I will give you some money for fixing up the man," Beau told her.

"What's he to you?" she asked. "If he is a friend, you shouldn't have dragged him here by the collar. His neck is bruised and he damn near choked."

"He is no friend, Mrs. Yeager," the mountain man replied. "It was my girl that shot him."

"You don't owe me for your daughter protecting herself," the woman said. "Shorty told me he was trying to rob some money from her." A flash went through his body as he realized what she'd said.

"I think it would make her feel a bit better if we gave you something."

"How old is this daughter of yours?" Mrs. Yeager asked.

The question caught him by surprise and he thought, *How the hell old did she say she was?*

"Is she a young'un?" she asked.

"Mary is ten and her brother Toby is eight," Beau said, remembering their first meeting.

"Ten is good," she said. "Your son is eight, hmm. I'll have to check on that."

"Check on what?" Beau asked.

"I got clothes that was give to me over the years when I made folks' children bigger ones," Mrs. Yeager told him. "If you got a need, I might have a few things that will fit them."

Appreciating what he was hearing, Beau said, "If you do, I can pay you for them."

The woman pointed to a cabin below the fort. "I live down there. Come by tomorrow and bring the young'uns."

"I will do that, Mrs. Yeager," Beau said, with a feeling of exhilaration going through him. Then a thought came to him. "If things go bad to the fellow Tooley, don't tell Mary."

"You don't have to keep calling me Mrs. Yeager. The name's Gertie." Laughing loudly, she turned and headed for her home.

The mountain man went to the store to see if anything had been put out yet. He noticed some books sitting on a shelf, covered with dust from lack of use. The gruff store owner was busy with two men who were going over a list if supplies they hoped to get.

Picking up the top book, Beau dusted it off on the back of his pants. It was a story about the '49 Gold Rush. He was placing it back when he noticed the author Walter Johnston on the next book. Its title was *Beaver in the Rockies*. Smiling, he took that one, figuring Mary would like reading it.

* * *

The next morning, the fort was abuzz about a young girl shooting a man. Beau avoided taking the children into the fort as they headed for Mrs. Yeager's cabin. They found her at the pump in front of the building, filling a bucket to water her stock.

Setting it down, she put her hands on her hips and loudly said, "So these are Mary and Toby."

In return, Beau said, "Children, this is Mrs. Gertie Yeager."

"As soon as I finish my chores, we'll go inside and see what I can find," the robust woman said.

"Can I do the chores for you, Gertie?" Beau asked.

Laughing, she said to the children, "It's nice to have a man around now and again." Then, to Beau she said, "After you water and throw hay to the stock, I could use some wood split."

The woman had two milk cows and a small, black and white piebald horse in the barn behind the cabin. There was a sturdy corral built on one end of the barn. A door on the back of the barn led to the manure pile. Next to the door was a wheel barrow, a fork and a shovel. Seeing that the barn needed attention, the mountain man set to cleaning the barn right after watering and feeding the stock.

He turned the small horse out into the corral and noticed a nice-sized garden to the north. A hoe and plow sat near a split log bench. Beau headed for a lean-to that held her firewood. He had split and carried several arm loads to the front of the cabin when the door opened and the children came out, each carrying a bundle of clothing.

Mary looked happy enough to burst. "I been trying on all kinds of clothes, but I only took ones that would be okay for traveling." Her brother had his clothing, but did not show the same excitement.

"What is it that I owe you, Gertie?" Beau asked.

"I am not sure," she said. "I ain't had so much fun in a long time."

Then she looked at the horse in the corral. "I see you put out Spot."

"I figured the mare could use some fresh air," the mountain man told her.

"The man that sold her to me said she come from good stock near 16 hands high, and would be a good draft animal," Gertie said. "She was just a pony then and I figured the horse would be good for plowing and dragging in firewood. She is hardly over 14 hands high and slight built, making her a little light for both."

"It looks like an animal that would be good for a lady to ride, or pulling a courting buggy," Beau said, agreeing with her.

"A boy up the valley rode her plenty," she replied. "She's as gentle as a kitten and about as strong." Gertie slapped her knee and let out a loud laugh at her own joke.

The mountain man's mind was working. He began to wonder, and then proposed, "I got a fine mule back at my camp that would work well for plowing and pulling. Would you be interested in trading?"

"I'd want to see this mule," she said. "I already bought one pig in a poke, and don't need to do it again."

Beau took no offence to her being skeptical, and the four of them headed for the camp. While the woman looked the mule over from top to bottom, Mary whispered, "That's pa's mule. What will Toby ride if you get rid of it?"

"Toby will ride behind me on the chestnut," he told her. "The small horse will be yours, and you will ride it."

"Really!" she squealed.

Returning from checking on the mule, Gertie said, "Sounds like you told her it would be her horse."

"That I did," Beau replied.

"I think you got a deal," she said, "but only if you let me throw in a saddle and them clothes are included in the trade."

Grinning from ear to ear, Beau told her, "You drive a hard bargain, but you have a deal."

By that evening, the animals had been swapped and the horse came with the saddle and saddle bags. Not an hour later, Mary was fitted to the stirrups and riding the horse around the camp. Her father had let her ride their horse back in Iowa and she was comfortable from a trot to a gallop.

Toby was a little put off by his sister getting a horse. Beau told him that he would be able to ride with him on the chestnut as much as he wanted. It seemed to satisfy the boy. Looking at the packs near the fly tarp, the mountain man knew they would have to get rid of at least half of it and travel lighter, hopefully faster, for the rest of the trip to Fort Laramie.

CHAPTER NINE

The sun burned down on the rolling hills to the east of the fort as Beau reached down to pull Toby up behind him. Anything of value that couldn't be packed on the buckskin or in the saddle bags was given to Gertie. Most of the children's old clothing had been discarded. The wooden money box was also left behind. The money and papers it contained were now in a leather packet in his saddle bag.

The old woman had confided in Beau that the man Mary had shot would probably not make it. Infection had set in and Tooley was running a high fever. The mountain man figured that was another secret he'd have to take to his grave.

Mary rode abreast of the chestnut as they left the fort. She sat straight and was smiling from ear to ear. Without having to worry about the children hanging on to the packs, Beau kept the horses at a trot. He hoped to be at the South Pass in two weeks. By the end of July, he should make Fort Laramie.

Every hour, Beau would let the horses walk for a while. He even had the children dismount and the three of them would lead the horses. Once while doing this Mary asked him, "Are we supposed to call you pa?"

"What makes you ask that?" he inquired in return.

"Mrs. Yeager called us your children," she said, "and when you brought the wood she told us that our poppa was finished with chores."

Unsure how to answer her question, Beau walked for a few minutes. Then he told her, "What you call me isn't as important as how we feel about each other. I would say right now we are as close as family and I think it is my responsibility to take care of you and your brother. Whatever you feel comfortable calling me is okay by me. Right now, I think of you two as my children. While I may not call you and your brother daughter and son, the feelings inside are the same."

Beau had no idea if what he said made any sense, and he never wanted to have to repeat it. Evidently it did satisfy Mary and she reached up and took his hand.

It was a sunny day when they reached Soda Springs. The mountain man had gotten a can of peaches at the fort and saved it for this stop. The children scooped the bubbling water into their mugs and Beau poured some of the peach juice in to make the drink special.

A small troop of soldiers were camped at the spring and were going east as far as Fort Bridger. They were attempting to keep attacks by the Shoshone and Bannock in check. The sergeant invited Beau to ride with them as long as he and the children could keep up.

The presence of the soldiers was a comfort to Beau. While there always was a slight chance of being attacked, the probability of having the horses stolen was much higher. Camping with the soldiers made the possibilities of loss much less.

Mary had been thrilled when Beau showed her the second book by Walter Johnston. Each evening after their meal, she would read to her brother. The mountain man listened, recognizing much of it as the type of life he'd lived in the mountains. One chapter spoke of a burnt cabin and the trapper finding the resident killed by Indians. Later, the trapper found the man's horse. A situation like that was very familiar to Beau and it gave him chills.

The mountain man figured that this author Walter Johnston must have lived in the west and lived the life to have written so accurately about it.

Fort Bridger had fared much better than Fort Hall. It had gone through its trials over the years, being taken over by the Mormons, having been fought over in the Utah wars and now back in possession of the army. The army had appointed a sutler to run the fort's store. Sutlers would often follow the army, carrying and providing supplies for them in more remote areas.

At the onset of the War Between the States, soldiers had been sent east to fight for the Union. Those now manning the forts and protecting the routes were local volunteers. The sergeant attempted to recruit Beau as a scout for the army volunteers. He told the mountain man that he would find a place for the children to stay while they were on patrol.

Beau declined, telling the sergeant that he was headed east to join the war. The sergeant told him he had a long trip ahead and the war might be over before he got there. Then the sergeant said, "You are going to fight for the North, right? You kind of sound like you're from the South."

Making sure he didn't create a fight right here, Beau answered, "Of course I'm going to fight for the North."

The mountain man had pondered which side to fight for since reading the paper in Astoria. He had decided to make his final decision when he got to Fort Laramie. In the meantime, he would answer the question in the least conflicting way.

Riding out of Fort Bridger, Beau figured that it would be two days to the Green River ferry. He would then spend some time letting the children and horses rest. It was the dry time of year and the hills were parched with golden grass and sagebrush. The streams were shallow if not dried up. The horses grazed on the mature grass during the evenings.

Beau managed to knock down a pronghorn, which gave them fresh meat. The piebald, which Mary had renamed Princess, was startled when he shot and gave the girl a bit of a challenge getting it under control.

Sitting in the lonely stretch of land, Beau worried that they would come into contact with marauding braves. If they were Flathead, he could claim friendship with Elijah, the slave he'd run with from Arkansas and who was now a chief in the tribe. Others would look upon their horses and weapons as prizes. He wished that he had one of the repeating rifles to discourage them.

The Green River, or Lombard, ferry was sitting on the western bank when Beau and the children rode up. Normally the mountain man would have swam his horses across to save the fare charged by the ferry, but with the youngsters it was out of the question. He was thankful that the price going east was much lower than that coming west. Most often the ferry returned to the east side empty.

By late afternoon they were safely on the east bank. "I know a place that we can do some fishing," Beau told the children as he led them downstream to the location where he and a wagon train had once built their own ferry, to avoid having to pay the high prices charged during the gold rush and having to wait over a week for their turn to cross.

The rapids beyond the bend were much the same as Beau remembered them. They set up camp very near where they'd built the ferry. It had been twelve years ago and nothing remained after several spring floods.

Beau rigged up two fishing poles for the youngsters and helped them bait the hooks with worms he found under rocks along the shore. After an hour of earnest fishing, they had enough cutthroat trout for a hardy meal. As Beau carried the catch using a branch for a stringer, Toby talked excitedly about the big one that almost broke his pole.

While the children added wood to the fire and cleaned the fish, Beau cut several green branches, to broil the trout. "Fish guts are awful," Mary said as she pulled out a long string of intestines and dropped them on the ground.

"They are," Beau said, "but think of how good the fish tastes after it is cleaned."

The youngsters went down to the river to wash their hands while Beau put the fish over the fire to broil. Sitting and looking around while waiting for the fish to cook, he saw some of the graying stumps of the trees they had cut on the other side when building the ferry. He remembered everyone working together and it still gave him a good feeling.

That night drinking the last of the coffee, Beau listened to Mary reading to Toby near the fire. She did an excellent job of taking care of her brother. He had never had a sister or brother to grow up with. Maybe that was why he and his father had been so close after his mother had died. That night he lay in his blanket for a long time with thoughts of how quickly life can change and how people adapt to survive.

Another day was spent at the river, doing laundry and sitting in the sun while watching the birds sing and the clouds float by. The area was peaceful, making Beau consider coming back here and settling down in the future. The thought made him laugh inside when he remembered all the mountain meadows he'd seen and had had the same thought.

The children were slow to get up on the morning of departure. "Why can't we stay a while longer?" Toby asked.

"We have more places you need to see," Beau told him. "There is even a place where a giant animal once lived. When it was attacked it tore a large hole in a granite wall and escaped."

"Like in the first book?" Mary asked as she rolled up her blankets.

Grinning, the mountain man replied, "Yes. Like in the first book."

As they rode, he told them about the South Pass, where on one side the rivers and streams flowed to the west all the way to the Pacific Ocean, while on the other side they flowed east to the Missouri River and beyond.

"I think we were there before," Mary told him, "but pa didn't say anything about the rivers."

"That's because your pa was too busy driving the mules and taking care of two little dickens," Beau kidded her.

The horses would be climbing as they headed for the South Pass and along the way it was dry and hot in the day and very cool at night. They traveled with their canteens full of the sweet water of the Green River, but the animals would have to deal with the tepid water holes along the trail. They would get some relief when they reached the Big Sandy Creek.

The heat of mid-summer created a haze that obscured the grander of the mountains surrounding them. To prevent the children from dozing while riding, Beau tried to point out landmarks and provide them with stories related to them. Despite his attempts, all three were lulled into a stupor by the relentless heat as they rode east.

Toby was sitting in front of Beau and holding the chestnut's reins while the mountain man rested his burning eyes. "Indians!" the young boy shouted.

Blinking rapidly, Beau squinted in the sunshine, looking in the direction the boy was pointing. Five braves were riding hard in their direction! Desperately looking around, the mountain man saw a cluster of large boulders to the south. "Mary! Follow me!" he shouted.

The three horses broke into a gallop, Beau clinging to the lead rope of the pack horse. The braves were bearing down and attempting to cut them off. The mountain man feared that their only chance would be to make a stand, short of the boulders, behind the carcasses of their horses.

He released the lead rope of the packhorse, hoping some of the braves might go after it. Beau prayed that it might be enough of a reward so that the braves would be satisfied and go, avoiding a firefight. The pack horse stayed close, refusing to be left behind. The Indians began to fire at them.

It was evident that they would not make the boulders before being cut off. Beau was about to pull the chestnut to a stop and start killing the horses when he saw a cut in the sage brush and sparse grass. It was a dry river bed.

"This way, Mary!" he shouted, and turned the exhausted chestnut toward the gulch. Sliding down the steep bank to the dry creek bed, Beau swung off the horse, clutching Toby under one arm.

He looked up at the edge, terrified that Mary hadn't been able to follow him. Suddenly the small piebald appeared, descending in a cloud of dust and debris. The girl was clinging to the horse's mane for dear life.

Pulling the Sharps, Beau climbed to the edge and peered over. The braves had been intent on cutting them off before reaching the boulders and that had sent them wide of the dry creek bed. Precious seconds had been gained to get prepared.

All of a sudden, the packhorse loomed near Beau, almost hitting him as it tumbled into the gulch. Sliding to the bottom, the mountain man grabbed the lead rope of the struggling buckskin. The pack had slipped over to its side. Pulling his knife, he cut the straps, letting the pack fall.

Pointing to an undercut close to them, he shouted to Toby, "Try and tie the horses there and then you stay put!"

Mary had already tied her piebald near the undercut and was running back with her small pistol in her hand. Unable to wait to see if Toby could handle the other horses, he dug a second box of cartridges from the pack, leaving its contents spread on the gravel. He climbed back up the creek bed bank and placed the possible bag and box within easy reach.

The braves had stopped for a moment, determining the best way to attack. Mary came up beside him, carrying her pa's Hawken, possible bag, and powder horn. Sitting below the edge, she began to load the rifle.

"I don't want you poking your head out," he told her. "When you get the rifle ready, hand it to me and I'll shoot."

Her face was a mask of fear as she replied, "Okay."

Glancing over, he saw that Toby was with the horses, still holding the chestnut's reins. "Tie it to something, son," he called.

Then, talking to himself more than to the girl, he said, "I ain't going to give them time to plan how to kill . . ." Without finishing the sentence, he fired the Sharps at the braves.

They were still a quarter of a mile away, and he saw the dust spray up as the bullet hit short. "Take your time, you dumb bastard," he scolded himself.

As if the shot was a signal, two braves rode to the left and three to the right. Mary thrust the Hawken in front of him. He handed her the Sharps, and took aim at the two riders. They were closer to the creek bed that cut to the east.

Lining up the sights on a rider, he pulled the set trigger, and then touched off the other. The Hawken recoiled and smoke obscured the target. The Sharps was thrust in front of him. Without hesitation, Beau aimed at the lead rider going to the right. He fired, and not waiting for the results he opened the slant breach and slid in another paper cartridge. Closing it, he placed a cap on the nipple and swung it to the left. One of the horses was down and the other rider was low over the neck of his animal.

Taking a deep breath, Beau aimed just above the rider. Pulling the trigger, the Sharps sent a lethal bullet toward the brave. The barrel of the Hawken appeared in front of him. Handing the Sharps to Mary, he swung the Hawken to the right. One of the riders had pulled away and his horse was walking. Beau again lined up on the lead brave. Firing, he reached for the Sharps, handing her her father's Hawken to reload.

The attack had broken off and the braves were pulling back. On the left, a riderless horse was trotting away. From the sagebrush the brave who'd had had his horse shot out from under him rose up, caught the horse's halter and leaped on, riding away from the creek.

Suddenly, Beau's stomach lurched. He didn't notice Mary handing back the rifle. To the east, about a half-mile away were 20 or 30 mounted braves. The mountain man's exhausted horses would never carry them safely away when the attack came.

"Keep shooting, poppa," Mary encouraged him.

The braves who had initially attacked them continued going south toward the boulders. The Indians to the east began to spread out. Suddenly, around 10 braves rode hard to Beau's right. The mountain man figured that they were reinforcements who intended to make the dry creek bed to the south, work their way up and attack.

What appeared to be their chief sat on a silver-gray horse, holding a spear adorned with golden eagle feathers. Beau heard Mary ask, "What's happening, poppa?"

"Come up and look," he told her.

She came up beside him and whispered, "Oh, no."

They watched the braves riding toward the right. It looked like they were heading for the boulders that the attacking braves had just ridden behind. "Will your rifle shoot that far?" she asked, pointing at the waiting warriors.

"I can probably worry them a bit," he said, "but they are too far to do much good."

"Can we run from them?" Mary asked.

"Our horses are tired, but we will probably have to try a run," he told her. "Go get your brother and bring the horses here. We can ride along the creek bed for a while and then try and find someplace to fight from west of here."

Beau watched as Mary went to get the horses. She had been a great advantage during the skirmish. With her help, he'd been able to keep a pretty constant rate of fire. With two different rifles, they may have thought there were two shooters.

Then the mountain man heard gunfire coming from the boulders. It lasted around five minutes and then all was quiet. Mary stood below him with the horses. She had Toby sitting on the chestnut. He hardly heard her when she told him, "The buckskin is limping."

A group of warriors appeared from behind the boulders, driving two rider less horses and waving something in the air. "I bet they have scalps," Beau said, wondering what he was looking at.

The warriors reached the rest of the braves and rode among them. Beau could hear the cries of victory as they milled around, waving their bows or rifles. The leader remained still on his horse, looking in the direction of Beau and the children.

"One of two things are going to happen," Beau told Mary. "Either their chief will come down here and we will share a meal with him, or . . . they will come, intent on capturing us." He had almost said "kill us", but the girl didn't need those thoughts in her mind.

Lowering his spear, the chief walked his horse toward them. The rest of his braves remained behind. For the first time, Beau felt hope. These warriors might be Flathead. If the ones who attacked them were Blackfoot, they were a sworn enemy and then what he'd seen at the boulders would make sense.

Beau told Mary to stay put as he climbed up the bank and stood tall, watching the chief. He set the Sharps rifle onto the ground in front of him and then held up one hand, palm out with two fingers raised. It was a sign of friendship.

The chief returned the sign and brought his horse to a trot. From behind, Beau heard Mary. "I have my gun ready and will shoot him if he comes too close."

"Don't shoot, Mary," the mountain man said. "I think this is a friend."

It was a friend. As he got closer, Beau recognized Elijah, his long-time friend. "I didn't expect to see you this trip," Beau told him.

"We have a camp north of here," Eli said. "We were making medicine before our hunt and heard the gunshots. They were Blackfoot."

"I was guessing that," Beau told him. "I thank you for your help."

Eli dismounted and walked toward the mountain man. "It appeared that you," he said as he noticed Mary, "and the young lady had them on the run."

The chief motioned for the other Flathead to join him and they trotted across the sagebrush and sat mounted, staring at the three of them. Toby had climbed the bank to see what was going on.

Pointing down the creek bed, Beau told the warriors, "There is another Blackfoot on the ground over there."

Several braves broke into a gallop, intent on counting coup on the downed Blackfoot. Elijah smiled as they watched them go. "Success against this enemy will give us strong medicine on our hunt."

While collecting their horses and gear, Mary noticed that the piebald had been grazed by a bullet while they were fleeing the attack. "She's bleeding," Mary said, worry on her face.

The bullet had just grazed the left flank. Beau dug into his possible bag and brought out the small tin of salve. "A man gave me this and said it was good for man or beast. I am sure it will fix up your Princess."

Beau and the children spent two days with the Flathead. Elijah talked of problems they were having with the government and the Bitterroot Reservation. He told the mountain man that the area they now were hunting on was no longer authorized, but his people were hungry and needed the meat this area provided.

"What if the soldiers come?" Beau asked.

"They will send us back to the northeast," Eli told hm. "If we do not fight, they shouldn't hurt us."

"I haven't seen many soldiers," the mountain man replied.

"They have gone to the war in the east," Elijah said. Smiling, he added, "They are fighting to make me a free man."

"That is where I am going," Beau told his friend. "Seeing you has helped me decide which side I will fight for."

During the stay they had conversations about the war, but also reminisced about their time together trapping beaver. Beau told him about finding the children. They watched as Mary and Toby played with the young Flathead children. Elijah's children were with their mother at the Bitterroot Reservation.

After the short visit, it was time for the Flathead to go hunting, and Beau needed to continue east. They swapped the buckskin for an Indian pony. The buckskin's injury was not severe, but the mountain man needed a pack horse right away and couldn't wait for it to heal. Beau also gave Elijah some powder and lead.

* * *

When the three of them reached the South Pass, Beau stopped and again told the children about the waters running east and west. He said it happened at the Continental Divide. They were now less than two weeks from Fort Laramie.

A few miles east of the South Pass, Beau took the Seminoe Cutoff. He was able to avoid several crossings of the Sweetwater River and the Rocky Ridge. The downside was its lack of water. With only three of them to worry about, the few springs available should be enough.

There was enough pronghorn to keep them in meat, and every few days they'd pass some type of trading post or small mercantile to purchase a few needed items. One night they camped with a troop of soldiers. There was a lot of talk about the war, and from the conversations it sounded like the South was having the most victories.

Beau no longer wondered if he'd get there before it was over. Little progress was being made by either side. When they got to Independence Rock, Mary and Toby showed Beau where their father had chiseled in their names. There were two wagon trains at the rock with intentions of continuing west until they reached Fort Bridger. They asked a lot of questions about the trails, grazing, water holes, and cutoffs.

The mountain man took the children to Devils Gate and once again told them the story of the large beast that had cut through the granite with its great tusks. Toby listened wide-eyed while Mary just smiled at their poppa as he told the tale. They were camping near the Sweetwater River and had just finished a meal of fish when Beau was looking at the golden grass.

"It must be mid or late July already," he told the children. "Soon the summer will be gone and it will be fall."

Mary had a look of surprise on her face. "That means I am eleven. My birthday was on the 12th of July."

"Mine is in February," Toby said.

Truly feeling bad, Beau said, "I wish I had known. I am sorry we didn't celebrate your birthday."

"Oh, pa didn't do that," she told him. "He said it was just another day."

The mountain man reflected on his 45 years. He could only remember a few times that his birthday had been remembered. "When I get back from the east," he told the girl, "you remind me and we will do something special on your birthday."

"Mine too?" Toby asked.

"Yes, yours too."

* * *

It took two days to ride from Independence Rock to the sight of the old Mormon Ferry. Beau stopped at the small cemetery and was pleased to see that someone had continued to take care of the gravesites. An impressive moss-covered stone marked the spot where Jon Scott, a friend who had drowned crossing the Platte River, had been buried. The mountain man spent only a few minutes praying over the grave before climbing back into the saddle and continuing with the children to Guinard's Bridge, which now spanned the river, making the crossing simple.

"Why didn't we spend more time?" Mary asked him.

"Bad memories," Beau replied. "I lost a friend and then there was this lady." He gave her no more explanation than that.

Fort Laramie was unusually still in the midday sun when the three tired travelers rode in. With so many of the soldiers sent to fight in the east, the place was manned with a limited number of volunteers. Two men on guard duty near the open main gate watched the mountain man ride by.

One of them shouted, "If you're here to join up, I can take you to see the major."

Road weary and dust-covered, Beau ignored the offer and continued toward the Buffalo Hide Saloon. Stopping at the front, he lowered Toby to the ground and then swung down to help Mary. The door of the saloon opened and the mountain man looked up and smiled at his old friend Louie.

The owner looked at the three of them and asked, "Is that you, Beau?"

"It is, my friend," he replied. "We are tired, dirty, and hungry, and damn glad to be here."

Louie turned and called to his sister, "Lucy, we got company."

The owner took them straight through the saloon to the back. It was part of his and his sister's living quarters. Lucy followed them in and looked at the children. "Who have we here?"

Before Beau could answer, the young girl replied, "I am Mary, and this is my brother Toby."

"I'm Lucy," she told the children. "Why don't you come with me? I've got something for you to drink and then I'll let you clean up a bit."

Louie picked up a decanter and poured a drink for Beau and himself. "It is good to see you again. Your last trip here you talked of going to see some white bears. Looks to me like you found a couple of blond young'uns."

Tasting the brandy that the owner had poured, Beau replied, "I did see the white bear. The children were unexpected."

Beau told the grizzled, old saloon owner about finding the children and then about his need to find a place for them to stay while he went east to join the war.

Shaking his head, Louie told him, "Taking on the children, that is something I'd have to talk to Lucy about." The owner's brow furled and he looked at Beau. "What if you don't come back from the war?"

"Would it be so bad watching the young ones grow up?" the mountain man asked. Then he added, "I do have full intentions of coming back when the war is over."

Louie poured them a second drink. "Why don't you just stay here and join the volunteers? They need men and you would be helping with the war."

"It wouldn't be the same, staying here," Beau told his friend. "Going east is something I got to do. The children have some money to help pay for their keep. I'll save up my army pay and give you whatever additional is owed when I get back."

A flash of anger went across the grizzled man's face. Then he took a deep breath. "It isn't money I'm worried about. Lucy and I aren't that young anymore. If something happens to us and you don't make it back, what happens to the youngsters?"

"All good concerns," Beau replied. "Is it okay if I talk to Lucy and see what she says?"

Avoiding answering the question, Louie said, "Let me get a hot bath going for you. Leave your gear on the back porch and put your horses in the livery. Later, we'll talk to Lucy."

Leaving the saloon, Beau's stomach was tight. He wasn't sure how much of it was hunger and how much was worry. He hadn't thought that Louie and Lucy might not take the children while he was gone.

Leaving the saddle bags and items from the pack horse that they'd need, he led the horses across the open ground toward the livery. He looked at what remained of Louie's trading post. Little was left, other than stones that had been part of the foundation and a sagging shack that had been located at the back of the

154

original building. When Fort William had closed and Fort John on the Laramie had been built, Louie had closed his trading post. Now it was just called Fort Laramie.

When he finished with the horses, Beau went to Louie's boarding house, which had the bathing area. He could hear the children with Lucy in another room. Stripping off his clothing, Beau climbed into the metal tub and sank down into the warm water.

The brandy and the days of riding had their effect on him and he began to doze. The closing of a door woke him with a start. Confused for a moment, he looked around and saw that his dirty clothing was gone and clean ones had taken their place. Unsure of how long he'd dozed, Beau began to wash. It could not have been too long, because the water was still warm.

The mountain man dried off with a towel near the tub and then pulled on the clean, itchy long johns. There were some pants made from a canvas-type material and a wool shirt. Once dressed, he looked in the mirror at his scruffy beard and unruly hair. He'd have to see the barber at the fort.

In the next room he found the children impatiently waiting for him, all cleaned up. "What took you so long?" Toby asked. "We're starving."

Taking their hands, Beau replied, "Let's go see what Miss Lucy has for us to eat."

Louie was busy behind the bar with some customers while Beau sat eating with the children. The saloon was almost out of place for a frontier establishment. Its furnishings and dishes had been shipped in from the east. The bar was polished wood with a brass foot rail. The lanterns kept the room well-lit, displaying painting and other items hanging on the walls.

Lucy brought Beau some coffee and then poured a cup for herself. Taking a seat, she grinned at the mountain man. "Mary told me you would like to have them visit me for a while."

The mountain man needn't have worried about leaving the children with Lucy. It turned out she was thrilled at having them around. Beau told her about the money their father had had and insisted on leaving it with her.

After a couple of days enjoying Louie's hospitality and giving the children time to get to know him and Lucy, Beau went to the fort to find out about going east and joining up. He had read the newspapers that Louie had to catch up on what was happening in the war.

The major welcomed the mountain man with a broad smile. "I am Major Henry and I understand you are looking to join up."

"I want to join an outfit fighting in the east," Beau told him.

A flash of disappointment crossed his face, before he once again smiled. "You don't have to go all the way east to help," the major said. "You can do so right here at Fort Laramie."

"Quite frankly, major," Beau replied, "I intend to go east. The war won't come this way even if the North was to lose. I aim to be east to help them win."

Like any good recruiter, the major did his best to convince Beau that defending the frontier was as important as fighting back east. Standing firm to all of the reasons for staying that the major could come up with, it was finally decided that Beau would go east to Missouri with the next morning's troop detail, then take a train east to wherever the army decided to send him.

Both of the children were teary eyed as the mountain man told them he was leaving. Mary said, "You promised to come back for one of my next birthdays, poppa."

"I will do that," he told the girl. They both knew it wouldn't be the next one, but hopefully too many wouldn't go by before he was back.

He tucked them both into their bed in what would be their home for the foreseeable future, then went down to have one more drink with Louie. It was unexpected, but his throat hurt and his eyes began to sting as he left their room.

CHAPTER TEN

Beau and six other men rode in a crowded stagecoach on the way to the war. Two were already in the army and had requested a transfer from Fort Laramie. Beau and the other three had had a quick swearing in by the major. The mountain man had left the chestnut with Louie. Had he kept it with him, the army would have most likely taken it from him. He did keep his Sharps and Colt.

The stage would take them to St. Joseph, Missouri, where they'd be assigned to a regiment after some quick training. Most of their training would be done by the regiment they were sent to, depending on their needs and any special skills a soldier might have.

The stagecoach could travel about 60 to 70 miles a day and would take 10 days to reach their destination. The men had to endure the constant jostling, dust, and heat. Each night they spent at a stage station, which could be a finely built home or a rough soddy. The recruits were instructed to sleep under the stars or in the barns, leaving the more comfortable quarters to the officers or civilians.

The stage had just forded the South Platte River and pulled up to a station to swap horses. The men climbed out of the coach to stretch their legs. Needing some exercise, Beau helped with harnessing the fresh team. The driver of the stage was Bob Whalen and the man riding shotgun went by Lolly.

Rubbing his sore bottom, Beau asked the driver, "Would you mind if I rode on top of the stage?"

Laughing, Bob told him, "It ain't any softer on that coach roof, but you are welcome to climb up if you want."

Lolly rolled his chaw and spat. "If you are asking to ride up there so you can slip off when we ain't looking and run from your oath, I'd have to shoot you."

Taken aback by the statement for a second, Beau realized the man was kidding and the three of them got a good chuckle.

While it was even more uncomfortable on the stagecoach roof, being intertwined with the luggage, mail, and packages that wouldn't fit into the boot, Beau was happy to have the wind blowing in his face. He lay on his back, using his possible bag for a pillow and looked up at the clouds floating across the blue sky.

He thought about what Lolly had kidded him about. The truth was, he had given an oath to stay in the army for three years or the end of the war, whichever came first. Now if he changed his mind decided to go back out west, he would be a deserter and could be put in prison, hung or shot.

Beau had no intention of shirking his duty to the army, but he now fully realized he'd given up his freedom for three years. Vivid memories came back of working off the contract in Arkansas and being under the cruelty of the boss man Angus. Suddenly Beau thought about the wanted posters for him and Elijah that Angus had posted everywhere. He had been wanted for attempted murder of the mean boss and Eli for being a runaway slave. Smiling, Beau figured that it had been over 20 years since he'd left Arkansas. Enough time had passed to not have to worry about them.

A shout from the driver and the crack of the whip over the horses brought Beau out of his daydream and he sat upright. Lolly had his shotgun to his shoulder and was staring to his left, behind the stagecoach. The coach bounced severely on the rut covered road as the horses broke into a full gallop.

Closing quickly were over a dozen riders who had come up from below a rise near the river. At first Beau assumed that they were Indians, but, clinging to the roof rail, he got a good look and realized that they were holdup men intent on taking over the stage.

Lolly yelled at Beau, "Best keep your head down! We got raiders coming after our cargo!"

"You carrying gold on this damn stage?" the mountain man hollered back.

"Hell no!" the driver shouted. "We got Union soldiers they're looking to kill."

Beau realized that he was seeing his first Confederate soldiers. And if they weren't soldiers, they sure as hell were fighting for the South. The mountain man had heard about raiders working out of Missouri and Kansas, stirring up trouble. Many weren't soldiers, just sympathizers.

Lying on his stomach, keeping his balance by spreading his legs, Beau loaded the Sharps. The raiders began to shoot. The stagecoach, being a big target, was easy to hit. The mountain man heard bullets whining off as they clipped the coach.

"As soon as they get closer, they'll take down some of our horses!" Lolly shouted. "Then they'll sit out of range of our guns and pick us off with their rifles."

The mountain man realized that a few of the men inside the coach had revolvers, and one had an older muzzle loader. Lolly's shotgun had a limited range. Beau could see the glee on the faces of the pursuers and he lined up his sight on the closest rider.

Squeezing the trigger, he felt the familiar recoil of the rifle. The rocking of the coach caused him to miss his target, but a rider just to the left went down. Quickly Beau reloaded and fired again. One more rider went down, causing two horses behind him to pull away from the group.

The mountain man continued to fire along with an occasional shot from the muzzle loader in the coach. After firing several times, two horses had gone down, and three riders had been knocked out of the saddle. The remaining riders pulled up. Despite the distance, someone in the stagecoach emptied a revolver in the raiders' direction.

After letting the horse run for a couple more minutes, the driver slowed them to a walk. The raiders were now a mile back and had turned to help their injured comrades. Bob turned to look at Beau. "I sure as hell wouldn't want to be no Confederate when you're doing the shooting."

Lolly was muttering, "Got to get me a damn rifle."

"If they have been sending unarmed recruits from the west, you best convince the army to arm the men, even if the rifles travel back and forth each time," Beau suggested. "The South has brought the war to Nebraska and you got to let the men defend themselves."

"I think they been worrying that if the stage was held up, the raiders would end up with the rifles," Bob said.

"Yes," the mountain man replied, "and the recruits would be dead."

* * *

A smiling sergeant was waiting for them when they reached St. Joseph late in the morning. Beau tried to brush some of the dust off his new shirt and pants when the sergeant told him, "You're wasting your time, recruit. The first thing the army gives you is a fine uniform."

Being 45 years-old and listening to a 25-year-old sergeant call him a recruit kind of went against the grain for the mountain man. He bit his tongue and followed the sergeant past the stage station to an old wooden building. One end had an area that appeared to be a wash room. Several tubs of cold water had dippers hanging on the side and bars of soap sat on raised platforms. The wooden floor had holes drilled in it to allow water to run out.

"Strip down and scrub yourself good. There are razors and scissors to trim and shave with near the mirror. Keep your long johns and shoes. Then meet me in the next room for your uniform," the sergeant barked at the recruits.

After removing his clothing and folding them on a bench, Beau placed his possible bag and hat on top. His blanket and ground cover, the Colt in its holster, his rifle, and his boots were placed next to them. Filling a bucket with the cold water, the mountain man began to wash up. The bar of soap had a strong lye smell to it and all but took the skin off as he washed himself. He looked around and saw no towels.

The mountain man walked up to the mirror and drip dried while hacking away at his beard and hair. Looking at the results, he muttered, "Good enough for these bastards."

While pulling on his long johns one of the other recruits commented, "You must have done a might of fighting already. You got all kinds of scars."

Looking at the young man, he replied, "If you live long enough, you will have them too."

Men clad in their long johns began to file into the other room. Beau looked at his gear sitting near the bench and went back to get the possible bag, blanket roll, Colt, and rifle. After a moment's hesitation, he picked up the hat and put it firmly on his head.

The mountain man was the last to enter the room. The others were sorting through the clothing to find sizes that fit them. The sergeant glared at him. "What the hell you going to do with all that stuff? The army will supply you with what you need, and that will be *all* you will need."

Struggling to hold his temper, Beau replied, "I was told at Fort Laramie that I could keep the rifle and revolver."

"Did they tell you to keep all the other jumble you're carrying?" the sergeant asked. "Go back in the other room, and when you come back I don't want to see anything but you, your guns, and your boots."

Beau wanted to explain that the possible bag held items he needed, but chose to do exactly what the sergeant ordered. A time would come when they were in town having some rye and he'd run across the insolent man. Then the score could be settled.

It was hard for the mountain man to understand why the sergeant chose him to make an example of in front of the rest of the recruits. He had volunteered to come and fight the war and give his life if necessary. He had expected there to be discipline associated with army life, but what the sergeant was doing did not make sense.

After bringing the other items to the wash room, Beau returned to pick up his uniform. By this time all the other recruits were dressed and staring at the graying mountain man hurrying around in his long johns. Remembering his shooting from the stagecoach roof, not one of them made a comment.

After finding a shirt, pants, coat, and socks, Beau picked up a slouch hat and placed it onto his head. He walked over to a bench, holding his pants up with one hand, to put on the new pair of boots he'd chosen.

"Put on your old boots," the sergeant instructed. "I don't need a bunch of sore-footed recruits."

The sergeant handed the mountain man a leather belt with a prominent buckle with the initials U.S. raised on it. "I can't have my soldiers holding up their pants when marching into battle."

Beau took the belt and slipped it through the belt loops. Those were the first civil words the sergeant had said to him. Then there was another surprise: The man handed Beau a holster engraved with U.S. on it. It had a flap to secure the Colt. He also handed him a sling for his rifle.

"You'll need the sling for marching and a proper holster for the Colt," the sergeant told him.

The mountain man folded up the cuffs of the pants so they wouldn't drag in the dirt. The rest of the clothes fit his muscular frame quite well. While he was finishing up, the other recruits were directed to take Springfield rifles from the racks on the wall.

The sergeant then barked out, "I want you all to cock and squeeze the triggers and aim them around the room. They are yours for the rest of the war."

Most of the recruits had never held such a nice rifle or, in some cases any. For a few minutes they had fun acting up. "That's enough!" the sergeant barked. "From now on, if I catch anyone handling their rifle carelessly, you will be digging latrines. Your rifle is a weapon of war and your best friend. You will treat it as though your life depended on it."

During the whole demonstration, Beau stood with his rifle cradled in his right arm, unsure of what the sergeant was doing. The mountain man was impressed. The man had made his point.

"Fall out!" the sergeant shouted.

The men hurried out the door, wearing their brand-new uniforms and clutching their rifles. It was apparent that the midday meal had been forgotten. For the next four hours they drilled in the hot sun. By the end of the afternoon, the recruits were halfway decent at staying in formation and marching with their rifles.

The thirsty men were at the pump getting a drink of water when a wagon pulled up into the courtyard. Each man was issued a canteen, a tin cup, a mess kit, a knapsack, a haversack, a roll which contained a wool blanket, one side of a shelter, a gum rubber blanket, and a poncho. They also got a sheepskin lined cap box and cartridge box that would be worn on the belt. Both were loaded with caps and paper cartridges for the Springfield rifles. They also got a bayonet with a scabbard. The sergeant handed Beau one that would adapt to his Sharps.

In total, the men now had over 50 pounds of authorized gear they would be expected to carry during long marches. While the other men were busy looking over their new gear, the sergeant pulled Beau aside.

"Go into the wash room and get your cartridges for the Sharps and whatever else you think you will need. Remember every pound of extra gear you take, you have to carry," the man said.

"I appreciate that, sergeant," Beau replied.

"One more thing," the sergeant said. "Take one of the bags hanging on the wall and put in anything you want to send back to Fort Laramie. I'll give it to the stage driver."

Walking into the bath area, Beau realized that he'd just seen another side of the sergeant. He also figured it was probably a side he wouldn't see too often. Quickly, Beau went through his possible bag and put a few things into the haversack. One of the items included the clasp knife that he'd gotten out of the children's pa's pocket. When he came out carrying the bag, the sergeant motioned him to put it alongside the building. He then bellowed, "Fall in!"

After another hour of drilling with rifles and fixed bayonets, the men were marched to another building. By the smells emitted from the inside there was a promise of a meal. Their rifles were stacked in groups of three out front before entering. The taste of the food did not live up to its smell, but the men hadn't eaten since early morning, so there were no complaints.

After the meal, they were marched to a barracks. The sergeant set some needles and thread on the table along with a box of powder, some oil and some rags. "I want the pants hemmed for inspection in the morning and your rifles shining. Levesque, you're in charge."

Beau looked at the wooden bunks. They were missing any type of mattress. He heard the two army men who had come with them complaining that they shouldn't have to billet with the recruits and one of them should have been put in charge.

The mountain man figured that he should say something. "You men have been in the army for some time. I have done some scouting for the army, but that's about all. Once we get these new pants the right length, I'm going to need you two to show the others how to take care of their rifles. If we look good in the morning, the sarge just might be a little easier on us."

The powder was some kind of crushed rock and mixed with a bit of oil. It brought out the shine on the rifles. Having a rifle barrel that reflected light didn't make much sense to Beau. It would only give away your position to the enemy. More than once in his life a flash of light had saved his bacon.

The men were still busy at their tasks when the word came for "Lights out!"

In the dark a few men continued trying to finish things. The barracks was hot and the mattress deprived bunks were hard, so falling asleep took time. After a few hours of sleep, the sound of reveille woke the men. It was still dark. Confusion was the order of the day in the barracks as they attempted to dress, roll up their blankets, and pack their knapsacks. A half-hour after reveille there was the command, "Fall out!"

After an inspection and dressing down about their appearance, the sergeant told them they would be moving on to their company, commanded by Captain Lewis. The men were instructed to put their new boots and few loose items into their knapsacks. Included in the knapsack was one additional shirt and pants, and extra socks.

To say Captain Lewis was young would have been an understatement. He was barely in his 20s. His commission had been purchased by his wealthy parents. The only saving grace was that he did have experience under fire in one battle, and had had a good mentor prior to being given his command of a company.

For the next week the objective was to teach the company Hardee's Tactics and to work as a unit. They marched in formation, which would be used for going into battle. Staring straight ahead, they practiced firing by squad, which was volley firing at a common target. It required six commands to fire the Springfields, and then 10 commands and 17 motions to reload. They dry fired to conserve ammunition, and simply went through the motions to learn the moves. After a couple of dry firings, they would conduct a bayonet charge into straw dummies.

Fighting in lines, marching in close quarters, making oblique moves to spread out the rows to create a broader line did not make sense to Beau. All of this time they would be in the open and within range of the enemy. What the mountain man did not realize was that the tactics were from past wars and better suited to smooth-bore muskets with an effective range of less than 200 yards. Once the enemy fired they could close in with a bayonet charge. The bayonet had been the primary weapon of war, not the musket. They did not consider the longer range and accuracy of the rifle and Minié ball.

Beau kept his mouth shut, having to trust the experience of those who had actually fought in wars. He had been attacked by Indians, and even the Mexican army. Never had he or those with him stood in the open, in line, to defend themselves.

At the end of the day they would march several miles before setting up camp, sharing their half-section of tent with another soldier. Their rifles were stuck bayonet end into the ground. They took the place of tent poles. Then the two half-tents were buttoned together and draped over the rifles, creating a dog tent which was large enough for two men and their gear.

Fires were built and they would cook their own meals from the rations in they knapsack or haversack. They carried three days' rations, which could include items such as salted meat, side meat, vinegar, molasses, cornmeal, hard bread, salt, sugar, tea, and even fresh vegetables on rare occasions. Lights out came shortly after dark. Reveille was blown at 5 a.m. and they would strike camp and start drilling all over again.

During the second week the mountain man was assigned to a four-man group. They were called *comrades in battle.* They ate, slept, and drilled together. They were part of a skirmish line that would go out in advance of the main army. The skirmisher was to make contact, or harass the enemy, but not fight them. They were still required to maintain a line formation, not to exceed 40 feet between each man. They were allowed to use available cover.

Exhausted from the constant drilling, and tired of hearing the complaining of his fellow soldiers, one evening Beau wandered toward the stage station. Someone had built a bench under an oak tree, so he sat and tore a chew from his tobacco plug.

"What the hell are you doing away from camp?" demanded someone behind him.

Turning, he saw that it was the sergeant who had met them when they arrived. "Just trying to find some fresh air without all the grumbling," Beau told him.

The sergeant took a deep drag of his cigar. "I imagine they are complaining by this time. You best head back to the camp," he told Beau. "When you first get in, they are mighty touchy about where you go and might think you got deserting on your mind."

The mountain man got up and spat. "I figure you are right, sarge."

"Before you go," the sergeant said, "a friend of yours come through here. He asked me if I knew a man named Levesque. Said he was from the west."

"When you say come through," the mountain man asked, "was he joining the army?"

"He sure did," the sergeant replied. "He's assigned to another company. I'm not sure which one. Now, get your ass back to your company before you get in trouble."

Beau walked back toward his company, his thoughts spinning. Jocko came to fight? His friend had a wife and children to think about. The mountain man wondered if he'd said something that made Jocko think it was his obligation to join.

He had barely gotten back to his fire when the first sergeant came by. "The captain wants you to report to his quarters in the morning, right after marching in review."

The first sergeant turned on his heel and headed back toward his troop tent. Beau's mind was abuzz. Had someone turned him in for leaving the camp? Then his thoughts went back to Jocko. He had been told that they would get a pass to go into town come the weekend, and maybe he could locate his friend.

Reveille was sounded and Beau crawled out of the dog tent, which he shared with Joseph Riley. Joe was one of his comrades in battle. The first drill was in 30 minutes. It would be without knapsack and haversack, which wouldn't be packed until after the morning meal. With their rifles slung on their back, and with the cap and cartridge belts on, the men fell into their position in the line.

After drilling for an hour and a half, the men returned to their tent to have breakfast. Most of Beau's meals consisted of side meat and a type of bread. The men then took care of morning duties before hurrying to line up for guard mounting, or changing of the duty. Once the change was complete, the men marched in review with full packs.

With only 20 minutes before commencing the next drill, Beau hurried to the captain's tent. Two privates stood guard out front. "You here to see the captain?" the one on the right asked.

Feeling frustrated at even being summoned, Beau replied, "It was requested by Captain Lewis that I come here. I am Levesque."

The private on the left pointed out, "You are recruit Levesque, I believe."

For a half a second, the mountain man wished they were back at Fort Laramie and he could give a lesson to the arrogant pisher for reminding him of his rank. Before Beau could reply, he heard the captain call for him to enter.

Captain Lewis occupied the largest tent in their camp. On one side was what appeared to be a comfortable cot. There was a small table with two chairs in the middle, and a field desk with a chair on the other side. One other item Beau noticed was a small trunk with brandy and whiskey on it along with some cigars.

The captain was sitting at the table with a cup of coffee. He looked up and said, "Leave your rifle outside with the privates." Beau handed the rifle out through the flap, thinking, *The bastards could have told me to leave it with them.*

Once back in the tent and being unsure of the territory, plus having found few officers to his liking in the past, the mountain man stood across the table, doing his best to stand at attention. Beau fully expected to be asked about being away from the camp last night.

"At ease," the captain said, "and have a seat. Would you like some coffee?"

Slipping his knapsack off his back, the mountain man sat down. "Coffee would be good."

"Sir," the captain reminded him.

"Private, bring in another coffee," the captain called out.

The captain waited for the coffee to be brought in and motioned that it was for Beau. He then said, "Your name came up at a briefing last night. Something about the stage you were on being attacked and single handedly you drove the rebels off."

"They weren't rebels, sir. More like unorganized raiders . . ."

Captain Lewis held his hand up to silence Beau. "What they were is unimportant. What is important is you stopped a dozen or so men attacking the stage. One of the senior officers said you were a mountain man, Indian fighter, and also led a wagon train to Oregon."

A bit flattered with the praise and trying to remember his place in this conversation, Beau replied, "A man does many things in his life, sir."

"And yours has been a long life," the captain said, smiling. "You could have been my father, and I would have been proud if you were."

For Christ's sake, Beau thought, *he's going to tell me I'm too old and send me away.*

The mountain man was about to defend his being in the army when the captain said, "The army needs men like you. It is a waste having you in the infantry when we need experienced men in so many other places. It was even suggested we make you an officer."

At this point, the captain had Beau floored. He had no idea where this was going. Then Captain Lewis continued, "I doubt you would want to be an officer, but your greatest value is in your ability to survive and your skill with the rifle. I want you to try out as a sniper. Go from here to the ordinance sergeant. He will be expecting you."

"Would I still be drilling with the others, sir?" Beau asked.

Ignoring the question, Captain Lewis said, "We don't have authorization for snipers in our regiment. I have heard about successes with Berdan's snipers, so the plan is to find men from each company that can qualify and assign them to sniper duty. While that will be your duty during a battle, you will be classified as a skirmisher. When you are not fighting you can work with the ordinance sergeant and help those that need it with their Springfields." Then the captain leaned closer over the table. "Don't tell anyone, but we are heading south in two days. And if you shoot like I think you will, you'll be going as a corporal."

It was evident that the conversation was over, so Beau stood up to leave. The captain held up his hand, stopping him. "I have been reading some books about a mountain man. When time permits, I would like you to tell me about some of your experiences in the mountains."

Caught off guard by the request, Beau replied, "I would be happy to . . . sir."

The captain dismissed him, telling the mountain man to go directly to the ordnance sergeant to set up a demonstration of his shooting skill. Retrieving his Sharps, Beau headed for the wagon that served as the company's armory. An older man with sergeant stripes was working at getting two Minié balls out of a Springfield barrel.

Looking up, he swore. "Damn recruit rammed two loads in this rifle. He'll be digging latrines for the next two weeks."

No he won't, Beau thought. Then he said, "I was sent here to qualify for sniper."

"We ain't got no snipers," the old sergeant said.

Confused at the mixed messages, Beau told him, "Captain Lewis said when I qualify, one of my duties would be as a sniper."

"Why is it all you mountain boys think you can shoot the wings off a gnat?" the old sarge asked. Setting the rifle aside, he asked, "You got your 60 rounds in your cartridge box?"

"Yes sir," Beau replied.

"I ain't no damn sir, call me Sergeant Miller, Sarge, or Tom," the sarge said. "Follow me."

Walking behind the old sergeant, Beau heard him mutter, "Dad burn recruits."

The firing range had eight-foot wide walls to shoot at: One at 100 yards, another at 150 yards and a third at 200 yards. They were painted bright white and clay was put into prior bullet holes. To qualify for Berdan's snipers, the shooter had to put 10 shots into a 10-inch circle at 200 yards. It was a piece of information Beau did not know.

The sarge pointed to a plank lying on the ground. "You stay behind this board."

"What do you want me to shoot at?" Beau asked.

"Sure as hell not the first two!" the sergeant snapped. "See how close you can come to the middle of the third one."

"You're not going to put up a target?" the mountain man asked.

"I ain't so sure you can hit the furthest wall to begin with," the old sarge replied.

Beau was beginning to get a little angry. "Any man that can't hit a target at that distance sure as hell ain't going to be a sniper."

"Kind of mouthy for a damn recruit, ain't you?" Sergeant Miller growled. He then grabbed the slouch hat from Beau's head. "You go up and hang your hat on the wall. It can be your target."

Taking the nail and hammer that the old sarge handed to him, Beau walked toward the distant wall. "I am willing to bet the only hole that will be in that

hat is the one made by the nail," Sergeant Miller yelled at him.

The mountain man returned to the plank and opened the breech of his Sharps. He put in a paper cartridge and closed the breech, shearing the end of the paper off. He then reached into his cap box and removed one to put on the nipple.

Beau was mad clear through and his heart was pounding. If he hit the target, his hat would be full of holes. If he missed, the old sarge would have his revenge. Several soldiers in the area had come over to watch. It was obvious they were taking bets on his marksmanship.

"How many shots to you want me to take?" Beau asked.

"How about six?" the old sergeant replied, grinning at the mountain man.

He then saw his company being marched over to observe the shooting. "Let them all watch," Beau muttered.

"You will fire on command," the sergeant told him.

Giving a hard stare at the old soldier, Beau asked, "Is that what a sniper does? Waits for someone to tell him when to shoot?"

"What the hell," the sergeant replied. "Fire at will. It's your hat."

Taking his time, Beau rechecked his rifle. It was more to let his anger subside than the need to look things over. Then he raised the ladder sight and put the rifle to his shoulder. *"Damn waste of a good hat,"* he thought as he squeezed the trigger.

Taking his time, the mountain man reloaded and fired the Sharps. When he squeezed off the sixth shot, the hat fell to the ground. He had hit squarely on the nail. It had not been his intention, but Beau would never admit it.

The sarge took off to retrieve the hat, yelling back at Beau, "You only hit it once, recruit. And I figure that was just luck."

The old sergeant's return trip was much slower. He was pushing his fingers through the holes in the slouch hat. He was shaking his head and muttering, "I'll be damned."

A cheer went up from the soldiers and recruits surrounding the mountain man. Beau looked at the sarge. "Sometimes we're lucky and there's no wind."

"Maybe so," Sergeant Miller replied, a smile on his old, wrinkled face, "but you will be needing a new hat."

CHAPTER ELEVEN

Two days later the company woke to gray skies and the sound of assembly being blown. They pulled their boots on, the rifles out of the ends of the tents, and ran to the parade ground falling in at their assigned spot. Beau stood with five other men to the right of the company, who had been assigned to special duties. He had on a new slouch hat and his uniform had corporal stripes on his sleeve.

Captain Lewis rode up on his horse to address the company. "You were all expecting to receive passes to go into town this morning. I regret to inform you that there is an immediate need for our company with the Army of the Mississippi, for an upcoming battle. You have 30 minutes to strike the camp and assemble to march down to the waterfront. There we will board steamboats and proceed south. That is all."

The captain turned his horse and rode toward the docks. The first sergeant gave the order to strike camp and there was a mad scramble as the men got their gear ready for the march to the steamboat. If anyone was disappointed about not getting a pass to go into town, it did not show. Their company was on the move, headed to assist in a battle somewhere south.

It was the 13th of September as the company of 45 men marched to the port. Smoke puffed out of the stacks of two sidewheel steamboats with their forward gangplanks resting on the dock. Officers horses were being boarded on the aft gangplank. The officers themselves were already aboard and having breakfast in the dining room.

Beau looked to his right and left. There were at least 10 companies waiting to board the two boats, making up a regiment of over 400 soldiers. Their sergeant instructed them that they would be quartered on the aft part of the main deck. After 30 minutes of standing in formation, the companies were allowed to board the boat, the mountain man's being directed aft.

They would be traveling on the open deck, subject to whatever weather happened during the trip. They were told that two meals would be served each day. As it turned out it was some type of soup and a slice of coarse bread.

With the gangplanks pulled in, there was a shrill blast of the whistle and the boats moved away from the dock. Smiling, Beau was pleased to be on his way. A cold rain started falling late in the afternoon. The mountain man and his fellow soldiers huddled on the deck, wearing their ponchos.

Beau sat in the gloom, feeling the vibration of the paddles cutting through the water as he watched a gunboat that was escorting them. It had a 3-inch cannon mounted on the bow and it had a stern paddle.

That would allow it to beach on any part of the river and give support to troops. If engaging another steamboat, the paddle would be protected at the stern while firing the cannon.

Word slowly trickled through to the troops that they were heading for Corinth, Mississippi. Their company and brigade would be a part of Rosecrans' forces. Sailors on the steamboat entertained the bored troops with stories of the Memphis battle that had happened on the river earlier that year. The Union had defeated the Confederates 'cottonclad' boats, which were protected from enemy fire by bales of cotton lining their sides.

The only break in the monotony of the trip was when Beau was assigned to the watch at the rail. Both steamboats had twenty men standing two-hour watches around the ship at all times. When going on watch, or using the bathroom, Beau was given more freedom to move around the deck. The steamboat he was on had four companies onboard. He searched for a glimpse of Jocko. His short, stocky friend would be hard to spot among so many of the tall, young soldiers. He began to inquire if anyone knew of a man named Jocko in their company. He did find one young, strapping boy with that name.

To help kill time, the mountain man cleaned and re-cleaned his Sharps 1853. He had let the shiny finish required for inspections dull to prevent reflecting sunlight. He emptied and repacked his cartridge box, which now had 100 rounds. His cap box had twice that many nestled in the sheep's wool lining. Beau found himself gazing at the river shore as it went by. The smell and the feel of the South was around him. Soon he'd be only about 150 miles from the small cabin on Crowley's Ridge.

After five days of thin soup twice a day and huddling on the aft deck, rain or shine, the steamboat tied up at some docks that had several burned out and bombarded buildings that had at one time been warehouses. The mountain man stood in formation on the deck for an hour waiting for his company to disembark. He was able to watch as the officers' horses were taken down the aft gangplank, saddled and ready for their riders.

The first sergeant stood in front of their company. He gave them a stern warning. "Up until now, you have been drilling to be a soldier for the Union Army. When you step off this boat, you will be in enemy territory. At any time, from anywhere, the Confederates can come at you. If you are enjoying the birds, sitting on the latrine, or taking a nap on watch, when they come, you will not be ready and will quickly suffer the consequences."

Then moving to one side he snapped, "From this moment, you had better stay sharp! Companies disembark!"

The soldier standing next to Beau whispered, "Welcome to the war."

* * *

It was hot and humid in Mississippi when 400 men marched away from the river. They were to meet up with Rosecrans' Army of the Mississippi on the northeast side of Corinth. Corinth had been successfully taken over after a Union siege earlier in May. The fear was that the Confederates would attempt to take it back.

The Battle of Iuka had been waged on September 19th, driving the Confederate forces of Price south and west. Rosecrans' army then went to Corinth to reinforce the area against a possible attack from Van Dorn's Army of West Tennessee.

Beau and three other skirmishers were sent out about a mile in front of the marching regiment to provide early warning should they encounter any Confederate troops. While they resembled a comrades in battle group, they were not required to move forward in line. Beau and another man were at point in the lead, while two were back a couple hundred yards.

Should the men on point be pinned down or killed, the other two would bring the warning to the regiment. If a force was come across, and the skirmishers not discovered, again the two men in the rear would return to the regiment with the size and location of the enemy troops. The officers with the regiment would then decide whether to engage or set up a defensive line.

The mountain man knew that if the decision was to engage, he would find an advantageous place to observe the enemy and begin to eliminate their leadership. The regiment had been marching for two days and were now less than six days from joining up with Rosecrans. It was dark when Beau returned to his company.

One of the soldiers cooking over a small fire called him over. "I got water on for tea, and plenty of side meat in the pan. If you have some bread left we can have ourselves a fine meal."

Dropping his knapsack near the fire, Beau dug into it. "All I got is hard bread. I do have an onion that might go well with the meat."

While cutting up the onion, the mountain man introduced himself, "The name's Beau Levesque. I hail from the Rocky Mountain area."

"They call me Mac. Last name's MacKay," the man told him. "I also came from the west. I called you over because I met some folks at Fort Laramie that knew you. I told a man named Louie that I was going to join the army and he said that a friend named Levesque had just went the week before. I asked about you when I got to St. Joseph, but didn't find you. Someone come by when I was making my fire and said Levesque should be back any time."

Relief flooded over Beau. It was not Jocko who had asked about him. "The sergeant that had met us mentioned you asking about me." Putting the onions into the pan, the mountain man asked, "What part of the west are you from?"

The man hesitated as he stirred the onions into the side meat grease. "I been many places. Run off to California when they found gold. I was only 15 then. Wasted my time there. Spent a good amount of time in Montana."

Filling his mug with tea, Beau sat back. "It is good to meet someone from the west."

"The young'uns said hi," Mac told him.

"Young'uns?" Beau asked.

"The children you left with Louie," Mac said as he began to divide the meal into the two mess kit pans.

Thoughts of Mary and Toby raced through his mind. Smiling he replied, "I do miss them."

After the meal was finished, Beau spread out his gum rubber blanket on the ground. With his poncho protecting his wool blanket and using his knapsack as a pillow, he went to sleep with his rifle and Colt next to him.

Mac turned out to be a likable sort. Each evening when the marching ended, they shared a fire to cook their meal. While he was sketchy about his life out west, he had plenty to say about being in the army. Beau would have liked to have him as part of his comrades in battle, but they were assigned to different companies.

On the fifth day, scouts riding horses were sent out to locate Rosecrans' forces. Beau watched them ride away, envying them on horseback. He sure did miss riding the chestnut. That evening the scouts returned, letting them know that they should reach the Army of the Mississippi around midday.

The regiment was assigned to Hamilton's division, under Sullivan's brigade. It was September 24, 1862. Beau was amazed when he looked at all the soldiers attached to Hamilton's division. There were over 4,000 men preparing for Van Dorn's attack. What he didn't realize was that there were four other divisions with as many, or more, men. While the soldiers sat and wondered what their next move would be, those planning the battle were frantically trying to gather information and predict the Confederates' move.

On the 1st of October, three of the divisions, including Hamilton's, which Beau's company was assigned to, moved west of Corinth to set up a line. McKean's division was on the south end of the line, Davies' division was in the middle, and Hamilton's was on the north end of the line. They were to set up defenses in the outer rifle pits about a mile from Corinth. Van Dorn's Confederate troops were expected to attack from the west. On the 2nd, the skirmish line was set up. As part of the skirmishers, Beau was sent another mile west to the old Confederate entrenchments. They were to absorb the enemy's advance and fight as long as possible before falling back to the rifle pits.

That night they ate a cold meal of bread with molasses and water. The night temperature was in the 70s and they expected the next day to be in the 90s. It was humid and the men's uniforms were damp with sweat. Despite the discomfort, they had to drink sparingly from their canteens. Word had come out that the water in the area was contaminated, and dysentery had been a severe problem for the Confederates before they were routed from the area.

The next morning, Beau looked for some defendable high ground to set up a sniper nest. The sun was just coming up behind him when he settled in to await a target. It was hard to believe that less than a mile away Van Dorn's army was preparing to take back Corinth. Beau felt an advantage with the sun being at his back rather than in his eyes.

At 9:30 Beau caught movement to the southwest. Without taking his eyes off the area, his hands expertly went over his rifle, checking its readiness. The mountain man realized that the Confederates were lining up, preparing to attack. Any targets of value would be out of his range. He looked across the entrenchment, directly west. He saw nothing. He was sure that the attack would be coming from the far, left side.

Out on the frontier, Beau would have been on the move to meet the attackers head on. But in the army you stayed in your position until orders came to move. If the attack came toward Davies' division, to their left, he might get some action.

All hell broke loose at 10:00 a.m. as the attack came. It was impossible for Beau to see exactly what was happening, but it looked like McKean's division on the far left was the focus of the attack. It began with cannon fire, which spewed clouds of smoke into the air and drifted in on the westerly breeze. Then came the rebel yell as the line of Confederate soldiers maneuvered into battle.

For two hours Beau watched from his nest, praying that a target would come within range so he could help in the battle. Smoke from the weapons masked much of the battle, but Beau caught glimpses of men falling on both sides, struck by the lethal rifle fire, their bodies strewn across the battle lines.

Dirt flew as cannon balls hit the ground or earthen works, remaining trees were shattered and cannister shot mowed swathes through rows of marching soldiers. The mountain man saw Davies' division moving up toward the entrenchments. The sounds of war were deafeningly close, yet Beau could do nothing to help.

He watched as the Confederates broke through between McKean's and Davies' forces. The mountain man fought down the urge to stand and shout to try to get his division moving. Then the Union army to the left began to fall back, giving up ground almost to the redoubts, a half-mile from Corinth.

At 3:00 p.m. Hamilton's division received orders to attack the advancing Confederates on their left flank. Unaware of this order, Beau stayed put, sweat running down his body under his shirt as he watched the battle unfold. Then he heard shots to his right. Buford's brigade, part of Hamilton's division, was under attack. In the hot afternoon sun, Beau felt cold inside. These Confederates were finally within range.

The mountain man's first target was an officer astride a black horse directing the southern troops. Beau lined up the Sharps and fired. The officer went off the horse, wounded. For the next hour, Beau searched for targets through the smoke of battle, firing at anyone who appeared to be directing the Confederate attack.

Then two bullets hit close to his nest. The enemy snipers had spotted him. Beau worked his way out of the nest and looked for another vantage point to shoot from. It was shortly before sunset when the batteries went quiet. The only sounds were the occasional shot and the cries of the wounded begging for help.

Hamilton's division had not been able to assist Davies. A combination of miscommunication and the sudden attack by the Confederates on Buford's brigade had prevented action until it was too late. That night the Union army slept in the redoubts while the Confederates slept 600 yards away, having taken possession of two pieces of artillery.

Pickets stationed outside the redoubts could hear enemy movement as they prepared for the next day's attack. Beau was on picket duty for the last part of the night. Each picket consisted of a lieutenant, two sergeants, four corporals, and around 40 privates. The mountain man sat with the ordinance sergeant and stared out into the dark.

"How many shots did you take today?" the sarge asked.

"Sixty-three," Beau told him.

"How many kills?" the sarge asked.

The mountain man was truly unsure of the number of kills. He knew that he had hit 43 men. They had fallen within a second after he'd fired. "I don't know how many were kills, but forty some went down."

"Damn fine shooting," the ordinance sergeant replied. "Probably saved the lives of three times as many of our soldiers."

Beau sat staring, thinking, *I hope so.* It was possible that he'd made a lot of widows today and he hoped there was a benefit to the lost lives.

At 4:30 a.m. the next morning a battery of Confederate guns opened up, targeting the inner line of Union entrenchments. The flash of the cannons firing in the dark could be seen and the smoke filled the nostrils of the Union soldiers. The firing continued until just after sunrise. The men on the picket lines had had no place to run for cover, so they just had to sit tight and steel their nerves against the bombardment, praying that the cannons weren't turned on them.

When the guns fell silent, the Union army set up, anticipating an attack immediately follow the end of shelling. It did not come. The smoke drifted clear and the sun burned down on the battle field. Beau had found high ground to shoot from. He had gotten a hardy congratulations from Captain Lewis when the officer found out about his success the day before.

Due to illness and other problems encountered on the Confederate side, it was almost two hours before the attack came. This time it began from north of Corinth, with a division of Price's Army of the West engaging Davies' and Hamilton's divisions. Part of the delay had been when the Confederates moved their troops into the woods north of the town. Battery Powel was one of their objectives and was defended by Davies' division. By mid-morning the Confederate were able to rout the Union defenders and take the battery.

Meanwhile, other Confederate brigades attempted to enter Corinth from the northeast, which meant breaking through Hamilton's division. Beau had no problem picking out targets through the smoke of battle, with it being spread out in front of him. As the fighting continued to move, the mountain man moved with it, continuing to seek targets. Hamilton sent support to Davies and the battery and guns were retaken.

Beau could hear fighting behind him toward the town. Some of the Confederates had broken through while the battery was being retaken. Hamilton sent some of Sullivan's brigade, that had been held in reserve, toward the town. Beau was nearby at the time, replenishing his cartridges and he ran with them toward Corinth.

The Confederates were already in the streets and had not expected the strength that was thrown at them so quickly. Union soldiers took them on in the narrow streets. Beau fired once with the Sharps and then pulled the Colt. Sullivan's troops continued to put pressure on the Confederates, forcing them to pull back. Once pushed out of Corinth, they were caught in the crossfire of two Union batteries.

In the unbearable heat, Beau put the empty Colt back into his holster and knelt on the edge of town, loading cartridges into the rifle and firing at the retreating Confederates. Finally, sweat running into his eyes and smoke in the area made it impossible to sight in on any targets.

By 1:00 p.m. the Confederate army was in full retreat. Beau was back with his company on high ground, watching for any target of opportunity. It appeared that the fight was over. Everywhere the mountain man looked there were dead or wounded soldiers. Horses lay wounded, unable to rise, or dead across the battle field.

Beau filled his cartridge box, expecting the word to pursue the retreating Confederates to be given at any moment. It did not come. In the two days of fighting, the Union had 355 killed and 1,841 wounded. The Confederates had 473 killed and 1,997 wounded. The Union army had just over 1700 prisoners to deal with. Beau had fired over 250 shots and had no idea how many hits he'd had. He feared too many.

Pickets needed to be set while Rosecrans' army tended to the wounded and buried the dead. The mountain man volunteered to be on picket duty. The picket line was set up on the far side of the Confederate entrenchment. While they were getting water and rations to take with them, word came that Grant had sent McPherson with reinforcements from Jackson.

Everywhere Beau went he came across bodies. Elderly men and women had come out after the shooting stopped to help with the dead. A dazed Confederate who had been at first thought dead stood up and staggered among his comrades. Beau brought him to their camp to get him bandaged before having a couple of privates take him to the prisoner area.

A smile came to his face when he saw Mac with the other privates. "Glad to see you made it through the fight," Beau told him.

"They did some shuffling in the companies after the battle and I got assigned to Captain Lewis," Mac informed him.

It turned out that Private MacKay had been put into a skirmish group, replacing men who had been lost during the battle. One of the men lost was Joseph Riley. Beau wouldn't know about Joe for another week, when all the dead and missing were accounted for. Right now, the two new friends sat together happy and talking. They had survived the battle.

On October 5th there was pursuit of Van Dorn's Confederate forces by Grant's Army of the Tennessee led by Major General Ord. They encountered the Confederates about 25 miles west, near Pocahontas. Ord engaged Van Dorn's Confederates in a battle known as Battle of Davis

Bridge. Despite the hot engagement, the Confederates were able to escape across the Hatchie River.

Sullivan's division, which Beau's company was attached to, did not take part in the pursuit of Van Dorn. They remained in the Corinth area until called to participate in the Battle of Parker's Crossroads.

Confederate Brigadier General Forrest had been on a campaign of disruption in Tennessee. Beau's company was part of Sullivan's forces under Colonel Durham. They marched six days north to confront the Confederate general. They met at Parker's Crossroads and the battle started at 9:00 a.m. in the morning.

The mountain man was at a disadvantage, having the Confederates on a wooded ridge above them. Forrest's artillery pinned down his company. Beau moved along the Union line until he finally was able to see part of the artillery.

Lining his sights on one of the gunners, the mountain man fired and was rewarded when the man spun and went down. While he was unable to stop the cannon fire, he was able to keep some of the guns unmanned for short periods of time.

Durham was able to move his brigade back a half-mile and then aligned them to defend the north. Attacks on both flanks and the rear by cavalry and skirmishers continued to hamper the Union line, which had most of their strength on the center front. Word was sent by the Confederate general demanding an unconditional surrender.

Colonel Durham refused and started re-deploying his troops, preparing for another attack. Beau had moved into some trees that would give him cover and help him defend against the flank attacks.

That was when another brigade led by Colonel Fuller arrived, attacking Forrest's forces from the rear.

Like a trapped beaver, Forrest's troops fought both brigades surrounding them and managed to break out and retreat to Lexington, Tennessee. During the intense fighting Beau shot a cavalry soldier from his horse. With the smoke of battle clearing, he saw the animal standing in the trees, its head hanging from exhaustion.

Slowly the mountain man walked up to the animal. He saw several slight wounds on the horse that could have been from riding through brush as well as bullets or bayonets. Beau loosened the cinch and untied the saddle bags and bedroll. A quick look into the bags told him that there was little of value. One had some moldy bread and something greasy wrapped in paper. The other held personal items and ammunition for a rifle that was missing.

Colonel Durham's forces had lost over 200 men in the battle and then there were the Confederate soldiers who had been left behind, which numbered 500.

Pickets were put out to cover any return of the Confederates. Beau kept the horse with him when he went on picket duty. Mac looked the animal over and gave the mountain man his approval. Beau was well aware that the horse would probably be put into common stock and used as a pack animal, or to pull a wagon or cannon.

A half-hour later, a runner came looking for Beau. "The captain wants to see you," the private told him.

"Word travels fast," Beau muttered. "They've already heard about the horse."

Arriving at the captain's tent, the two privates on duty showed a little more respect than he'd gotten as a recruit. Handing his rifle to one of the privates, Beau said, "Corporal Levesque reporting as requested." He waited to be summoned inside.

After a couple of minutes he heard, "Corporal, come on in."

The captain was not alone. He had another company's captain sitting at the table with him. Both men had glasses of brandy. Beau stood at attention, waiting to be told to stand at ease or even invited to sit.

Looking up at Beau, Captain Lewis said, "At ease, corporal. Pour yourself a drink and take the chair from my desk."

All of a sudden the mountain man was anything but at ease. He was definitely in unfamiliar territory. Moving woodenly, Beau poured some whiskey into a glass and then moved the chair over to the table. Once seated, he said, "I take it this isn't about a horse, sir."

A moment of confusion was expressed on Captain Lewis' face. "I know nothing of a horse, corporal. This is Captain Adams. He's come to me with a situation and asked me if I knew of anyone that could help."

Taking a sip of his whiskey, the mountain man waited to learn what the situation was, and how he could help. Finally, Captain Adams said, "During the battle today, I had some of my men taken as prisoner."

It was not unusual that men be taken prisoner. They could be used for bargaining, or pumped for information. At the very least shipped off to a prisoner of war camp. Having men taken by the enemy was seldom considered a situation.

Anticipating that they were waiting for him to speak, Beau asked, "How can I help?"

Captain Adams replied, "I had six men taken during the fighting. I don't believe that General Forrest realizes the value of one of their captives. He is the son of one of the senators in Washington. He was being mentored to be an officer with his own company. He dressed as a private to keep his identity hidden."

Beau was quite pleased when his captain got up and refilled the three glasses. "Wouldn't being dressed as a private put him in more danger?"

Shaking his head, Adams replied, "He was assigned to remain close to me, . . . like the two privates outside this tent. We were instructed to keep him well out of harm's way."

"When we were attacked in the flanks," Captain Lewis said, "the private was being moved well away from the battle by five men in Adam's command. Once the battle was over, they were nowhere to be found. We fear the worst. We fear he has been taken prisoner by the Confederates."

The worst would be to have found his body, Beau thought. Then he said, "If you are wondering if I saw any prisoners being taken, I did not."

Captain Adams stood up, his nerves making it impossible to continue sitting. "I asked your captain if he had anyone that would be capable of finding the

Confederates and learning if they had prisoners, and if so, find a way to free them, or at least the senator's son."

"If I find them sir," Beau asked, "how will I know the son?"

"He has been given the name Rodgers," Captain Adams answered.

"Intelligence we have tells us that Forrest has gone as far as Lexington," Captain Lewis said. "From there we expect them to head east across the Tennessee River."

On their march from Corinth, they had come through Lexington. Beau knew the area somewhat and it was only 10 miles away. The mountain man figured it was time to bargain.

"I would be glad to help free the senator's son," Beau said. "In return, I would like to use the horse that I found after the battle. It was a Confederate cavalry animal. With the safe return of Rodgers, I would like to be allowed to keep the horse for my use."

Looking doubtful, Captain Lewis said, "I'm not sure I have the authority to let you keep a personal horse. I could try, but I can't guarantee that it will be allowed."

The look of frustration showed on Captain Adams face, "For Christ's sake, Lewis. Make him a cavalry soldier. They are allowed horses."

Realizing that his request had the two captains going at each other, Beau said, "I am ready to go after the senator's son whether or not I get to keep the horse. I will need it to go after Rodgers."

Smiling, Captain Lewis said, "Hell, Levesque. When you get back with Rodgers, you will be a sergeant in my cavalry."

Thanking the two captains, Beau said, "I will leave within the hour."

"You are authorized to take some men with you, if you think it will help," Lewis said.

Beau already had three days' rations in his knapsack and haversack. His cartridge box was full and he had powder and balls for the Colt. He had noticed a scabbard for a rifle on the horse and he could replace the bayonet and scabbard with a Arkansas Toothpick he had found after the Battle of Corinth.

Mac was eating some bread and molasses when Beau returned to the picket line. The mountain man asked him, "Do you want to go hunting Confederates tonight?"

Furrowing his brow, Mac said, "Stay in the safety of the picket, or make myself a target of the Confederates. Hmm, now that's a hard decision."

"You don't have to come," Beau assured him. "This mission is purely voluntary."

"Well . . . hell, I had no plans tonight anyway," Mac replied, laughing.

Beau saw the lieutenant in charge of the picket station and let him know that he and MacKay would be going on a raid at the request of the captain. He also let the lieutenant know that MacKay would require a horse.

It was just getting dark when the two men rode south toward Lexington. It would take about two hours' riding to reach the town and then they would have to locate Forrest's camp. Beau knew that returning with the prisoners would be another story. They would all be on foot and it would take a little over five hours to walk back. That is, if all the prisoners were able to walk.

As the mountain man rode the cavalry horse, he was impressed at the smooth gait. It would be a good horse for Toby if he was able to bring it back west. Beau thought about his orders while riding toward an armed enemy camp. The only prisoner who the captains wanted back was Rodgers. If they took only the one man with them, he and Mac could take turns riding double and be back to the safety of the Union camp well before daylight. Beau knew he wouldn't leave any of them behind unless he had no other option.

The moon was in first quarter and gave a pale light to the surrounding landscape. Mac rode without talking, which was a good thing. Sometimes sound can travel a long way in the night. Beau was confident that they could ride without meeting Forrest's men most of the trip. If the Confederates had put out pickets, they would be within a mile of Lexington.

They were riding over a ridge when they caught sight of the town's lights. The two men swung off their horses and continued to lead them toward the town. Beau had removed his Colt from the holster and put it into his waist band. They passed a small clearing short of Lexington and left the road, tying the horses out of sight, in some pines. Beau debated taking his rifle and decided to leave it, depending on his knife and revolver. Mac carried his rifle with the bayonet fixed.

Suddenly, Beau had an idea. He went to the horse's saddle bags and fished out a Confederate shirt and pants. "You stay here with the horses, Mac. I talk southern and if I am dressed like them, maybe I can find out where they're keeping the prisoners."

"If you are caught," Mac warned him, "they will hang or shoot you for being a spy."

"Then I best fool them really good," Beau replied. Once dressed, he looked at his hat. He decided that he'd have to hope the darkness would cover for the color. Beau had no emblems on the hat to give him away. As a sniper, he didn't want anything that would reflect light.

He looked at the prominent buckle on his belt. That would have to be left behind. Fortunately, the pants were a little tight and that would help keep them up. Beau then changed his mind and took the Sharps, putting a few cartridges into his pockets.

He headed down the road toward Lexington, humming a southern hymn. He saw the picket station before they saw him. Calling out to prevent them from shooting, he began to talk about the night reminding him of Crowley Ridge, and about wanting to go back there when the fighting was over.

As luck would have it, one of the men on picket duty was from Arkansas and was quite familiar with the ridge. They talked for a bit, reminiscing of their younger days on the ridge. Suddenly one of the men asked, "Is that a Sharps breech loader you got there?"

"You damn right it is," Beau said proudly. "Took if off a Union fellow that didn't have a need for it anymore. Left my Enfield with bayonet sticking in him as a trade."

The four men guarding the road got a good laugh from Beau's story of the trade. Then one of the men noticed he was not wearing a belt. "You're going to lose your damn pants. What happened to your belt?"

"Put it on the leg of a man that was bleeding bad," Beau replied.

There was a brief silence as the men thought about the wounded. Then the mountain man said, "I am supposed to help watch the prisoners, but don't know where the hell they put them."

The man familiar with Crowley Ridge said, "They are in the barn just down the road on the left."

"Well, y'all have a safe evening," Beau said as he headed down the road. The cool air coming in from the north was starting to create fog. *It will help*, the mountain man thought.

He passed two other soldiers as he walked down the road. By the sound of their conversation, they had just been relieved from guarding the prisoners. Once the barn came into sight, he ducked into the woods and came up behind the building. He had glimpsed some soldiers at the front of the barn, and as he looked between the boards on the wall, he could see two men sitting on bales, playing cards on a nail keg. They were using a candle stub for light.

After watching for a half-hour, Beau was able to determine that the six men were in one of the horses' box stalls. Moving as quietly as the fog surrounding him, Beau worked his way around the unguarded parts of the barn. Another set of doors in the back were barred, but the small door used to throw out the horse manure was not.

The mountain man wondered if there would be any benefit to going back to the clearing and getting Mac. He decided that trying to free the men would be best done by one man. Taking his time, Beau pushed open the small door. The leather hinges made no noise.

He carefully set his rifle onto the inside wall. Then, holding his knife and Colt close to his body so they wouldn't bump against the door frame, he stepped into the barn. Once inside the barn, he felt totally exposed. Beau stared away from the candle so he wouldn't be blinded if he had to move quickly.

The barn floor was littered with straw, broken handles, and pieces of some kind of machine. Praying that the two card players wouldn't look to the back of the barn, Beau slowly moved across the floor, seeking cover next to the stall. One of the barn floor boards creaked as he put his weight on it. The mountain man froze, ready to draw his Colt.

"Wind must be picking up," one of the men said. "The old barn is talking to us."

Just as Beau got next to the stall, the front door opened, allowing fog to roll in. "Y'all best keep sharp!" the man snapped. "Fog's coming in. Damn Yankees would have to bump right into us before they'd see us."

The door slammed and the man went back out. "He's worrying for nuthin," one of the card players said. "We whupped the buggers today and they ain't looking for no more fighting. They're sitting, hole up, licking their wounds."

"Harry got killed today," the other player said. "His mama lives on the farm next to us and I'll have to write her a letter."

"Lots of good men getting killed," the first player replied. Then the two men were silent, with only the sound of their cards being heard.

Beau realized that he would probably have to kill these two men to get the prisoners out. The letter to Harry's mama would never be written. The mountain man crouched next to the stall, struggling to control his breathing.

Suddenly, there was a gust of wind and the small door swung the rest of the way open and slammed against the wall. "What the hell . . ." He heard the keg fall over and the candle went out. The two men moved to the stall and were kneeling in front of it.

The gusts of wind continued to swing the small door. "It's just the manure door," one of the men said.

"You don't think anyone come in?"

"How the hell could they come in? We would've heard 'em."

Beau was less than five feet from the two men, just around the corner of the stall.

Then the mountain man heard, "Go light the candle, I'll shut the damn door."

There was shuffling in the straw as one man went back for the candle and the other began to feel his way toward the door. In the gloom of the barn, Beau saw the outline of the man appear in front of him.

Now or never, Beau thought as he swung the rifle barrel at the outline. There was a grunt and the man hit the floor.

"Did you fall, Tuck?" the man getting the candle called over.

"Yeah," Beau said, trying to match the man's voice. "Hit my damn knee."

There was a laugh from his comrade. "Don't be trying to get out of standing watch."

The match flashed as the man attempted to light the candle, just as Beau struck him with the butt of the rifle. The flash blinded the mountain man as he blinked his eyes to try and clear them. He saw that the match was starting the straw on the board floor on fire. Stomping it out, he turned to head for the stall. He could see nothing.

The brief light had made him night blind. He whispered, "Rodgers. Rodgers, are you in here?"

He was feeling his way to the stall as he heard a faint, "Yes."

"I am here to get you men out of here," Beau said. "Can you all walk?"

"Got one man wounded," a voice said.

"You ain't leaving me!" the wounded man said, a bit louder than was safe. "I can walk."

There were eight men crammed into the stall. They stumbled out, bumping into Beau. He swore, "You damn buggers best move quietly or the guards out front will he filling the barn with bullets."

It seemed to take forever before the prisoners were out of the barn. Once outside, the heavy fog gave them the cover they needed to move away from the barn and travel parallel to the road as they made their way to the clearing. Beau was constantly warning them to keep quiet and watch where they stepped. The mountain man felt that they sounded like a herd of cattle moving through the woods.

It was only the wind and swirling fog that save them from being discovered. Beau hit the road before the clearing. When he got there, he had no idea if he was beyond the clearing or not. "Who's the senior man here?" he asked.

A corporal came forward, "I am. The name's James, Dick James."

"Take these men up the road," Beau told him. "Keep quiet and near the edge of the road. I'll find the horses and be right along."

"We got horses?" one of the privates asked.

"No," Beau replied. "I got a horse, you have a long walk."

CHAPTER TWELVE

Beau did not become a sergeant after bringing the senator's son back, but he was transferred to the cavalry and got to keep the horse. Mac also was able to get a transfer. Generally, it took months of training to become a cavalry soldier because riding and shooting weren't common skills held by those joining the Union. Both Beau and Mac were well-versed in both.

Years before the cavalry had been an offensive force, but after the development of the rifle that could start hitting men and horses at 300 yards, they'd become a defensive force. Scouting out enemy positions, cutting off communications, and destroying transportation were some of the key responsibilities of the cavalry.

The first action Beau saw as a cavalry soldier came during the Battle of Vicksburg. While the cavalry wasn't directly involved in the battle, they were assigned to disrupt and conduct raids in Mississippi and Louisiana. The mountain man rode tall in the saddle as they left Tennessee on their mission.

Col. Benjamin H. Grierson led the troops with orders to destroy anything that would support the Confederates. It was a week before they found their first opportunity. A slow-moving train was spotted, consisting of several cars loaded with supplies destined for the South. It was climbing a long grade, the engine spewing clouds of black smoke.

Stationed on top of the cars were Confederate soldiers armed with Enfield rifles. It was assumed that additional soldiers were riding out of sight in the train cars. Beau's company was given the word to attack and disable the train.

Splitting the forces, part of the cavalry was sent ahead of the train to lie in ambush. They were instructed to take out soldiers on the car roofs, and disable the engine. Those waiting, which included Beau, would then come up from behind the train, keeping in the trees for cover to prepare for battle.

Suddenly there was rifle fire from the ambushers as they opened up on the Confederate soldiers. Several were knocked off the roofs with the first round of fire. The remaining Confederate soldiers lay flat on the train cars and began returning fire. Rifles quickly appeared at the car windows and doorways.

Adrenaline rushed through Beau's veins as the order to attack came. He spurred his horse toward the train searching for a target. Almost immediately rifle fire came in their direction. Saddles were emptied around him as men were killed or wounded. The mountain man fired at the unseen enemy inside the cars.

The train began to slow to a stop, confirming that those attacking the engine had been successful. The cavalry had been trained to dismount once contact had been made with the target and assume infantry tactics. Beau swung off his horse, making use of whatever cover was available and began firing in volleys on command.

They were quickly able to take over the train, taking the remaining guards prisoner. The train was loaded with small cannons, food and other supplies for the Confederate Army. They were ordered to destroy anything that Grierson's brigade couldn't use.

While charges were detonated under the engine and cars, leaving them ablaze, the wounded and dead were attended to. The carnage was left behind as Beau and the others rode away, looking for their next target.

Several times during the campaign they came up against Confederate troops on the move. Their strength was too small to take them on, but they did attack their flanks and their supply trains, which consisted of wagons stretching out miles behind the army. It made Beau think of about how wolves would take down an elk, never going for the throat while the animal was strong, but rather grabbing it from behind, a bite at a time, wearing the animal down.

They moved fast, taking down telegraph wire wherever they found them. Factories or mills that could provide food or equipment for the Confederates were disabled. When forward scouts found larger troop movements, they were avoided, but dispatches were sent to alert the Union.

There was talk that the Confederate cavalry led by Forrest was looking for them. If they were confronted by Forrest, it would be a battle for survival. He was a formidable foe. For over 17 days Beau's company spread destruction and chaos for 800 miles, helping to keep the Confederates', focus off General Grant's main objective. In early May, Beau and the cavalry arrived in Baton Rouge.

Beau sat in front of his dog tent, cleaning his Sharps. Mac came over carrying a tin plate of beans. "They got a pot going near headquarters," Mac told him. "Said for us to help ourselves."

Smiling, he looked at his comrade in battle. "Do you realize we destroyed two trains, took down miles of wire, met the Confederates a half-dozen times, not to mention all the factories we shut down, and all in less than a month?"

"Hell yes," Mac replied. "We done all that and word is we will be off to help General Banks take Port Hudson."

"I wonder if we will be joining up with Grant at Vicksburg?" Beau asked. "That's a bigger target than Port Hudson."

"Well, all I heard," Mac said, "is that the South got two places on the Mississippi that prevent our boats going up and down the river. They both have to be taken to open it up."

"Hell," Beau replied, "if we do that, we cut off Louisiana, Texas, and Arkansas from the rest of the Confederate states. The war will be over before you know it."

Mac poked at his plate of beans for a moment before asking, "Ain't it Texas that the Confederates get their beef?"

"Maybe so," the mountain man said. "I sure could use a nice beef steak right now."

Setting down his rifle, he asked Mac, "Where'd you say those beans were?"

* * *

That night, Beau lay in the dog tent thinking about the end of the war. He decided that when it ended, he'd first go back to Crowley Ridge and see if his small cabin was still standing. Maybe he'd do some black bear hunting. There was still a market for the oil that could be rendered from the animal.

If things were good in Arkansas, he could even send for Mary and Toby. The three of them could make their home near the ridge. He had sent two letters to the children and was due to write another. It was doubtful anyone was still looking for him in Arkansas and Elijah wouldn't be a runaway anymore because there wouldn't be any slavery.

The fight for Port Hudson lacked the quick victory that was anticipated during their march from Tennessee. The port was well-defended and two unsuccessful attacks were attempted before Banks decided to set up a siege on the port. It lasted a month and a half. The hot, sticky, mosquito infested area made life miserable. Mixed rumors of the battle for Vicksburg continued to be spread, giving hope to its swift end and then dashing them as the battle dragged on.

There continued to be small skirmishes in the area, which kept reminding Beau how quickly a soldier could go from a fighting man to a dead one. Disease was also taking its toll on the soldiers. On July 4th Vicksburg finally surrendered to General Grant. Within five days, Port Hudson followed suit and the Mississippi River was free to Union boat traffic and the western Confederate states were cut off.

To the soldiers, these accomplishments saw little change in their day-to-day existence. After a few days of revelry, they marched away to their next place of battle. Beau and the cavalry were to ride directly toward Chickamauga, Georgia, 400 miles to the east to assess the Confederates' strength, destroy communications lines and generally harass the enemy prior to arrival of the infantry.

The battle at Chickamauga was a disaster for the Union troops. Coming off victories in the west, Rosecrans' Army of the Cumberland was able to push Confederate General Bragg's army east and out of Chattanooga. The resulting battle along the Chickamauga Creek should have been another victory for Rosecrans, but mistakes were made, leaving a gap in the Union line that allowed Bragg's forces through. Beau watched from his dismounted position as the Confederate soldiers began to outflank them. Rosecrans' retreating army was being decimated by the deadly fire of the Confederates. The only recourse was to pull back to Chattanooga.

Back on their horses, the cavalry attempted to give whatever cover they could to the Union troops. Several times, Beau dismounted and fired the Sharps toward the advancing Confederates, only to be forced to leap back onto his horse and fall back. Knowing his cartridge box was almost empty, the mountain man and much of the cavalry rode for Chattanooga with hopes of resupplying.

The Union army found itself besieged in the city by the Confederate Army of Tennessee. Their supply line was cut off by raiders or sharpshooters on Missionary Ridge, Lookout Mountain, or by Confederate pickets along the river stringing out toward Alabama. Beau and Mac found themselves on duty, across the river from the Confederates, short of cartridges and food.

It was a dark, cloudy, October night as the two men huddled behind a makeshift barrier.

"I never saw so many men fall so fast," Mac said. "I swear the river was red with our boys' blood."

"I'm just wondering how a gap ended up in our line, letting them flank us," Beau complained. "I swear we had their backs to the wall, and then there was Confederates all around us."

"Word is," Mac confided, "the supply wagons coming have repeater rifles for us."

"You mean, the wagons that can't get to us," Beau replied. "We sure as hell could have used them today."

Across the river a man was putting a pot to heat over the fire. No doubt his intention was to aggravate the hungry Union forces. Raising his rifle, Beau took aim at the cookpot. "Get your heads down," he told those around him.

Squeezing off the shot, the mountain man was rewarded, seeing the pot go over. He ducked just before the volley of shots came for the other side with searching fire toward the flash of his rifle.

"Kind of gives us the strength of their forces across from us," Mac said.

"Well, at least they'll be doing their cooking a bit farther away," Beau replied with satisfaction.

After days of hunger for both man and beast, the sound of fighting was heard. Additional Union forces had arrived and were opening a way to get supplies to the besieged city through Browns Ferry. It was dubbed the Cracker Line plan, bringing in the much-needed supplies. Word also came that Rosecrans had been relieved and replaced by Maj. Gen. George H. Thomas.

Through November the battle was fought with the Union taking control of the area and opening the way to Atlanta, the stronghold of the Confederates. Major General Sherman's made this his next objective. For the duration of the Atlanta Campaign, the cavalry company Beau was assigned to supported that effort.

Christmas of 1863 was a cold, drizzly day. Beau and Mac sat under a shelter made with the mountain man's gum rubber blanket. Despite the gray day, the two men were in good spirits. Mac had killed a small wild boar and it was roasting over their fire.

"The captain wants us ready to ride in two days," Beau said, making idle conversation while watching the juices drip from the pork.

"We'll both be looking for another horse," Mac replied. "Mine has a bruised hoof."

"At least you were able to ride it in," Beau said. "A damn sniper shot mine out from under me in the last skirmish."

"If he'd have shot a little higher," Mac pointed out, "You wouldn't have needed another horse."

"That's a damn lot of comfort," Beau snorted. Then the mountain man laughed, "Worse yet, I wouldn't be enjoying the hog you shot."

Then both men got serious for a moment. There had been too many lives lost on both sides in the past months. Beau and Mac had watched men riding beside them, fall from their horses, mortally wounded. They both wondered how long their luck could hold out and the incoming bullet or shrapnel would be for them.

Two days later the weather was still dreary as the company prepared to ride. The two men had no problem getting another animal. Men had been killed in the last skirmish and that made the needed horses available.

The captain told them that they would be disrupting Confederate communications and supply lines to help weaken the South as Sherman pushed toward Atlanta. Their orders were to destroy with fire whenever possible to permanently put factories and mills out of business.

The pace at which the captain pushed his cavalry was exhausting. The constant riding stretched from weeks into months. Beau hoped that the destruction they were causing was actually helping the effort and not just hurting those who depended on them for a living.

With the chill of winter behind them and everything in full bloom, the company was camped near Snake Creek Gap. Beau was brushing his latest horse. Mac came by and kidded him, "You making it look pretty so the snipers won't want to hurt it?"

"Just down the road are Johnson and his army," Beau replied. "Brushing the horse helps my nerves."

The enemy were entrenched along Rocky Face Ridge. The cavalry would be going in to attack the Western & Atlantic railroad. Right now, the company was waiting for McPherson's columns to arrive. They would then go south through the gap.

On May 9th McPherson's troops arrived and they headed through Snake Creek Gap and on toward Resaca. Riding ahead, the cavalry found that the Confederates were entrenched around Resaca and rode back to inform McPherson. Beau and Mac sat on their horses, adrenaline racing through their bodies as they anticipated the order to attack.

Fighting could be heard as other columns engaged the enemy near Buzzard Roost. Beau knew that the Confederates were aware that they were coming and the longer they waited to attack, the more casualties the Union army would sustain.

Suddenly the word came that they were pulling back to wait for additional support. The captain slapped his boot with his riding crop. The cavalry was designed to engage in lightning strikes and then depart, having inflicted the maximum amount of damage on the enemy. Pulling back would only give the Confederates more time to harden their positions.

After a nervous night of waiting for the attack to start, Sherman's forces joined McPherson and they marched on Resaca, only to find the enemy gone. The week-long Battle of Rocky Face Ridge was considered a Union victory, even though General Johnson and his Confederates managed to avoid defeat by slipping south from Resaca, Georgia.

Two demoralizing, Union defeats followed at New Hope Church and Pickett's Mill. An attack led by Major General Howard, on the exposed right flank of Johnson's forces at Pickett's mill found the Confederates ready for the Union, allowing them to inflict high casualties.

The cavalry that Beau was with remained assigned to Major General McPherson and was preparing for an upcoming battle near the Big Kennesaw Mountain and Little Kennesaw Mountain. Beau and four others were tasked with providing reconnaissance on Johnson's army. The mountain man liked the security of being in the hills. They had just crossed the Powder River Road when they met up with the picket line of the 14th Kentucky Volunteer Infantry.

It was late afternoon and Beau was having some coffee and giving what information he had to their lieutenant. Beau's group had caught sight of a Confederate force to the east and would be going back to estimate the strength. They were just about to leave when rider came, warning the pickets of a force headed their way. Beau and the four men with him left to seek higher ground to offer the Kentucky Volunteers additional fire power and cover their withdrawal.

It was June 22nd, and the beginning of the Battle of Kolb's Farm. At 5:00 p.m. Hood's corps attacked the picket station, pushing the Kentucky Volunteers and the New York Infantry back. Beau and his men fired down on the Confederates until the withdrawal was complete and then abandoned their position.

While Hood was able to push back the pickets, parts of his Stevenson's division sustained considerable damage and were forced to pause. The remaining Confederate troops reached the open area of Kolb's Farm and faced the waiting artillery of the Union. Forced to retreat, Stevenson's troops fell back to a ravine that was covered with additional Federal artillery, causing a final defeat.

The mountain man was again confident of the strength of the Union Army with the success at Kolb's Farm. The next conflict he encountered was the Battle of Jonesborough on August 31st. The cavalry poured in sniper fire at the approaching army, then attacked the rear and their supply train, depriving the Confederates of much needed items.

After the two-day battle, General Johnson and his Confederates were forced to abandon Atlanta. A few days later, in September of 1864 the Union took over the city and opened the way for Sherman's March to the Sea.

* * *

While Sherman's forces were pushing east, a concerted effort was developing near the Mississippi. Raiders were busy attempting to develop a second front, hoping to split the Union forces. Cavalry companies were needed to hunt down and defeat the fast-moving raiders. The company that Beau and Mac were attached to was reassigned and found itself on a train heading west.

It was October and Beau was back in the familiar territory, west of the Mississippi. He and Mac were part of Major-General Samuel R. Curtis' Army of the Border. The Confederate raider Price's cavalry was operating in Arkansas, Missouri and Kansas. After the Confederate loss in Atlanta, Price's intention was to try and increase the size of the conflict, creating bad news on the progress of the war, and hoping to help defeat President Lincoln in the upcoming election.

Beau was riding a new horse after losing his in the last skirmish. The tall dun could carry him swiftly into battle, and quickly back out to safety during their hit and run tactics. While in Missouri, the Union troops could be attacked from all quarters due to the state having many Confederate sympathizers.

Spies had brought word that Price was headed toward Westport, Missouri. Due to illness, desertions, and battle losses, Price's Missouri Expedition had dwindled from 12,000 men to 8,500. Union forces led by Curtis had a strength of 22,000.

Westport was an area that Beau knew well. He rode with the cavalry, confident that victory would be theirs. They were armed with repeater rifles that held seven shots, and their horses were in good shape, having just had a rest with adequate feed.

On October 23, 1864, he felt the dun surge under him as the cavalry swept down on the Confederate fortifications. He saw Mac look back at him, shouting, "Let's get the bastards!"

That was the last thing the mountain man remembered about the battle.

CHAPTER THIRTEEN

It was dusk and a chilling rain was falling. Beau was confused as to where he was. His first fear was that he had overslept and was supposed to be on watch. Then he heard someone ask, "Are you dead yet?"

He opened his eyes and the world spun above him. "I ain't dead," Beau replied, lying still with his eyes closed. Turning his head slowly and using one eye, he looked toward the voice. It was Mac, sitting up against the carcass of his horse. He was holding Beau's Colt in his hand.

"What happened?" the mountain man asked.

"We was hit with a case shot," Mac replied. "It landed next to me, blowing up, killing my horse and knocking us into you. You hit your head pretty hard and have been lying there for hours. Your horse is just yonder, grazing like nothing happened."

Beau tried to get up and nausea hit him. He retched, his head pounding from the effort. The ache in his head was so severe that he couldn't help but cry out. "Hurts, don't it?" he heard Mac say.

"Oh! God help me, it hurts," Beau moaned.

"I don't hurt at all," MacKay replied. "From belly button down, I feel nothing. I'm coughing up blood."

Despite the pain Beau was in, he felt dread for Mac. No doubt his back was broken. Maybe shrapnel, or a rib, had punctured his lung. "Can you move at all?" the mountain man asked.

"Enough to drag myself to get your gun and back here," the man said.

Lying with his eyes closed, Beau pleaded, "Don't shoot yourself. Maybe it was only the shock of the shell made your legs numb."

"Oh, it ain't me I got to shoot," Mac said. "I got to shoot you."

Beau lay on the cold, muddy ground, silent. He had heard what the man had said, but it made no sense. The mountain man wondered if Mac was hurt so bad that in his confusion he thought Beau was a Confederate.

In a soft voice, Beau asked, "Why?"

Mac coughed and spit before answering. "Family," Mac replied. "You killed two of my cousins back in Oregon and I was sent east to kill you if I found you. Others went to California, and some to Canada."

"We been together for a damn long time," the mountain man said, feeling a bit of anger. "Why the hell you just getting to it?"

"I met the Allan children in Fort Laramie. Didn't I tell you that?" Mac asked. "They sure took to you. I told Louie we were friends. He said you had already gone to the army. I followed and finally found you. I ain't a killer like some of my kin. I can't just shoot a man in the back. I figured you were bound to get killed on the battlefield. Maybe I would too. I already got the letter in my pocket to be sent home saying you were dead. I'd send it if you were killed. Others would send it if I was killed. It wouldn't be a lie, though. I was sure you'd be killed before the war was over."

"Now you will have to kill me," Beau told him.

"I tried before," Mac replied. "Once in Corinth. There you were in the sniper's nest, in plain sight. I shot, but missed. I was glad I missed. As I got to know you, it got harder to think about killing you. I even prayed that the war would do it for me."

"Your prayers might just have been answered," Beau said. "I am in a damn bad way here."

"Hell, I'm all busted up," the man said. "If I start slipping away, I got to shoot you. It's part of the clan code."

"MacKay and Brodie," the mountain man said. "You come from the same clan in Scotland."

"You heard of us?" Mac asked.

"My father liked to read and talked of the clans back in Scotland and Ireland."

"Then you know I got to kill you."

Beau tried to move his head, causing shooting pains through his skull. He gritted his teeth, refusing to give the man the satisfaction that he was hurting. For just a moment, he wished Mac would pull the trigger and make the aching stop.

"Life sure is funny," Mac said wistfully. "I left Westport, Oregon to find you and here we are in Westport, Missouri, where it will end."

"I considered you a comrade in battle," Beau said. "That is more than just a friend. It is someone I would give my life for."

"And I you," Mac said. "I didn't mean for it to happen, but it just did."

"You're going to die," Beau told him. "If it helps settle things before going to the other side, then shoot me."

MacKay began to cough. "Damn," he said.

The mountain man heard the Colt being cocked. "I'll be waiting for you," Beau warned.

The gunshot caused the mountain man to flinch, only adding to his pain. Then there was only darkness.

* * *

"We got to kill him," a girl's voice said. "He's a damn Yankee."

"We don't kill people, Ellie," a second feminine voice said.

"You just turn your head, Corky, and I'll do it."

Beau was sure he was in Hell. The hereafter was just one person after another wanting to kill him. He wanted to say *"Do it,"* but his mouth and throat were so dry that all that came out was a croak.

He then heard the angry voice of Corky. "If you shoot this man, I will not be your cousin anymore!"

Trying to reason with her cousin, Ellie said, "If we don't, he'll be out there killing southern men. Maybe our husbands."

"The other one looks like he shot himself," Corky said.

"He's covered with blood all over," Ellie replied. "He was probably hurting so bad he couldn't stand it."

The sound of horses caught the cousins' attention. "The damn Yankees are coming back," Corky hissed. "They'll think we done this and kill us."

Then there was the sound of horses all around Beau. He opened his eyes and the light sent spears of pain through his head, then the blissful unconsciousness returned.

Bumping along the road brought Beau back to the world of his pain. Each movement caused the constant ache to increase. He was lying on hay, or straw, on the bed of the buckboard and there was a wool blanket covering him. Any light amplified the ache in his head, so he lay there with his eyes closed.

"This is a damn mess," he heard Ellie say. "I can't believe you told them Yankees that we would take care of one of theirs."

"They give us his horse," Corky told her. "More than likely he's going to die from banging his head and then we can just keep it."

"I'll give him a bang on the damn head," Ellie said. "What are folks going to think when we got a man, a damn Yankee in our house, while our husbands are out there risking their lives fighting the buggers?"

The morning sunlight shined off the cousins' red hair as they debated their situation. When the cavalry had returned, seeing Mac's body sprawled over his dead horse and Beau looking as good as dead, they had realized that nothing could be done until the battle at Westport was over. Finding the two girls kneeling over the mountain man had given them a solution.

They'd asked if the girls could care for the downed soldier until arrangement could be made to take him to one of the temporary hospitals that would soon be set up. When Ellie had told them that they had no way to move him from there, one of the sergeants had said that they could take the horse and use it if they had a wagon.

That was when Corky had stood up and said, "We have a fine buckboard at the house and can use that."

While Ellie glared at her cousin, the soldiers had stripped the men and animals of their ammo and the repeater rifles. Then, as quickly as they'd come, the cavalry thundered away, leaving Ellie holding the reins of Beau's dun.

As the two cousins approached their house, Corky suddenly said, "Annabelle! We can ask Annabelle to take care of him."

Brushing a wisp of red hair off her face, Ellie replied, "We can't just dump this damn Yankee off on sweet, old Annabelle."

"Well, she is the closest thing we got to a doctor around here," Corky countered. "Annabelle has delivered most of the babies in the area for the past 20 years."

"And now you want to deliver a Yankee to her doorstep," Ellie replied.

Giggling, the cousin replied, "It will make good company for her."

Drifting in and out of awareness, Beau listened to the girls. He could feel the warm sunshine on his face but didn't dare to try to open his eyes. No one had thought to pour a sip of water into his mouth. Try as he might, moving his tongue around, he couldn't get enough saliva to wet his parched throat.

Finally, the painful movement stopped. He heard Ellie say, "We got to clean him up some before we bring him to Annabelle."

With a cousin on each side, they got Beau off the wagon and dragged him into the house. He lay on their kitchen floor, looking more dead than alive. Corky went to get a bucket of water, while Ellie got a fire going in the cook stove.

Beau tied to open his eyes a crack. The dim light of the kitchen didn't make his head ache any harder, but he saw double and the room spun, bringing on a wave of nausea. Squeezing his eyes shut, he prayed the feeling would pass and he wouldn't begin to retch.

Lying on the floor, he could hear the sounds of the girls preparing to clean him up. He also heard a sizzle and then the smell of side meat frying. His stomach burned with hunger and finally the saliva glands were stimulated enough to wet his mouth just a bit.

"You get his clothes off," Ellie told her cousin.

"All the way off?" Corky asked.

The two girls laughed, and then Ellie replied, "At least enough to clean him up."

As Corky began to remove Beau's shirt, he whispered, "Water. Water."

"I think our man here is alive," Corky said. "He's asking for water."

"Oh, hell," Ellie said. "We plumb forgot about that. I bet he's thirsty."

Corky held Beau's head up. "What are you doing with that block of wood?" she asked her cousin.

"If he jumps up and tries to hurt us when we're giving him water, I plan to conk him and put him back down," Ellie replied.

The dribble of water into Beau's mouth caused him to choke and cough as he struggled to swallow. Rather gently, the cousin put his head back down. Finally, the mountain man was able to swallow and speak.

In a raspy voice he said, "I ain't going to jump up and do anything. I can't even open my eyes without being sick."

"You just stay put until we clean you up," Ellie said. "You stink something awful."

For the next hour, Beau suffered the indignities and comments of the cousins as they cleaned him up. Helpless to do for himself, he lay on the kitchen floor naked as he heard Corky say, "Now don't be looking at him like that."

Once he was dressed, they tried sitting him up, but the pounding in his head forced him to beg to be laid back down. One of the cousins got a pillow and put it under his head, which didn't help the ache but did make him more comfortable overall.

"We put some of my husband's clothes on you," Ellie told him. "I figure it was a fair trade for the horse."

"I'm hungry," Beau replied.

"We got some soup on for you," she said. "Corky's gone to get Annabelle. We'll give you some soup when she gets back."

Then he felt her breath as she leaned close to him. "If you get sick on this kitchen floor, I'll give you a bang with this here stick. We already cleaned up some pretty awful stuff from you."

The sound of Corky returning was a relief. Beau didn't fully trust Ellie. He was sure she wouldn't hit an injured man, but her threats sounded mighty real. Someone came close and he felt a soft hand on the side of his face.

"I'm Annabelle," a gentle voice said. "The girls have asked me to take care of you."

Her hands moved around his head touching the split area that had come in contact with the ground. Beau moaned. "You took a terrible fall," she said. "Can you open your eyes?"

"No," Beau replied.

The three ladies moved away from him and Beau could hear them talking softly. He lay there thinking, *Where is the soup?*

* * *

After some of the soup, Beau was put back on the buckboard. While he didn't dare open his eyes, he was able to walk with the assistance of someone on each side. His head still ached, but it was somewhat more tolerable. Each bump in the road still caused shooting pains.

Once he was in Annabelle's house, the cousins called goodbye and let the screen door slam behind them. The sharp sound was painful. Beau was sitting in a cushioned chair and could hear Annabelle collecting some items. Then there was the sound of her light footsteps returning.

"First off, I need to know your name," she said sweetly.

"The name is Beauford Levesque," he said, his voice still sounding raspy. "Folks call me Beau."

"Well, Beauford, the first thing I need to know is what makes your head hurt?" Annabelle asked.

"Light is the worst," he told her. "Loud noises and bouncing in the wagon will get my attention."

"Anything else?" she asked.

"In the dim light, when I can open my eyes, everything spins, making me feel sick."

"Are you seeing double?" Annabelle asked.

"I think so," Beau told her. "Everything spins when I try and look."

Annabelle came up behind him and reached around his head. She put a soft strip of cloth over his eyes. "There," she said, "now you can open your eyes and light won't get in. You also won't be able to see double."

Slowly, Beau opened his eyes. The thick strip didn't allow any light in. "That worked," he told her. "Now, do you have anything that will help the aching in my head?"

"Prayer and time will take care of the ache, Beauford," she assured him. "Now, I need to clean and rebandage the split you have on the side of your head."

He could smell the carbolic as she opened the bottle. Beau braced himself for a new source of pain. Even Annabelle's gentle touch could not dampen the sting as she swabbed the wound. Finished with the immediate care, Annabelle led him through the house, cautioning him about each piece of furniture. Beau still felt unstable as he slowly shuffled, holding her arm.

After moving into the pantry off the kitchen, she said, "I put a cot in here and this will be your room."

She sat him on the small bed and described shelves with canned venison and vegetables, and the other things that were around him. "If you stay to the right when leaving the room, the wall will guide you to the parlor. Straight ahead a few steps are the chairs. If you need to use the toilet, it is out of the kitchen door. Let me know and I will bring you."

The mountain man continued to have problems with nausea, mostly due to the constant ache in my head. When it got more severe, it would affect his stomach. Slowly, the worry that this would last the rest of his life began to creep in and he began to wish Mac had followed the will of the clan.

Most days, Beau would sit on the front porch, often wrapped in a blanket. Annabelle believed in the power of prayer and fresh air. The days tended to run together with the same routine, except for Sunday when he was carefully guided to church. They sang Christmas hymns and the sermons centered around the birth of Christ. It had been years since Beau had celebrated Christmas, and in his dark world he was finding it most satisfying.

Saturday night was bath night. The sound of Annabelle working the kitchen pump could be heard throughout the house. Pots of water were being heated on the wood stove, to be dumped into a large bronze tub for a good soak. She would bathe first, then it was Beau's turn.

The Saturday before Christmas, she had finished her bath and called to Beau. The constant ache was almost gone, but the occasional migraine headache had to be endured. His eyes were still sensitive to light, and to prevent an unwanted headache he continued to keep them covered at all times.

Moving through her small home had become much easier. Annabelle had moved all the items that could trip the mountain man. Feeling his way through the house, he placed his hand on the edge of the bronze tub. Slowly he removed his clothing.

"Let me help you in," Annabelle offered and she took his arm. He felt her naked body brush him as he climbed into the warm water.

"I am going to shave you and cut your hair after your bath," she told him. "I am thinking you are a handsome man under those whiskers."

She took the soap and began to gently bathe him. While she had always helped him during bathing or dressing, Annabelle had never been this helpful. The warm bath and her gentle caressing relaxed the mountain man, and for the first time, he felt no ache in his head. He was also having some other feelings he hadn't had in some time.

"The stress has left your face," she said, rubbing a soapy cloth across his chest.

"The bath relaxes me," he told her. Then, after some hesitation he asked, "Tell me, are you wearing some kind of clothes?"

"Does it matter?" she asked. "You can't see and I didn't want to get my dress wet."

As she worked her way down his body, Annabelle suddenly stopped. She placed the soap and cloth in his hand and said, "You better finish areas under the water. I'll get you a towel."

"I think I'd better sit right here and soak for a while," Beau told her. "Just leave my clothes and the towel beside the tub."

Christmas was a special day. As though a gift from heaven, Beau was able to keep the cloth off his eyes while in the house. Annabelle had made a patch to cover one of his eyes, which helped the double vision. The snow-covered outdoors was still too bright and forced him to keep something over his eyes.

While waiting to leave for church, the mountain man saw two haversacks and a knapsack near a small fireplace in the parlor. "Are these my things in the parlor?"

"They are, Beauford," she told him. "One of the bags was from the young man that was killed, but the army took his knapsack."

Adjusting the patch over his eye, Beau began going through the haversacks. In Mac's bag he found the letter addressed to his people in Westport, Oregon. He also found his Colt in his haversack. The cousins, or the army, had not taken it. It still had blood on the barrel from Mac's last act.

After Christmas was over, he'd send the letter to Mac's family. He would also add a line about MacKay's death on the back of the envelope. The letter should stop the clan from looking for him and Beau had no intention of ever going back to Oregon.

Beau and Annabelle sat with Ellie and Corky at the church service. The mountain man looked around the plain country church and had a warm feeling. For the first time he was able to see the people around him, including an old gentleman who sang very loud, with great pride, and had no sense of tune.

Annabelle put the folded scarf over his eyes before they left the church. The cousins were joining them for the Christmas meal. Their voices surrounded Beau as he took in the brisk air and the crusted snow crunched under their feet. These were happy times.

With the church hymns still running through his mind, Beau sat in the living room, smelling the aromas of the meal being prepared. Ellie and Corky were busy in the kitchen with Annabelle. He could hear them laughing and kidding Annabelle about having a man in the house. The tea they had brought him was almost gone. Right then he would have done about anything for a glass of rye and a chew of tobacco.

He glanced at his packs. Beau was sure there was some chew in them.

The mountain man would move the patch from one eye to the other, hoping to keep them both working well, but he kept it mostly on the left side, keeping is shooting eye free. He missed having the repeater as he thought about how easy it was to load the next shot. He was glad he'd found the Colt. The cousins must have kept it out of sight, or the returning cavalry would have taken it with the rifles.

Beau glanced at a two-day old newspaper while waiting for the meal. It talked about Price being beaten and driven out of Missouri. Also, that Lincoln had won reelection and the worries of a broader front were over. Beau figured that if his eyes started working right, he would most likely be transferred east for the rest of the war, or he could request a discharge due to age and his injury.

While bringing the food to the table, Corky stopped a moment in front of the mountain man. "You sure do clean up nice."

"You'll have to thank Annabelle for that," Beau replied. Then Corky and Ellie broke into a round of laughter.

The four of them sat at the table with a meal in front of them, the likes of which Beau had never seen before. Annabelle said a lengthy prayer for the ending of the war and safety of the soldiers. Ham, root vegetables, sweet breads, and many other good things were enjoyed at the feast. Ellie and Corky kept referring to things spoken of in the kitchen that kept Annabelle blushing.

Annabelle was older than Beau had guessed by her voice and touch. Her white hair was put up on her head and framed her smiling face. She wore a festive dress that accented an attractive figure. Both Ellie and Corky were a pleasure to look at and appeared to be having the time of their lives. The cousins had received letters from their husbands, confirming that they were alive and well.

With the meal finished, two presents were placed in front of Beau. Removing the loose wrappings revealed a bottle of rye and a pipe with tobacco. "Now I don't expect you to drink too much of that whiskey at one sitting," Annabelle warned him. "It could bring on the headaches."

The pipe was one of her husband's, who had been killed at the beginning of the war. Nothing was said of which side he was fighting for. It might have even been during a local conflict, which there had been many of.

"Thank you very much," he told her. "I didn't get you anything and wish I had been able to."

"You have brought life into my house and a purpose for me," Annabelle said. "I needed nothing more."

The sun was about to set when the cousins left. Annabelle watched the buckboard drive away. "They really like that horse of yours," she said. "All their stock was taken by raiders for the war."

Beau thought back to all the businesses and farms they had raided, never thinking about the results. They had just figured it was for the good of the Union. The mountain man felt a slight ache as he thought about the fighting. He needed to get his mind elsewhere.

"Do you mind if I light the pipe?" he asked.

"I was hoping you would," Annabelle replied.

Taking his time, Beau filled the pipe and then broke a match from the block and put the flame to the tobacco. He drew on the pipe and soon had it properly lit. Annabelle closed her eyes, letting the smell bring her back to better times.

Suddenly, she stood up. "I think we should have a toast to the holiday." She went to the kitchen and came back with two glasses. She poured some whiskey into each and handed one to Beau.

"To a speedy end to the war," she said, and they both drank.

The whiskey warmed Beau's stomach and he was again relaxed. Annabelle began to tell him about the Christmases of her youth. They talked late into the evening, having another drink to good health.

Annabelle got up and put out the lamps in the front room and kitchen. Beau went out to the little house to relieve himself one more time. The ice-cold air reminded him of the mountains. In the dark he stared at the stars. He could see Annabelle's shadow move across the windows as she got ready for bed. He would miss talking to her when he left.

He entered the warm house. The smells of the meal and the pipe still hung in the air. He pulled back the curtain from the doorway of his small room. He decided to add a bit of wood to the stove before going to bed. He heard footsteps behind him. Then he felt her arms around his waist.

"Would you mind coming to bed with me tonight?" she asked. "The night is going to be cold."

Arm in arm, they walked through the parlor into Annabelle's room. Unable to think of any of the right words to say, Beau commented, "It is cool in here."

With a perplexed look on her face, she replied, "Do you think more wood in the stove would be the best solution?"

* * *

For the next two months, the pantry was only used to store canned goods. The headaches came less often and only the brightest winter days bothered his eyes. Beau still wore the patch over his left eye. Annabelle had begun to call him her pirate.

Another book written by Walter Johnston showed up in the small town and Annabelle had surprised Beau with it. In the evenings they would take turns reading about living in the mountains. She would often ask Beau questions about being a mountain man. He told her it was pretty much like what was written in the book.

The letter had been sent to Oregon and another went to Fort Laramie. In the letter to the fort, he did mention being wounded and away from his company for a while. Lucy sent a letter telling him that the major in the fort had received a letter inquiring about two children who might have been left there. The mountain man now wished he had opened Mac's letter and read it before mailing it.

For the Union, the war had gone well. It was the end of February and Beau figured the snow would be gone in Arkansas. A few weeks earlier, he'd visited the local army headquarters. While they'd had no record of him, the captain had decided to give him some back pay, along with traveling orders so he could make his way to Memphis and from there to the east. Using the pay, he purchased a team of horses and presented them as a gift to the cousins, in exchange for his dun. While they pretended to be disappointed about losing a fine horse like the dun, their smiling eyes told a different story.

He had built a fire in the small fireplace and Beau and Annabelle sat in front of it. The mountain man had his pipe lit and held a glass of rye. Annabelle had poured a little rye into her tea and was tapping the edge of the cup with her nail.

"I get the feeling you are about ready to leave," she told him.

"I am," Beau replied. "It bothers me that I am not being fair to you after all you have done for me. I want to visit Crowley Ridge and have another look at the old cabin I had there. For all I know it has completely fallen to ruin."

"And then where will you go?" Annabelle asked.

"I will have to go east to muster out of the army," Beau said. "The war is drawing to a close, and with my double vision I can't be much help. It is time for me to get out."

"How about the children?" she asked.

"My guess is someone from Oregon will show up at Fort Laramie to take them west," he replied. "I don't plan to send any more letters to the fort. They know that I was wounded. I am sure she will work it out, letting Mary and Toby know what they need to believe if someone comes."

"Even if she has to tell them you might be dead?" Annabelle asked, surprise on her face.

"If they come from Oregon for the children, it will be best," Beau replied.

For a long time, they sat in silence and watched the wood slowly being consumed by the flames. It appeared that nobody was getting what they wanted and Beau had no idea what his next move would be after leaving the army.

CHAPTER FOURTEEN

On March 3, 1865, the mountain man rode away from the small house near Westport. Annabelle stood on the porch with a shawl wrapped around her shoulders to protect her from the cold wind. Clouds of breath hung in the air from the dun as it snorted, excited to be on its way.

Most often, Beau would have ridden away without a look back, but something about leaving Annabelle forced him to turn the horse and wave. "You take care of yourself, Beauford," she called to the mountain man.

Turning away, Beau brought the dun to a trot. The wind was cold on his bare cheeks. Drops of water from his breath formed on his full moustache. He was not wearing a uniform, to prevent any folks still fighting the war in the hills from looking at him as an easy target. He was traveling close to the route he and Elijah had taken years ago.

While the weather was still cold, he had a warm blanket and the half tent that would work well as a fly tarp. Beau did wish he had a rifle. If he met danger at close range, the Colt would be adequate for defense, but should he find himself attacked by a more distant foe, the revolver would be useless.

It would take two weeks of steady travel to reach the cabin area of Crowley Ridge. The mountain man was actually riding there to determine if that was the area he wanted to settle down in after the war. There was a good chance that he wouldn't have any direction pulling him after the war was over, so Arkansas just might be the answer.

The second night on the trail, there was a damp, two-inch snowfall. Beau lay under the fly tarp, trying to hear the sounds of the night. Snow clinging to branches would cause them to snap. The mountain man had often heard these sounds in the past, but for some reason they now sounded more like danger. He sat up in his shelter and cradled the Colt in his lap.

He no longer felt comfortable with his choice of campsites. He should have found an area that wasn't as open, maybe within some windfall to provide more protection. The dun snorted, which caused him to break into a cold sweat. Beau scolded himself for having the feeling of fear. There was no reason why anyone would be stalking him.

After a sleepless night, the mountain man broke camp and rode away before daylight. While he felt that someone was out there coming for him, it made little sense. At Annabelle's in Westport he hadn't had these feelings. Then he did recall, when using the little house at night, he would rush back into the house, unsure of his safety.

Years ago Beau would have the same feeling in the mountains, especially if there had been a conflict with one of the tribes. But in those cases he had been able to sort out the sounds and, with the help of his horse's actions, he would become comfortable with the night.

"You're just getting old and spooky," he muttered.

For the rest of the ride south, he couldn't shake the feeling of danger. The only time he felt safe while riding was on high ground. At night he would seek out a dense thicket in which to make his camp. He wouldn't burn a fire after dark, and those he did light were small and put out quickly.

Beau spent the night in Carthage, Missouri. Confederate raiders had torched most of the town the fall before. A tavern with rooms to rent was still open. They had a small barn in the back that he put the dun in. The tavern had a few local customers nursing their drinks. The wooden structure had a low ceiling and six small rooms to the back for sleeping. The portly bartender claimed the raiders didn't burn his building because it was the only place in town where a man could get a drink.

The place served a thick stew that was mostly rutabagas. Beau took a seat at a table with his back to the wall. The bartender set a bottle of whiskey and two glasses onto the table. Noticing, Beau told him, "Just one glass."

"Hell, man," the bartender replied, leaving the glass, "little later a few ladies will be coming in and you just might want to share a bit of that bottle with them."

"I appreciate your kind thought," the mountain man said. "Fetch me a bowl of that stew."

The stew was surprisingly good, and the bread that accompanied it was freshly made. The tension that Beau had felt for days ebbed away in the surroundings of the building. It made no sense to the mountain man. Here he was, drinking in a town ripe with raiders, and he felt comfortable.

Well after dark, the *ladies* came in. They appeared to have lived a hard life, more than likely the results of the war. One woman with her hair tied back and a shapeless gingham dress came to his table and sat down.

Giving him a crooked smile, she asked, "Is one of those glasses for me?"

Beau picked up the half-full bottle and poured her a generous measure of the amber brew. "What should we drink to?" he asked.

"You sound like a local boy, but I am betting you lost that eye fighting for the Yankees," she replied. "We'll drink to them."

Without waiting, she poured herself a second drink. "You know, we beat your asses in '61. Now there are just a few boys out there still fighting . . . and dying."

The woman continued to make small talk, pretty much rambling from one subject to another while she slowly finished a good part of the whiskey. Beau tried to be a gentleman and nodded in agreement with most of what she said. She had been one of the women who had followed the armies, doing laundry, cooking, and giving comfort to the soldiers for some spare money. For a while she had followed the Confederates, and later the Union because they had more money.

"Do you have a room here?" she asked suddenly.

Unsure of how to answer, the mountain man asked, "Do you have a place away from here?"

"Yes, but it is just a shack," she replied. "This tavern has the nicest rooms around." Then she laughed and added, "And the only rooms around."

Beau took a couple of coins from his pocket and pressed them into her hand. "I won't be staying with you tonight, but this money is for the company you have given me this evening."

Looking at the coins, she suddenly jostled him, grabbing and scratching, then snarled, "God damn Yankees think they are too good for a woman like me." Shoving her hands into her dress pockets, she staggered away into the dark street.

A man playing cards at the next table leaned over and asked, "Are you a damn Yankee?"

Beau put his hand on the butt of the Colt in his waistband and replied, "I am just an old soldier coming home."

"Ain't we all," the man laughed and then went back to his card playing.

The room had a solid wooden door and no windows. Beau put a chair under the knob to prevent entry. Preparing for bed, the mountain man noticed that the woman had stolen some things from his pockets. Some money and his travel orders were gone. Despite the discovery, Beau was exhausted and slept deep that night. By daylight he was back on the trail. Soon the feeling of pending danger had returned. Beau swore at himself, thinking, *Damn you out there, shoot me already*.

Arriving near the ridge, Beau found that the plantation that he'd worked for had the look of neglect. The slaves were gone and the fields lay fallow. Not much additional land had been cleared since he had left. It appeared that things had stopped after Horst Weber had died.

The only places where Beau saw snow were up in the shaded areas on Crowley Ridge. The air remained cold and he pulled the blue wool coat closed in the front. The coat would identify him as a Union soldier, but he had removed the brass buttons and replaced them with flat black ones when he was assigned as a sniper.

His haversack and pack were tied on the back of the saddle, wrapped in the ground tarp. His shoes were the issued brogans, and he had a black felt slouch hat with a flat brim to keep the rain and sun off him. His shirt and pants were not army issued. They were the ones given to him by the cousins and could get him hung as a spy if caught by Confederate raiders.

Riding past the plantation, Beau knew that there was no way he could be mistaken for anything but a Union soldier. He had gotten away with it at the tavern with the help of the low light and having his coat off. Beau adjusted the Colt in his waist band and he walked the dun along the base of the ridge. He still hadn't shaken the feeling that he was being watched. Inside he felt that someone would burst out of hiding at any moment from behind the slightest amount of cover.

The mountain man swung off the dun near the area that had once been the start of the trail up to his cabin. He could see crocus pushing up through the dead leaves ahead of him. Soon the grass and ferns would appear, followed by budding leaves.

Beau's legs ached with fatigue as he climbed the slope. "You're showing your damn age," he muttered.

Suddenly, the horse pulled back as it was startled by a grouse flushed in front of them. "Easy there," Beau said rubbing the side of its neck. "That was just my supper getting away."

He stopped short of the cabin. Beau was surprised to see that the roof had been replaced at some time. The leather hinges were now metal. He looked back at the delta below and the familiarity of the place washed over him. The smell and feel were comforting. He tied the dun to an evergreen near the cabin and lifted the new latch, pulling the door open.

The rusted metal hinges complained as they creaked on opening. A musty smell came out of the dark interior. Beau stepped inside and stood waiting for his eye to adjust. There was the sound of small residents scampering along the log walls.

Finally, he was able to make out the furnishings. A double bunk had been built along the right wall. His original table was still next to the door, but the stools had been replaced with handmade chairs. The shelves and fireplace were pretty much like he'd left them. The floor was still packed dirt. The cabin was in surprisingly good shape and had been left clean by the last occupants.

"This will do just fine," he said as he turned to rearrange the rocks for the firepit. It was mid-afternoon and he had eaten some cold biscuits and water for breakfast. It felt right putting the sticks together for the fire. Beau realized that he'd missed this place. It had been the first home that he'd built and lived in after his father had died.

The spring just up from the cabin still flowed clear with good water. Filling the coffee pot, he returned to the fire and set it to heat. Beau had never owned an animal when living here and he quickly realized that there was very little for the horse to eat. Stripping his gear off the dun, he led it to a grove of aspen. The tender shoots would have to do for now.

After slicing several pieces of side meat into the blackened frying pan, he put it on the fire and went back into the cabin. A smile broke across his face. Whoever had been here had left his old pots that had been used to render oil from the bears. He found one that hadn't rusted through and put water into it in preparation for making a large pot of beans.

His coffee and side meat were done first, and the mountain man sat on a rock and ate some while watching the pot of water beginning to steam. He planned to put some of the side meat into the bean pot and make a fine meal that would last a couple of days in the cooler weather.

Looking around, he decided that one of the first things he'd do was build a proper bench for the front of the cabin. He could sit there in the evenings and watch the sun set beyond the delta. He closed his eye and thought about the many times he'd done that in the past.

Beau wasn't kidding himself. He knew his stay here would be short. He had to get to Memphis and catch a train for the east and finish up with the army. But right now he was feeling very much at home. The thoughts that he was being watched had drifted away with the security of the small cabin. He was in familiar terrain and safe.

Finding grazing for the dun and hunting fresh meat for his meals became Beau's only job at the cabin. He spent time in the morning and evening sitting on the new bench he'd made and watched the delta. Flocks of white birds would fly out in the morning and then back in the evening. Twice he caught sight of bigger game, but with only the Colt they could only be watched. A bear with its cub had played for hours just below him one of the days.

At the end of two weeks he knew he had to leave. He hadn't received any news on the war, or even spoken with anyone. The cabin was isolated, just like he liked it. Beau put the cabin in good order before leaving. In the back of his mind he had every intention of returning in the future.

He wondered about the family he had met over the ridge. Homer Franks would be in his sixties, if he was still alive. The wife was a little younger and he remembered there had been five children. He decided he'd ride over the ridge and visit them. Memories of the confrontation over the bear Beau had shot came back. Homer had been reasonable and had come up with a plan that had worked for both of them.

Later, when Beau had to run from the area, Homer had loaned him a mule to help him get ahead of anyone chasing him. As the dun picked its own way over the ridge, the mountain man recalled that Homer had married the woman and made a frugal home for her and her children. While he had little, he had given so much.

Beau discovered that the two-room cabin had been expanded to double its size. Additional out buildings had been added. Land had been cleared below the small farm and was tilled in preparation of this spring's planting.

He could hear the voices of youngsters as he walked the dun toward the farm. Smoke came from a metal stove pipe near the center of the roof. A middle-aged man was coming from the barn as Beau swung down from the dun.

"Can I help you?" he called out.

The mountain man stepped away from the horse. "My name's Beau Levesque," he replied. "Twenty years ago, I met a man named Homer Franks that lived on this place."

"That would have been my father," the man said. "I am Karl Franks."

The man stood and watched as Beau walked towards him leading the dun. "I see you won't be needing to borrow a mule this time," Karl said.

Smiling, Beau replied, "You remember that. I never did know, did the mule make it back here?"

"It did," the man said. "We never heard from anyone on the other side of the ridge looking for you. We heard talk in town that you had taken a bunch of slaves north. I went to your cabin and helped my father get the bear meat. I been keeping the place up and using it for hunting. Seems to have more game on that side of the ridge."

"Are your mother and the rest of the children still here?" Beau asked.

"Mother's buried next to father to the north of the house. Lost one of my brothers in the war and the other is still fighting. The sisters live in the Memphis area. I married and have young'uns of my own now," Karl said proudly.

"I heard them at play," the mountain man replied. "It was a good sound."

"Martha has some venison stew on," Karl told him. "You are welcome to join us."

"I'd like that," Beau replied. "I'll put the horse near the barn."

Tying the dun on one of the corral rails, the mountain man looked around the barn yard. The buildings were well laid-out and displayed the skill of the builder. He followed Karl into the house. There had been many improvements since the stark, two room cabin where Beau had shared a meal the first time.

The two men stopped at the woodshed and got an armload to fill the wood box in the house. "I never took slaves north," Beau said. "I did travel with one that ran. We went west and did trapping and hunting. Elijah was the slave and the son of Horst Weber. Now he's a Flathead chief and has a family of his own."

He watched as Karl picked up the last stick of wood. He wondered what his reaction would be hearing that Beau had helped a runaway. The farmer smiled. "So you became a mountain man."

Martha was a good-looking woman, wearing a plain dress and her hair put up in a braid. She smiled as the mountain man walked in and said, "So who is this, Karl?"

Her husband told her briefly about the meeting years ago, leaving out the fact that Beau was running. "It is his cabin that I hunt out of," he told her.

"It has a fine view of the delta," she said. "I can't believe you ever left it."

While the meal was not fancy, it had a wonderful taste of good home cooking. Their three youngsters sat quietly eating, just a bit shy at having a stranger in the house.

"Where did you go after leaving here?" Karl asked.

"From Missouri Eli and I went west. We had decided to become mountain men, but our only problem was we knew nothing about living and hunting in the mountains," Beau told them. "Fortunately, luck was on our side, and we met the right people that taught us how to survive and for the past 20 years it has been my life."

"What made you come back east to fight the war?" Martha asked.

"I guess all I can call it is mixed feelings," the mountain man replied. "I started east to fight for the South that I grew up in, and got here agreeing with the Union cause and joined them."

The mountain man was sure Karl's brothers were fighting for the South and Martha probably had family dying for the southern cause. The conversation shifted away from the war and settled on the weather, farming, and plans for the place.

After the meal, the two men went outside to have a chew. "Everything about this area is familiar to me," Beau told him. "I don't understand the uneasy feeling that seems to dog me. Many nights I wake up sweating, sure that I heard something out in the dark. It never comes, but I am sure it is out there."

"My father was in the war of 1812 and fought it in the south. He was wounded once and had lost friends, and killed more that a few of the enemy," Karl replied. "He spoke of the same kind of things. He told me once that before he met my mother the neighbors found him sitting on top of a shed, rifle loaded and looking for those that were after him."

"What did he do?" Beau asked. "I met your father before I left and he didn't seem to have any problems."

"He told me that he thought drinking might help," the man said. Smiling, he continued. "It wasn't the solution. Father said it just made things worse. I guess he just accepted what he felt and everyday he had to wake up and remind himself that there wasn't anyone out there coming for him."

Beau stared thoughtfully at the ground and spat at a wooly caterpillar. "What you say is probably good advice. Until the war is over, it will be hard to shake it though."

Then the mountain man headed for his horse. "I do want to thank you for the meal, and you have a real nice family there."

"You are welcome to spend the night," Karl offered. "My wife reads from the Bible every night and then a bit from the book about mountain men to help settle the children down. They would love to hear some stories from a real mountain man."

Smiling, Beau replied, "Just have her read the book. It seems to cover my life."

"The good book?" Karl asked, kidding.

Shaking his head, the mountain man replied, "I wish it was, but no."

* * *

The mountain man was three days from Memphis. It was near the end of March 1865. He hadn't heard much news of the war since leaving Westport. All he knew was that the Confederates were being pushed hard and Sherman was marching to the sea. The war was pretty much over in the area where Beau was traveling, but not everyone had stopped fighting.

Realizing it was probably just his nerves, Beau still camped the first night in a cottonwood thicket. Keeping his fire small, he just made coffee and had one of the biscuits that Karl's wife had sent with him. Again, he wished he had a rifle. It is unlikely it would have helped with the feeling he had, but just holding it would have been comforting.

It was hot and muggy when Beau woke up the next morning. The dun stood in the evergreens, slapping the flies that buzzed around its back with its tail. Warming last night's coffee near the fire, Beau began slicing side meat into the frying pan. He looked around, smelling the air and the feel of the place. Just a day's ride south had left the feel and comfort of the small cabin behind.

Beau kept to the trails in the hills when he left the camp. He feared that riding along the road would leave him too exposed. He had to remember that he still looked more like a Union soldier than a Confederate, and the patch over his left eye wouldn't buy much sympathy if he ran into raiders.

In the late afternoon, he was riding along the railroad tracks that cut through two hills. Scattered on both sides of the tracks were discarded ties and bent rails left over from prior attacks by Union soldiers. The sun cast dark shadows from the ridge to his right. Out of these shadows rode three men. A heavyset man carried a rifle across the saddle, while the other two men had revolvers in their holsters.

The mountain man looked around quickly and realized that there was no way of avoiding the men. He continued riding, keeping the dun on a path directly at the men. "If they move to the side, horse, we should be okay."

The riders spread out just a bit and stopped. Beau pulled the dun up 30 feet from them. "I'm headed for Memphis," Beau told them. "Can you give me way on the trail?"

"Tuck here has taken a liking to your horse," the heavy-set man with the rifle replied.

"I would say Tuck has a good eye for horse flesh," the mountain man said. "This is a fine animal."

Beau sat on the dun with his coat unbuttoned and his hand resting on the saddle horn, inches away from the Colt that was just out of sight in his waistband. The rider called Tuck said, "What my friend means is I'd like to have the horse."

Keeping his voice casual, Beau replied, "If you are looking to swap horses, I believe we could come up with a deal. How much money you got?"

The two men riding with the heavy-set man appeared to be kin. The one furthest left replied, "You look like Union trash and the horse you're riding is too good for you. It's more fit for Tuck here."

"You best do what Billy says," the brother named Tuck warned. "He's got a pretty short fuse."

The man with the rifle began to swing it in the mountain man's direction and never saw the quick move that brought out the Colt. Fire spit from the barrel and the .36 caliber ball flew toward the man's torso. The bullet hit the rifle action and ricocheted up, tearing a ragged hole in the side of the man's face.

As he fell backwards, blood spraying from his cheek, the other two brothers reached for their revolvers and froze when they saw the Colt leveled at them. The man who had the rifle lay writhing on the ground with his hands over the wound on his face, blood running through his fingers. The damaged rifle rested next to him, the breech dented and the hammer missing.

The two brothers froze, their hands in the air. "Don't shoot us," Tuck cried, "we was just kidding you."

"My ass you were kidding. I killed a lot of you boys in this war and saw a whole lot more killed by others," Beau said. "It is days from being over and it don't make no sense in getting yourselves killed. Now toss your guns on the ground and get off those horses."

The two men stood by their horses, fearful that the angry man on the dun was about to shoot them. "Your partner over there needs help," the mountain man said. "I want you boys to bring the horses and revolvers to me. Make sure you hold the guns by the barrel."

The shot from the Colt had done enough damage to the breech loader, so Beau figured it was useless. He stuck the two revolvers into his waist band. With the reins of their three horses in one hand, and the Colt in the other, he rode by the would-be robbers.

"I want you to heed my words: The war is over and the fighting has to stop. Go home, boys." Then, tapping the dun with his heels, he rode away along the tracks, keeping the animals as a prize. Beau was still a long ride from Memphis, but he decided that with the help of the raiders' horses he could be there by dark. He would sell all four horses and take a train east to Washington.

Memphis hadn't suffered much damage from the war. It had been used to house and treat 5,000 wounded Union soldiers. They also had a prison that held southern sympathizers. Riding through the streets, Beau looked for a place to put the horses up. He was almost to the far side when he saw a weathered sign the said, "Livery: Horses Bought & Sold"

In the shadows of the large building, Beau caught sight of a white-haired man. He was kicking some hay into a stall. The hostler saw him and hurried out through the wide bay doors. The mountain man noticed he was missing an arm. Missing limbs had become an all too common sight as the result of the war.

The white-haired man smiled, showing tobacco stained teeth. "The name is Smutty."

Before Beau had a chance to reply, the hostler started looking at the horses. "You got yourself a bunch of horses there."

"I come on a couple of extra just a day ago," the mountain man replied, and then said, "The name's Beau."

"Well, Mr. Beau. It is a pleasure to meet you." Then Smutty asked, "You wouldn't be looking to sell a couple of them, would yah?"

"If the price is right, I just might be," Beau said.

For the next half-hour, Beau and the hostler dickered over the price. Smutty was thrilled to find out all four horses were available, as well as the saddles. "I sure could use all four," he said, shaking his head. "Money is kind of tight right now in Memphis. To be truthful with you, I had too much of mine in Confederate."

"Just let me know what's your best price," Beau replied. "To be honest with you, there might be some fellows looking for three of these horses."

The old hostler's eyes lit up upon hearing this. "Then we just might be able to do business."

Beau turned to get his saddlebags off the dun when the left eye began to itch. Removing the patch, he was about to rub it when he noticed that he wasn't seeing double. For the past couple of mornings, he had been able go for short periods without the patch, before the double vision would return. This was the first time that he had no problem late in the day.

Smutty had walked back into the shadows of the livery and was returning with a bottle of rye in one hand and a piece of paper under his stump. "If what I writ on this paper is okay, we'll have a drink to seal the deal."

Then he looked at Beau. "Weren't you wearing a patch when you come in here?"

"I was," the mountain man said, as surprised as the hostler. "Seems the eye got better."

Beau had never sold horses so cheap, but considering he had only invested in one, he did all right. The rye used to seal the deal hit the spot. The mountain man walked away with a warm glow inside and enough money in his pocket to keep him in groceries until he reached Washington. And, best of all, the patch was in his pocket.

Smutty had recommended that he get a room above the saloon rather than staying in one of the army barracks. It was a place frequented by Union soldiers and had a decent kitchen that offered southern fried chicken most evenings.

The Union headquarters occupied one of the finer hotels in the area. Beau knew that he had to check in or he could end up being considered a deserter. A clerk with the rank of private sat at a small desk covered with stacks of files. Beau explained that he'd lost the copy of the orders that he'd been given in Westport.

The clerk pushed a visitor log at Beau and said, "Put your name, rank and company on the next line. If you can't write, put an X on the line and I'll fill out the rest."

As he filled out the information, Beau said, "I'll be needing transportation to Washington. At least that's what the folks in Westport told me."

"I'll be telling you where you'll be going!" the clerk snapped. He then pulled the log to him, noticing that the mountain man had finished filling out the information.

The cocky clerk wrote down the information onto a piece of paper and then disappeared into another room. After several minutes, he came back still carrying the paper and with a confused look on his face. "We got you listed as dead."

"When exactly was I supposed to have died?" Beau asked.

"It was in Westport, Missouri," the clerk said. Then he got a suspicious look on his face. "You ain't one of those Johnny Rebs that are trying to get money by switching sides?"

"I sure as hell ain't," Beau growled. "I've been fighting this war for the past three years and as you can see I ain't dead."

Standing his ground, the clerk countered, "You know anyone in Memphis that can vouch for you?"

It appeared that when the cavalry had come back and collected the weapons they had misreported that both Beau and McKay were dead. He wondered if the travel orders that were stolen would have even done him any good. Beau followed the clerk into the back room to review lists of soldiers that were currently in Memphis, hoping to find a familiar name.

For two frustrating hours the mountain man poured over a stack of records, looking for anyone he might've served with. After Westport, his division had been sent to Kansas. While he searched, the clerk had left the list of killed in action with his name, Cpl. Beauford Levesque, in plain sight. What really bothered him was the note next to his name: "Notification sent to family."

After exhausting the names of active duty in Memphis, Beau began to go through lists of those in the hospital. Suddenly, a name jumped out at him: Sergeant Thomas Miller. It just might be the old ordinance sergeant. Calling the clerk over, Beau showed it to him.

With doubt in his face, the clerk said, "The hospital records tend to be outdated, and some on the lists have died or been sent back home. And then it just could be another Tom Miller."

"Well, we won't know until we go to the hospital," the mountain man said, getting pretty tired of the insolent clerk.

"I'll have to check with my sergeant to see if I can go," the clerk replied.

After another half-hour wait, Beau and the clerk were headed for the hospital. With all the wounded housed in Memphis, it was no small task locating the Sergeant Miller found on the list. They were finally directed to a large room with dozens of beds filled with wounded soldiers.

A tired, overworked nurse led them into the room. The air smelled sour from the scores of weeping wounds. Competing with the sour smell was the odor of urine. She slowly walked through the ward calling out, "Sergeant Miller. Sergeant Thomas Miller."

There was finally a response from someone in a bed in the far corner. Beau looked at the emaciated man lying on stained sheets on a small cot. His clothing was tattered and a scarred stump protruded from one pant leg. He looked old enough to have been the man, but in the dim light the mountain man couldn't recognize the sunken, whisker-covered face.

The nurse noticed the shocked look on Beau's face upon seeing the deplorable conditions the man was living in. She quickly defended the spectacle. "We been trying to get him off the cot and clean him and the bed up, but the old cuss won't let us."

"Your name is Miller?" Beau asked.

"I'm Sergeant Miller," the wounded man said. His face twisted into an excuse for a smile, as he added, "Got me a spot with a window so I can see outside. They keep trying to take it away, but I won't let them."

The impatient clerk said, "This man look familiar to you, Levesque?"

Beau began to shake his head no when the old man suddenly piped up, "Levesque! Is that you, Levesque? You still have that hat I made you shoot at?" Then old sergeant began to laugh, which caused him to start coughing. Finally, he wiped his mouth and asked, "You still a sniper?"

The clerk broke in, "I ain't got time to talk about the good old days in this stinking place. I'll leave you two to it. I'll have your paperwork in the morning to transport you to Pennsylvania." Before Beau could reply, the clerk was gone.

"It was supposed to be Washington," the mountain man mumbled. Having nothing better to do, Beau found a chair and sat down to visit with the old ordinance sergeant. He saw the nurse a short distance away.

"If I help you guard this spot, will you let them clean you and your bed up?" the mountain man asked.

"You got your rifle with you?" the old sergeant inquired.

"I got my Colt with five shots," Beau replied. "That will hold anyone off."

Summoning the nurse over, the mountain man told her that the sergeant would like to be cleaned up. He told her he'd wait right near the cot until the man got back.

Beau stood to the side while a young girl stripped the cot and put on a fresh, less-stained sheet. "It should make his night better with clean covers," he told her.

She looked at Beau with sad eyes. "When he was hit, it did something to his stomach. He can't eat hardly anything. We expect to find him gone any day now."

"I'm sorry to hear that," he told her. As she walked away, Beau wondered how someone so young handled all the mangled bodies and death in the hospital.

Shortly, the sergeant returned, dressed in a clean uniform. The pantleg was pinned up over the stump. Beau assisted the nurse, getting him back onto the cot. It was like handling a skeleton. With a strained smile, she said, "He's dressed for traveling."

Late into the evening Beau stayed and visited. It was obvious that his old friend wasn't going to be around long enough to tatter his new clothes. The loss of the leg and the rigors of war had taken the fight out of the old man. He did have his window overlooking the Mississippi River and asked for nothing more.

CHAPTER FIFTEEN

The mountain man's stay in Memphis was short. The next morning the clerk had orders waiting for him to take a train to Camp Union, near Philadelphia. Beau's new assignment was to provide rifle training for recruits coming into the army.

It made little sense to the mountain man, with the war being almost over, to send him east to train recruits. All the newspapers were predicting that the war would be over in a matter of weeks, possibly even days. Beau arrived in Philadelphia on April 3, 1865.

Beau was assigned to infantry rifle training. The only bright side he saw was that he was going to be training with new repeater rifles. He had hardly gotten settled in when Lee surrendered to Grant on April 9th.

There was confusion at Camp Union as to whether new recruits should be mustered out and sent home, or if their training should continue. There was a tavern a short distance from the training camp named Kelly's. An Irishman with the same name owned the tavern and catered to those involved in recruit training. The clapboard building had a long bar on one wall and several tables for card playing. It smelled strongly of spilt whiskey, tobacco smoke, and sweat from the Union troops that called it their home away from home.

Access to the second floor could be gained by a stairway at the back of the tavern. It had several rooms that could be rented by the night or week. Most of the patrons rented one by the hour for entertaining the sweet-smelling ladies that worked for the tavern. Kelly's philosophy was that everybody won. He made money from the rent, the ladies made money from the men, and the soldiers made out.

It was Friday night and Beau sat at one of the tables sharing a bottle of whiskey and cigars with two other soldiers who were trainers at the camp. "With the war over," the mountain man said, "they'll be mustering old men like me out in a hurry. It's been three years since I had to worry about my next meal."

'Right," a stocky man named Leon replied. "You were getting your arse shot off, but you ate good."

The other man named Ralph, with a shrapnel scar across his jawbone, laughed, "And it was even tasty if you liked weevils and maggots."

"You guys are being kind of tough on the folks making our chow," Beau told them. "There were times in the mountains we got so hungry we would be boiling our boots for a meal. And that was after we ate every critter that crawled or scurried around the shack we was in."

The men kidded back and forth about the quality of their vittles until Ralph asked Beau to tell them about trapping and eating beaver in the Rockies. The mountain man thought for a moment and then began to regale them with a story of mountain living.

Beau was an experienced teller of tales and of repeating Indian lore. He had the knack and had been doing it around campfires and winter camps for over twenty years. He would embellish if it helped make the story more interesting for the listener, but always tried to keep a good degree of truth.

It was late when the mountain man and Ralph headed back toward the troop tent the three of them shared. Leon had stayed behind to entertain one of the ladies. Beau was feeling a nice glow and had to take care of where he stepped so as not to trip over his own feet. Ralph continued to ask the mountain man additional questions about mountain life.

Ralph went into the tent and flopped down on his narrow cot. Telling stories of his life in the mountains always made Beau yearn to go back west. He sat on the small, canvas camp stool in front of the tent and looked at the small, cold firepit. An empty pot sat on one of the flat stones. He would really have enjoyed some coffee right now.

Taps had already been blown and the array of tents around him stood silently in the dark. The only activity he could see was near the commissary, where the night bakers were busy preparing for the next day's meals. For a minute he thought about staggering to the mess hall and see if they had coffee on. Shaking his head, he mumbled, "Too damn much effort."

Tomorrow would be modified drill. The trainers and recruits would be finished by noon, being given time to clean equipment, do laundry and any necessary mending. Only those on duty around the camp, guardhouse and picket stations would follow the normal daily routines.

Beau had been assigned to picket duty next weekend and would have 40 recruits reporting to him. Being so far from danger, and with the war over except for a few raiders who were being mopped up, it made little sense to be setting up picket stations around the camp perimeter, but it was all part of the recruit training.

After watching the star-studded night sky for a few more minutes, Beau retired to his cot, lying on top of the covers, still fully dressed. He had decided to rest for just a moment before removing his uniform. Moments later he was snoring, deep into a drunken slumber.

There was the shrill sound of a bugle. The mountain man groaned and rolled over. It couldn't be reveille yet. As the sound of the bugle cut through his foggy brain, Beau suddenly exclaimed, "What the hell! They're blowing to arms!"

* * *

In the dark, the camp was in turmoil as Beau exited the tent. Half-dressed recruits were running in all directions, clutching their Springfield rifles, attempting to get to their assigned stations. Beau was still feeling the effects of the whiskey. He grabbed his Spencer repeater rifle and stumbled toward the armory.

The blowing of To Arms was done only if there was a threat of an imminent attack by advancing enemy. Every man in the company had an assigned defensive position and they were to go there ready for battle. Beau's assignment was the armory, or ordinance building, to distribute weapons and ammunition as needed to runners of the infantry troops, and the cannon batteries.

Sweat ran off the mountain man's temples as he shouted orders to the recruits assigned to him while helping them drag out the needed ammunition. Beau's head had started pounding as he quickly sobered up. Within only moments the camp was quiet except for the occasional order or the sounds of metal on metal as bayonets were fixed on the rifles.

Beau's secondary station was in a church bell tower just south of the camp. Captain Waters was in charge of the armory and he called the mountain man over. "We're pretty well set here, corporal. You go ahead and take the first sniper watch in the tower and I'll send someone to relieve you come daylight."

"What the hell's going on, sir?" Beau asked.

"Nobody knows," the captain said. "Word of some kind of emergency came into headquarters and the order was given to get everyone on station."

Grabbing some extra cartridges and the Spencer, Beau wondered what the hell he was supposed to shoot at. He had a powerful thirst and stopped by the water bucket. He filled the dipper several times, drinking the life-giving liquid before heading for the church tower.

Access to the bell tower was on the outside of the church. The narrow ladder had barely enough space to get a toe hold as he climbed. Then he had to go head first through the tower opening to get in. The space was cramped and had the strong smell of the cedar used in construction. The mountain man attempted to get comfortable between the bell and ropes as he set up to shoot. Below him, across the town, were several lights burning in the houses. In the distance he could see a brightly lit tavern with some of its patrons sprawled out in front of the building.

From what he could tell, only Camp Union was concerned about whatever impending threat was coming. His legs were cramped and the water he'd drank had done little to slake his thirst. He wished he had taken a canteen. Then came the need to relieve himself. "You are one damn miserable soldier, boy," he scolded himself. Taking a look around the town, he placed the rifle and cartridges near the window and began the task of climbing out of the church tower.

With his immediate needs taken care of behind the church, Beau cut through inside to get back up the tower. The pastor knelt near the altar, praying. "I hope my climbing up and down the tower didn't disturb you," the mountain man apologized.

In the dim candle light, Beau saw a stricken look on the clergy's face. "Someone just came in to pray," the pastor said. "He told me the president was shot."

The words made no sense to Beau and told him nothing of where, or how badly. In shock from the pastor's statement, the mountain man climbed back into the tower and stared out into the town. The war was over. Who would want to shoot Lincoln? Maybe it was just a rumor. Many a general had been reported killed in action and turned out to be alive.

Beau saw a beautiful sunrise over the town. He heard someone climbing the ladder to the tower. Looking down, he saw it was the pastor. "I have some coffee for you."

The mountain man took the metal container of coffee from the clergyman's outstretched hand.

Thanking the pastor, Beau screwed the top off and poured some liquid into it. The tin top was hot, but Beau clutched it tightly. He was not going to lose the hot brew. "Thank you, lord," he mumbled.

The morning was bright as the sun bathed the town. The coffee was hot and strong, just the way he liked it. But Beau was numb to everything around him, and then a sudden chill went thought him, causing his hand to shake, spilling some of the coffee. *The president has died*, went through his mind with dreaded certainty.

In mid-morning a young recruit called to him. "The captain sent me to get you."

"I'll be right down," Beau replied. "Any word on the president?"

"He died this morning," the recruit said. "They are going to call us to church in a little bit."

The mountain man got another cup of coffee from the commissary, but had no appetite for the flapjacks they were serving. The first one he saw when returning to the tent was Leon. He was doing his best to clean up after a rough night upstairs at Kelly's. Ralph was still on watch someplace.

Beau had just finished washing his face and shaving when the bugle sounded call to church. The services were held on the parade grounds. The men stood at attention while the major updated them on what was presently known about the assassination. They were told that an actor named Booth was being searched for. The secretary of state had been attacked but not killed. He also said that the camp would be on alert until all those involved with the attack had been caught.

The major then ordered the men at ease and allowed them to sit on the ground. The Camp Union chaplain then addressed the men. It appeared he might have been weeping. Beau could hear several men around him sniffling. Inside, the mountain man felt cold and angry. His first prayer was that Booth would come north and he would have the opportunity to get him in his sights.

The chaplain's sermon lasted about an hour. It was an angry sermon that condemned those who had carried out the plot on the president. The service ended with a hymn that sounded more like a dirge than a song of hope.

The captain ordered Beau to take 12 men from the cavalry, along with provisions for three days, and station themselves on a bridge five miles south of the camp that crossed the Delaware River. He was instructed to stop everyone crossing the bridge and verify their identity and purpose for crossing.

The road on the north side of the bridge was lined with oak trees. Beau had the detail set up camp a quarter-mile north of the bridge in a small clearing. He set up four-hour watches of three men with their horses standing by. Brush was removed from both ends around the bridge and defensive trenches were dug on the north side. Each man had a Spencer and 100 rounds.

For twelve days the soldiers stopped everyone and questioned them. During that time, four people were detained for further questioning at Camp Union. Late on the twelfth day word was received to break camp and discontinue the watch. They learned that John Wilkes Booth had been found and killed.

Beau missed seeing the train procession that carried the president's body back to Springfield, Illinois. It was said that millions had lined up along the

1,700-mile route to see it go by, and Lincoln was mourned by people from both the North and South.

The mountain man was glad to be back at Camp Union. Living on the trail rations sent every three days made a man look forward to a meal of commissary stew. With the shock of the president's death waning, and most of his killers caught, things began to get back to normal. Again, the talk was about when the new recruits would be sent home and the older soldiers mustered out. Word was that there was a need for soldiers in the West to help control the Indians.

Beau was enjoying a hearty bowl of bear stew at Kelly's one afternoon when a big bruiser entered the tavern. The man was a sergeant and had the look of having been in a few battles. Beau saw him looking around, trying to decide where he would sit. The mountain man waved him over.

"Have a seat with me," Beau said. "They are serving a damn good stew here today."

The man's head and knuckles displayed the scars of many fights. "I thank you," the sergeant said. "My name's Bart Nevell."

"I am Beau Levesque," the mountain man replied. "Can I buy you a drink? I'd buy us a bottle, but I got duty tonight."

The bruiser displayed a crooked smile and said, "I best just have a beer and some of that there stew."

Kelly brought the sergeant the beer. "Just beer today, Bart?" the owner asked.

"Just beer and some of that stew," Bart replied.

A look of relief came over Kelly's face as he hurried to get the stew. "You been here before?" Beau observed.

"Busted the place up a few times," Bart admitted. "While I love it, whiskey ain't my friend."

"Been in the army long?" the mountain man asked.

"In and out for a lot of years," the bruiser said. "I'll am supposed to head south to help sort things out down there. After that I'll be getting out."

"I spent twenty years in the mountains," Beau said. "I figure to head back that way."

Taking a close look at the mountain man, Bart replied, "You look like a man that would be suited to be in the mountains. You don't have the look of a family man."

"And you look like a man that should stay in the army," Beau replied, smiling.

Taking a drink of the beer, the bruiser said, "At least we got each other figured out."

The men finished up the stew and ordered another beer. Kelly placed two mugs on the table and collected the dirty dishes. Beau was surprised that he didn't stay a moment and chat. He figured it had something to do with past dealings Bart had referred to. "I take it you're a mountain man," the bruiser said.

"That I am," Beau replied. "I got there before the beaver run out and then stayed and hunted bigger game."

"You hunt buffalo?" Bart asked.

"Not if I can help it," the mountain man replied.

"I been west to Colorado. Followed a man there that needed killing," Bart said. "Even scouted for a wagon train back in the '40s."

"I led a wagon train to Oregon in '50," Beau recollected.

"Did you drop down to California to see if you could find any gold?" the bruiser asked.

Shaking his head, the mountain man replied, "I have no need for gold. Never figured it would give me much pleasure. For that you got to live in the mountains."

"I know very little about the mountain life," Bart admitted. "I run across some books on it that were pretty good, but reading them don't make me a mountain man."

"I read a couple myself," Beau told him. "One writer, Walter Johnston makes the life sound a bit more exciting than it is."

The name caught the bruiser's attention. "Almost had a chance to meet that Walter Johnston in Washington a year ago," he said.

"What stopped you?" Beau asked.

"Whiskey," Bart replied. "Took one drink before going and woke up three days later with an awful headache."

Both men laughed at the confession. "I would like to meet him someday and straighten him out on a few things," the mountain man said. The truth was, Beau wanted to find out where the man had gotten the stories.

"You ever have a family?" Bart asked.

"Not really," Beau replied. "Had a couple children with me for a while, but my guess is they are back in Oregon. I left them at Fort Laramie and the fort got inquiries about their whereabouts."

"Had me a real nice lady once," Bart said, a shadow crossing his rugged face. "Things happened and then she was gone. Never found another."

"Some of us ain't cut out to be family men," Beau said. "Life in the army or away from others in the mountains suits us better."

Bart stood up to go. "The stew was a good suggestion. I got to meet with some folks that are putting a division together to head south and start the process of getting both sides of the country back together."

Beau watched the bruiser leave the tavern. It was surprising how fast things changed from trying to kill each other to finding how to work together. Kelly came to the table carrying two cups of coffee. Setting one in front of Beau, he took a seat.

"You know Bart very long?" the owner asked.

"Just met him," Beau replied. "He seems like a man that would have been good to have alongside during the war."

"Maybe so," Kelly said. "But, you wouldn't want to have a drink with him after a battle. He tends to want to fight everyone around him after a few whiskeys."

* * *

The mountain man was promised a promotion to sergeant if he stayed in the army and went west to help with conflicts with the Indians. When he declined they countered with a scouting job with the army out west. They recognized Beau's knowledge of the tribes out west and were anticipating problems as the flow of the emigrants increased now that the war was over.

Disappointed that he didn't sign on to one or the other, the captain let the mountain man know that he would be mustered out soon. They needed him to stay until the excess recruits were sent back home.

Finally knowing what his future was, Beau wrote a letter to Louie, letting him know that he'd be passing through that way the end of July. The mountain man figured to spend the coming winter in the Yellowstone area. His mustering out pay should set him up with needed supplies.

Beau had little to do with the mustering out and furloughing of the recruits. He kept track of the return of weapons and ammunition. He was no longer in the duty rotation and stood no watches. He began to put his gear together for the coming year. One of the soldiers wanted to sell his horse and Beau got the gray with a saddle, at a good price.

He repaired discarded Springfield rifles and managed to make a few dollars on them, keeping one for himself. Beau's haversack would make a serviceable possible bag. His 1851 Navy Colt had been swapped out for the newer Colt Army Model 1860 cap and ball, which was a .44 caliber and held six shots. While it fired a larger caliber ball, the design allowed for a lighter weight revolver.

Each day Beau worked on preparations for his life after the army. Several times he was joined by Bart at Kelly's for their noon meal. The mountain man learned that they had both grown up in the South and had chosen to fight for the northern cause. The bruiser talked of the period of time he'd been a slave owner in Texas and about taking them to Kansas so they could live in a free territory.

Beau was busy packing some rifles for shipment when a young private came by with a letter for him. The mountain man held the envelope out at arm's length so he could read it. The letter had come from Fort Laramie. While it wasn't written on the envelope, Beau was sure that it was a reply from Louie.

He pulled his Arkansas toothpick and put the 14-inch blade to the edge of the envelope when he was startled by a shout. "Levesque! Get your horse saddled and come with us! We got raiders west of town!"

The man shouting at him was Bart Nevell. Beau shoved the letter into his haversack and grabbed his Colt and a Spencer. The gray was tied behind the armory with the cinch loose on the saddle. Quickly, the mountain man slid the rifle into the scabbard and tightened the cinch. He then strapped the Colt and holster around his hips. Pulling the reins loose from the ring post, he swung into the saddle.

A half-dozen men led by Bart were near a creak just below Camp Union. They were all part of the cavalry stationed at the camp. "They hit two farms northwest of town and were last seen heading toward the mercantile," Bart said. "There is only one bridge to cross the **Schuylkill River** when they head back south. We're going to try and beat them to it."

"Anyone recognize them?" one of the soldiers asked.

Bart had a grim look on his face. "It's believed to be Wil Thornton's bunch."

The mountain man heard another soldier ask, "What the hell is he doing this far north?"

In a cloud of dust, the troop headed for the bridge, with Bart in the lead.

Years of drilling in cavalry formations had the band of seven riding two abreast behind the leader, ready to split right and left if confronted by those they were pursuing. Fifteen minutes later they arrived at the bridge. All was quiet in the area. Bart had the riders disperse in the woods.

Beau knelt near a cottonwood and waited. The Spencer was loaded and he had the flap open on his holster, exposing the walnut butt of the revolver. His knife was in its scabbard on his hip. The mountain man caught the sound of running horses. Soon a ragtag bunch of riders appeared around the bend of the road.

Bart sat on his horse, blocking access to the bridge. The soldiers with him had been instructed to hold their fire unless fired upon. As the leader of the ragtag bunch raised his Navy Colt to fire, the six soldiers in the trees opened fire. The bruiser jumped off his horse and using it for cover, he fired at the rabble over his saddle.

After emptying the Spencer at the riders, Beau reached for the Colt and continued to shoot. He was reloading the Spencer when the last raider was shot trying to cross the river upstream of the bridge. In the space of a minute, the five raiders lay dead or dying as the dust of their horses drifted across the river.

Bart quickly went from one to the other, tossing their weapons away and checking if they were dead or alive. Beau went into the river and dragged the dead raider back to the shore. He had been hit four times and his horse stood wounded on the far bank. The mountain man reloaded the Colt before joining the others.

"Was it Wil Thornton?" Beau asked.

"No. No, it wasn't," Bart said, a look of relief on his face. "I think we got a bunch of locals that were just thieves and hoped their bad deeds would look like southern raiders."

Two of the ragtag group's horses had to be put down due to severe wounds. The bodies of three that were killed were dragged to the edge of the road to be brought back to Camp Union later. The wounded men were put on two of the horses to be brought back for a trial and probably a hanging. Two of the soldiers were left to watch the dead while the other five escorted the prisoners back to Camp Union.

Bart rode toward the back with Beau, who was leading the extra horse. The buckskin had only minor wounds and would probably become part of the stock at Camp Union. Suddenly the bruiser said, "I have a brother that rides with Wil Thornton."

Surprised by the statement, Beau thought about Bart ordering them to fire if fired upon. If it had been Thornton's raiders, he would have ordered the death of his own brother. The mountain man wondered if that was why Bart made himself the first target in front of the bridge.

"Did you know it wasn't Wil Thornton's raiders?" Beau asked.

"I hoped they weren't, but couldn't be sure until they were all down," Bart replied.

The group rode in silence the rest of the way to Camp Union. The prisoners were turned over to be seen by a doctor and then put into the stockade. A wagon was dispatched to collect the bodies of those killed. Bart went to headquarters to write up reports on the capture. Beau put the gray and buckskin behind the armory in a small lean-to. Stripping the saddles, he gave them both a rubdown, water, and hay. In the morning he would get them some grain.

Once he was done, it was too late to do any more work in the armory so he locked the doors and headed for Kelly's. His thoughts were with the men they had killed today and with Bart and his decision. It took a damn disciplined soldier to do what he'd done at the river. Beau had no brother, but he still wondered what he would've done if the roles had been reversed and he'd had to give the order.

The mountain man ordered a beer and a shot. He still wore the Colt but had left the rest of his gear at the armory. He was drinking his second shot when he suddenly remembered the letter in the haversack. "Damn fool," he muttered. "You received damn few letters in the past three years and couldn't remember to read this one."

Kelly came over with a bottle to fill Beau's glass and poured one for himself. "I figured you could use some company. It will give you someone else to talk to other than yourself."

"I got a letter today and forgot to take it with me," the mountain man complained.

"If it's from a girl, she is probably telling you she found someone else and the you needn't come home," Kelly said, smiling. "If it's from anyone else, it can wait. Hell, if it's from a girl it can wait also."

The owner raised his glass and tossed it down in one gulp. "I heard about the men you guys stopped at the river. Talk is they were from a town just west of here and were trying to steal enough for a good drunk."

"They used raider tactics and it got most of them killed," Beau said, staring at his empty glass.

Holding the bottle up, Kelly said, "Here, let me buy you one more. We got wild boar for supper tonight. Will you be staying?"

It was late evening when the mountain man staggered toward his troop tent. Leon and Ralph were already sleeping. Beau had hoped the whiskey would take away what he was feeling about today's killings, but there was probably not enough whiskey at Kelly's to do that. Others had come in during the evening, talking about the raiders being quite young.

CHAPTER SIXTEEN

The morning was gray when Beau woke to reveille. His stomach felt sick and his head was aching. Soon he would be out of the army, and when he drank too much he would be able to sleep in. He would still feel the effects, but at least it would be later in the morning. The air was humid and a drizzle was hitting the tent canvas.

Beau sat on the edge of his cot, his head pounding as he bent down to put on his boots. Before leaving the tent, he put on his slouch hat and headed for the commissary. He walked past the recruits who had fallen out for their morning drill before having breakfast. By the time the week was out many of them would be headed home.

A few of the noncoms were having morning coffee. One of them was Bart. He watched the mountain man get his coffee and slump down into a chair. "Hard night?"

"I believe the whiskey got the best of me last night," Beau admitted.

"I been there too often in the past," Bart replied. "My only problem is it didn't end in a one-night drunk. Hell, I could lose a whole week."

"I got another month in the army and am looking forward to putting the three years behind me," the mountain man said. "I'd like to find a place where there is a lot less killing."

"Could I recommend becoming a monk in your advanced years?" Bart asked, laughing.

"I got to get back to the mountains," Beau replied, unsure how he felt about the bruiser's mocking.

The conversation lapsed and Beau concentrated on his cup of coffee. After a few sips of the hot brew, he muttered, "I got a letter."

Bart looked at his hungover acquaintance. "You got what?"

"A letter," Beau replied. "I got a letter yesterday and haven't read it."

"Are you expecting bad news in this letter?" Bart asked.

The mountain man looked up. "No. I don't think so."

The bruiser got up and refilled his cup. "I think you should read it, then."

"It's in the armory in my haversack," Beau told him.

"What's it doing in your haversack?" Bart asked. "A soldier doesn't get a letter every day and usually reads it right away."

"That business we had with the raiders yesterday happened just as I got the letter. When we got back, I stopped at Kelly's and then it was today,"

Beau said, rubbing his scalp. "I think the head is clearing."

The cook brought out a pan of cornbread and a bowl of butter. "Help yourselves, men, before the recruits eat it all."

It was another hour before Beau got to the armory. His first task was to tend to the horses. He had put some salve on the buckskin's wounds and they were looking better. It was a good animal and he was hoping to make a deal with the army. It would complete his outfit for heading back to the Yellowstone.

Four recruits were walking up as he unlocked the armory. They were carrying their rifles, cartridge belts, and bayonets. Beau got the book out and logged in their names and the items being returned. One of the sandy-haired recruits shook his head as he handed the Springfield to Beau.

"I sure was hoping to take a shot at one of them Rebs with this here rifle," he said. "All I got to do was carry and polish the damn thing."

Beau almost dressed the young recruit down for thinking that killing a man was something to look forward to, but he decided to get the stuff checked in and the damn recruits out of the armory so he could dig out the letter.

Finally, he had a moment to himself and got out the letter. Using his knife, he slit it open and took out the neatly written letter. It was written by Lucy.

Dear Beau,

We can't tell you how happy we were to receive your letter. After you wrote about being wounded, we got word that you had been killed in Missouri. Mary and Toby cried for days. When Louie came to the Inn waving the letter from you, I made him take me straight to the school to let the children know.

I have been trying to get Louie to take me east so I can visit our cousin in Philadelphia and I want to do some shopping. This morning he told me that we would be going. The children started packing when they got home from school.

Stay safe, Lucy

Beau sat, staring at the letter. His mind was racing. *The children didn't go back to Oregon!* Then he realized that someone was calling to him from out front of the armory. Poking his head out, he saw that Bart had ridden up. "For Christ's sake, Levesque," the bruiser said. "I was beginning to believe you were sleeping off your hangover."

Quickly folding the letter, Beau put it back into his haversack. Walking out of the armory he asked Bart, "What are you doing on this beautiful day?"

"Beautiful, hell," the bruiser snorted. "Damn gray and clammy day. You must be feeling damn bad to think this is beautiful."

The mountain man smiled, realizing that his headache was gone. "I got a good letter from Fort Laramie."

Looking at the heavy cloud cover, Bart shook his head. "No letter could bring sunshine to this weather," he growled. "Get your horse saddled. The captain wants us to follow up on the raiders we got yesterday. The two wounded boys have family an hour west of here."

"The captain wants me to go with you?" Beau asked, surprised.

"I volunteered you," Bart said. "I figured you'd be useless here in camp after seeing your condition this morning."

The drizzling rain had stopped by the time they rode away from the camp. The heavy cloud cover remained, with the constant threat of a downpour. Beau told the bruiser about the children coming. The two men rode in silence past the bridge where they had stopped the men.

Once on the other side, Bart said, "I take it you won't be going to the mountains now."

The statement caught Beau off guard. The excitement of seeing the children had clouded any other thoughts of their future. Mary and Toby needed to go to school. They needed to be around other children. Most of all, they needed a place to call home. Following him in the Rockies would give them none of this.

With a frown on his face the mountain man replied, "I guess that is something I will have to ponder."

Giving him no relief to the problem, Bart said, "It would be best to leave them with the folks at the fort, if they will keep them."

Anger flashed through Beau. He did not appreciate the unsolicited advice from a man who had never had any children. He held his tongue, not wanting to ruin the day and the news the letter had brought him. The rest of the way to the wounded boys' homes the two men rode without talking.

With tear-filled eyes the boy's mother told them about her son falling in with some wilder boys who had been riding roughshod over the area. His father had been killed in July 1863 on Little Round Top during the battle at Gettysburg.

The men found a similar story at the second farm they visited. Bart and Beau then headed back toward Camp Union. Their moods were as dark as the sky above them. The grief they saw in the families of the two boys who had not been killed would not match that of those who had lost sons. But, Beau felt that the families had suffered enough and hoped that Bart could make a case for the two wounded boys to prevent their being hanged.

Suddenly Bart said, "I shouldn't have told you the children would be better off with the folks at the fort. It ain't my business."

"No, I suppose it isn't," Beau replied, "but you sure did get me thinking. Do I choose the life I want, or the life they need?"

The mountain man was glad to be back at the fort and in the solitude of the armory. He took the letter back out of the haversack and read it again. It didn't give him the same excitement that the first reading had. His brooding over the problem was finally broken when a group of recruits came to turn in their rifles.

The next morning Camp Union woke to bright sunshine. The muddy parade ground would soon be dry and the source of windblown dust. The mountain man's mood was much improved. He had come up with a plan that might work for everyone.

He would continue to travel to the mountains to hunt and trap. Before the snow got too deep, he'd return to Fort Laramie to be with the children. He wouldn't have to return to the mountains until late summer and would have several months with Mary and Toby. The only question that remained was: Would Louie and Lucy be willing to keep the children while he was gone?

Beau even figured that he could hunt buffalo some years, which would allow him to be gone for fewer months. Hunting buffalo was hard, smelly work, but the mountain man felt that he was up to it. He talked with Bart about his plan and was pleased when the bruiser agreed it might work.

"You can live with Louie and his sister, and that will make a home for the children," Bart said.

* * *

It was the end of June when Beau left the army. He had managed to keep the buckskin along with the gray, and had a nice nest egg saved from his army pay. Beau had to turn in his Spencer repeater. He had received a telegram from Louie, letting him know that they would be arriving on July 2nd and that they were looking forward to spending July 4th with their cousin Richard.

Beau found a boarding house in Philadelphia that would be appropriate for the children to stay at. The only clothing he had was his army uniform. It was in excellent shape and he had no desire to get rid of it. Beau did want proper clothes to take the children around the city with, so he purchased a coat, waist coat and matching trousers. They were all of the same material and called a *ditto suit*. Two linen shirts, a bowtie, and bowler hat completed the outfit.

The day before the children were to arrive, he took a long, hot bath, followed by a haircut and shave. He kept the full moustache and sideburns. When Beau was fully dressed, he looked at himself in the mirror and felt dread. The old dandy looking back at him had no resemblance to what the mountain man thought he looked like.

Beau had also taken to using spectacles when reading. His distance vision was still excellent and he could still shoot the wings off a gnat at 100 yards. Grinning, Beau thought, *Well, maybe something a bit bigger.* He had also purchased a pocket watch. That was something he had never needed in the mountains. There were stars at night and the sun during the day to let him know the time. In the cities, everyone worked to the minute.

He arrived an hour early at the train depot. Beau was one of the few people on the platform. He walked up to the ticket window and a white-haired station agent with a visor looked up. "Can I help you, sir?" the man asked.

The mountain man was about to explain that he wasn't a *sir* but decided to ignore it. "Is the west train on time?"

"That would depend on which west train you are referring to, sir," the polite agent said.

Glaring at the man, Beau held out the telegram with the arrival information. "It says at 11:30, but doesn't tell me which train."

Aggravation was showing on the white-haired man's face. "I'll check to see what time it left *Detroit!*"

Quickly the man turned and shuffled some papers. He had put more emphasis on the city than was necessary, but today was too important of a day and Beau chose not to reach into the window and pull the cocky bugger up short.

The station agent had collected himself by the time he found the paper he was looking for. Returning to the window, he very politely said, "The Detroit departure was 30 minutes late. We can expect the train to arrive here at noon."

Thanking the man, Beau strode out onto the platform and looked at his new watch. Then taking out his spectacles, he looked again. It would be another hour and 15 minutes. He looked across the street and saw a small tavern. He then looked at the hard, uncomfortable benches on the platform. Adjusting his trousers and waist coat, he headed across the street.

The place was dimly lit and heavy with cigar smoke. The familiar smells of rye and sweat tagged it as a working man's tavern. After ordering a drink, Beau carried it to a vacant table. The straight-backed wooden chairs offered little more comfort than the benches, but here he had something to warm his insides.

The men at the next table were talking about the railroad line being built from Council Bluffs, Iowa to meet up with one being built from Sacramento, California. It appeared that the man talking was a train engineer and had just come in driving a train from Iowa.

Unable to help himself, Beau asked the man when the building was supposed to start. The man spat into a spittoon nearby and replied, "It's been in the works since 1862. Those in California got a jump on us. It will be a race to see which end gets to build the most."

Then the engineer looked the mountain man up and down and asked, "Would you be interested in investing some money in the project?"

Surprised by the question, Beau replied, "I just got out of the army and wouldn't have money to invest, but I may be able to offer other services to the railroad."

The engineer smiled. "I didn't mean to imply anything, but you do look like a man of means in that ditto suit. If you're heading west, they will be looking for lots of manpower."

The time until the train came rumbling into the depot went quickly as Beau learned more about the expansion of the rail system. Thanking those sitting next to him, the mountain man hurried across the street to the depot. He dug out his specs and pocket watch. The train had made part of the delay up and was only 15 minutes late.

The once empty platform was now crowded with people coming and going. Packages and luggage were being tossed onto carts to be moved away from the train and people were pushing to get closer to meet those arriving. Beau stood above average height, but with all the top hats in front of him he could not see those getting off the train.

Every time he gave way to let a lady by several other people would push past him, leaving even more bodies in front of him. About then he wished he had the Colt on his hip. One or two shots in the air would have scattered the unruly crowd.

Finally, he spotted Louie and Lucy. They were talking to a man who resembled Lucy a bit and must be the cousin Richard. Beau could not see the children. No doubt they were engulfed below the crowd.

Fighting to keep his temper, the mountain man continued to duck, dodge, and sidestep the hordes of people as he worked his way to Louie. "Aloysius!" Beau shouted. "Over here!"

Louie looked in the mountain man's direction, but stared right past him. Finally, Beau was within a few steps of Louie and Lucy. He called, "It's me. Beau."

Surprise showed on the grizzled man's face and then there was recognition. "Beau, is that you?" he asked. "You sure look cityfied."

Beau was finally close enough to shake Louie's hand and give Lucy a hug. Smiling, he said, "It's the three years in the army and these damn new clothes."

"Did you see the children?" Lucy asked.

"No, I didn't," the mountain man replied.

"They had to have walked right by you," Louie said, looking beyond Beau. "There they are," he said, waving to them.

Beau turned and saw a beautiful young lady in a full skirt, and a top with pagoda sleeves, walking toward him, followed by a lanky boy. "Is that you, poppa?" she asked.

Without waiting for an answer, she ran and threw her arms around him, crying with joy. Toby was tall for an eleven-year-old and looked like he felt very awkward in the presence of the man that had saved them on the trail to Oregon.

Reaching his arm out beyond Mary, Beau said, "Come over here Toby, and let me hug you."

Stepping back with tear-covered cheeks, Mary said, "We walked right by you and didn't know you."

A bit shy and looking down, Toby said, "It was those glasses you're wearing."

Without realizing it, Beau had left the specs on and had been looking over them when looking for the children. Suddenly the crowded platform was empty again, leaving the mountain man with his company to get reacquainted. Richard was a pleasant man, dressed much like Beau. He was staying at a much more upscale hotel than the boarding house, and he invited everyone to join him in the dining room for a midday meal.

As they retrieved the luggage, Beau couldn't take his eyes off Mary. At 13 she was a young woman. He wondered what had happened to the tough, young girl who had shot the man at Fort Hall. Toby stayed close to Beau, almost as if he expected the mountain man to disappear in the next few moments.

Richard had two carriages waiting in front of the depot to take everyone to the hotel. Louie, Toby, and Beau rode in one. It followed the carriage with Richard and the two ladies. Finally, Toby managed to shake some of his shyness and asked Beau, "Are you still a mountain man?"

"Yes, I am," Beau replied. "Being a mountain man is something that is in your heart and not in the clothes you wear."

"We thought you were dead," the boy said.

"I was wounded and it took a long time to heal. I must have looked pretty bad because they wrote down both me and the man that was killed near me as dead."

"I'm glad they were wrong," Toby said. Beau saw the shine of tears in his eyes. Putting his arm around the boy, he replied, "I'm glad too." All three of them, feeling awkward at the show of affection, laughed.

The hotel was impressive, with a large lobby area and a grand stairway leading to the rooms on the second and third floors. The dining room with fine settings was beyond the stairs. There were only a few businessmen dining when they were escorted into the room. Two waiters hovered near them at all times, providing them with their every need.

Despite being dressed to the nines, Beau felt out of place in the room. He didn't dare pick up a piece of the silverware at his setting until someone else at the table used theirs. He grinned, thinking of all the times his knife was the only thing required to eat.

Knowing their places in this situation, both children remained quiet unless spoken to. Beau had a thousand things he wanted to ask about or tell them, but this was not the place to do it. Polite conversation was used around the table. Richard ordered wine for the table, including some watered down for the children. Beau sipped it along with the others, wishing it was whiskey.

Toward the end of the meal, Lucy's cousin began to talk about his work with the expansion of the railroad. He was one of the buyers for Union Pacific Railroad. Times had been tough during the war, with little expansion being done, but now that it was over he anticipated brisk business.

Richard began to ask Beau about the west and about his days as a mountain man. His real curiosity was what the conditions would be like laying the rails across the plains and into the Rockies. He also wanted to know about the Indians they would be dealing with. Soon Beau found himself doing most of the talking, relating conditions of the existing trails, the various obstacles that would be encountered, and the moods of the various tribes.

Several times Richard jotted notes down on a small pad of paper he kept in his coat. Toby's eyes were shining as he listened to his poppa, and Mary smiled, playing with her food. When the meal was finally over, Beau was more than happy to abandon the padded chair that somehow had become uncomfortable with time. While he had eaten several petite courses, he left the table hungry and in want of a drink.

It was decided that Toby would stay at the boarding house with Beau and Mary at the hotel with Louie and Lucy. There was a play at 8 pm in a nearby theater and Richard had purchased tickets for everyone. Lucy was thrilled with the prospect of seeing a play. With the meal over, Mary was a bit sad and gave Beau a peck on the cheek before leaving to go to her room. The mountain man could hear Lucy telling her that they had to hurry and change out of their traveling clothes and into something proper for tonight.

Louie followed Beau and Toby to the front of the hotel. "Richard is good for Lucy," he said. "Fort Laramie doesn't offer her many of the things we grew up with."

"I am happy for her," Beau replied. "I have never been to a play before. I've just seen a few troupes that travel from town to town."

"Richard asked me to order you a carriage," Louie told him.

"That's not necessary," the mountain man said. "The boarding house is less than a mile away. I could use the walk to help break in this suit." Toby nodded in agreement.

The day was a little warm for the suit and Beau began to open some buttons as they walked. The first questions Toby asked were, "What was it like in the war? Did you have to kill anyone?"

Beau talked of the hours of boredom and drilling in the army and the short spurts of activity when in battle. He did his best to speak in general terms, and then he saw a sign that would change the conversation: "Fussell Ice Cream".

"Have you ever had ice cream?" he asked Toby.

The young boy replied, "I've heard of it, but never had some."

The truth was that Beau hadn't ever had any either, but still being hungry after the fancy meal he guided Toby into the establishment. The two of them were soon sitting with large servings in front of them. The cold, creamy concoction was most satisfying.

With bellies full, the two arrived back at the boarding house. Toby's bag had been delivered there by one of the carriage drivers. Beau took him and his bag up to their room. It didn't have nearly the splendor of the hotel, but the room was clean with crisp curtains, a double bed, and a table with a wash basin. There was a shared bathroom at the end of the hall.

Beau sat on the single chair while Toby chose the edge of the bed. Both of them were uncomfortable in the fancy clothing. They had three hours before they had to be at the theater. Beau looked at the boy in his knickers and jacket. The young man was picking and tugging at them.

"Do you have more comfortable clothes in your bag?"

"Yes, I do, but Miss Lucy told me not to change before going out tonight," Toby said.

"Well," Beau replied, "I have two horses in the barn behind the hotel and I think we should change and go for a ride."

The young man's eyes got big as he asked, "Can we?"

Starting to pull his suit off, the mountain man said, "Yes we can."

Quickly they changed into comfortable clothing and were out the back of the boarding house and saddling the horses. "This buckskin is sure a nice horse," Toby said.

"I'll be using it as a pack horse some of the time," Beau told him, "but you can ride it when I'm not hunting."

The mountain man led the way through the narrow streets while Toby followed, sitting as tall as he could in the saddle. Beau was leading the way to a trail along the Schuylkill River. It felt good to get out of Philadelphia. While the city offered every type of store, it had few open spaces. Space is what Beau craved.

They rode past the bridge where the young men had been shot. Beau brought the gray to a gallop as they left the area. Toby was cheering behind him as they rode through the trees. He slowed to a walk a half-mile up the trail and the two rode beside each other.

"Will we be riding the horses back to Fort Laramie?" Toby asked.

"That would be a two-month trip," Beau pointed out.

"The others could take the train and coach," the boy said, "and we could ride the horses. I'd be back in time for school."

Beau felt his stomach tightening. Evidently Toby thought they would all be living together in Wyoming. Bart's words about them making their home at Louie's was a fly in the ointment. The children would have a home there, but he would just be a visitor who came and went. His only home would be some type of shack or shanty in the mountains.

The mountain man had done a lot of pondering about their future, but most everything was up in the air again. He had begun to think about working on the railroad, but the tracks wouldn't even reach the fort for a year or two.

Could he even take care of the children? Mary was now a young lady and couldn't be dragged from one end of the rail town to another. Suddenly, Toby asked, "Can I lead the way for a while? I always lead when Mary and I go riding."

"You go ahead and lead, but we have to turn back soon," Beau told him.

Watching the boy on the buckskin should have brought joy to the mountain man's heart, but instead he started to feel sadder and sadder. He thought about what he had to offer Mary and Toby. Beau owned two horses, a rifle, a revolver, and was living out of his saddlebags. He barely had enough money to purchase supplies for the winter and, without a good hunt, could end up skinning buffalo next summer.

Since he'd left Crowley Ridge as a young man that had been sufficient. A few brushes with romance hadn't gotten far enough to even make him begin to change. In a few years Toby would be old enough to take into the mountains, and by that time Mary would most likely be married. It wouldn't be fair to lead Toby in that direction. The mountains offered a bleak future for any man. In time even the high peaks would be settled and offer less freedom.

By the time they got back to the boarding house, the two had less than an hour before they had to be at the theater. Beau decided that he'd brush the horses later that night. His mood was dark due to the realization that there was no way he could take proper care of the children.

Toby noticed his mood and asked, "Did I do something wrong?"

Forcing a smile onto his face, Beau replied, "You did everything right. I guess I'm just a bit tired. I'll be fine. Now we better get dressed and over to the theater or we will be in trouble."

Louie was waiting in front of the theater when they arrived. "The ladies and Richard have already gone inside. I have our tickets."

Richard had reserved a box seat, so they had a prime view of the play. Beau's thoughts drifted to President Lincoln and his wife. They had been in a seat much like this when he had been shot. The play didn't grab Beau's attention. He kept running various scenarios of how he could spend most of the year with the children. Every one of them kept him away for months at a time. By the end of the last scene, the mountain man was glad to be up and moving. He could not have told anyone much about the play. To be polite, he did tell Richard that he enjoyed it.

They left the theater and stopped in a café for a light supper before everyone headed for their beds. Toby insisted on helping Beau brush the horses back at the boarding house. He talked of riding the mountain man's chestnut and about Mary getting a side saddle for the piebald. Half listening, Beau continued to nod and smile while the boy went on about life at Fort Laramie.

Exhausted, Beau lay on the comfortable bed, unable to sleep. He couldn't shut down his mind. He heard the soft breathing of the young man and envied how quickly the boy had fallen asleep. The innocence of youth had few worries. Louie and Lucy had planned two weeks in Philadelphia. The mountain man knew that he had to get them alone and talk about the children's future as soon as possible.

If it was decided that the children would stay with them, Beau knew that he should then leave immediately, because additional days with Mary and Toby would only make it harder on everyone. Each morning they would meet for breakfast at the hotel and plan the day's adventure. Richard continued to ply Beau with questions about the west.

The 4th of July provided a festive day in Philadelphia. For a while, Beau forgot about his problems and enjoyed time with Mary and Toby. The excitement they displayed could only be shown by the young. From the parade to the fireworks, their joy was infectious.

The youngsters insisted that Beau compete in the rifle competition. The prize was a .56-56 Spencer repeater. The mountain man went back to the boarding house and got the Springfield and his haversack. The rifle had been sighted in for 200 yards and Beau had often put 10 shots within a 10" circle, which was the requirement for an army sniper.

A plank had been set up at 150 yards and a 20-inch paper target had been affixed to it. There was a total of 48 men who paid the $3 to compete. The proceeds could have purchased three or four of the rifles. They were told that the extra money would purchase supplies for the hospitals housing the war wounded.

Each man was told to fire three shots at the target, and 20 closest to the center with their group of shots would go to the second round. Each man had 90 seconds to shoot their three rounds. Beau realized that it would be a long afternoon unless he was eliminated in the first round. The mountain man overheard Toby telling another boy that his poppa had been a sniper in the war. Pressure was on Beau to make it to the final round or maybe even win. He sure missed having a repeater rifle.

The mountain man was the 28th to shoot. He would be starting with a loaded rifle, and the 90 seconds was plenty of time to fire three shots. One shot had to be free standing, and the other two could be sitting, kneeling, or prone. Several ahead of him had had difficulty loading and firing from the sitting or prone positions within the time frame.

Beau chose to remain standing. He brought the 9-pound rifle to his shoulder and took aim. Squeezing the trigger, smoke belched out, sending the .58 caliber **Minié ball** at the target. With the commands to reload running through his mind, Beau loaded the Springfield. While he didn't need to go through the commands, they helped him stay calm while loading and firing.

Placing a cap on the nipple was done by feel. He didn't have time to put on his specs to see it clearly.

Again, he brought the rifle up and fired. A man with a spyglass watched the target and shouted out, "Score!" for every shot that was close to center. The crowd began to cheer Beau, most recognizing that he had been in the army by the moves he made to load. Ignoring the crowd, the mountain man loaded by the commands and placed a cap onto the nipple. Raising the rifle, he squeezed the trigger. Nothing! The rifle didn't fire. Beau lowered the rifle, and removed the faulty cap. Without rushing, he placed another on the nipple.

Unable to see the time, he felt an urgency to rush another shot. During the war, Beau had seen many a nervous soldier load and fire without hardly aiming, only to be killed by a much calmer enemy facing him. The mountain man set himself, took aim, squeezed the trigger and sent a final shot at the target. He was rewarded by the spotter's shout, "Score!"

Beau joined Toby and Mary to wait for the results of the first round. He overheard someone in the crowd say, "That old fella just made the third shot by a few seconds." The mountain man knew better than that. He had been timing recruits at Camp Union and most could load and fire three rounds in a minute. Beau figured that the delay put him just over a minute.

There were two more rounds before the final. Three men were left, which included Beau. The targets were placed on three planks, 200 yards out. They could fire the three shots in any position they chose. All three still had to be fired in 90 seconds. They would also be firing at the same time.

He was going up against a Sharps slant breech and a Whitworth rifle with classic iron sights. The best sniper rifle of the three was the Whitworth, and if the man had had a scope often used by Confederate snipers, Beau was sure that he would have won hands down. With all three firing at the same time, it would be more like action in a battle and tend to make the shooter rush. Behind them the crowd would be cheering, sounding a whole lot like a bunch of rebels.

Toby stood by Beau as the Springfield was loaded for the first shot. "You can beat them, can't you, poppa?" the boy asked.

Smiling at the worried youngster, the mountain man replied, "The man with the steadiest hand and the best eye will win this. The only difference between the three of us will be possessing a Spencer repeater. Other than that, you are looking at three of the best riflemen in all of Philadelphia."

The spotter had a wrought iron triangle he would hit to start the shooting. The mayor was keeping the time. You could hear a pin drop as the crowd watched for the signal from the mayor. Upon his signal, the spotter struck the triangle, the crowd roared, and the rifles fired. The wind was blowing the to the left, causing the smoke to drift past Beau. The noise around the mountain man was deafening.

He held his Springfield for the final shot, his target obscured by the others' smoke. Suddenly the crowd grew quiet, watching Beau. Somebody shouted, "Shoot! You got to shoot." Then the people started chanting, "Shoot. Shoot. Shoot."

Suddenly the target was clear, and Beau put the rifle to his shoulder and fired. Only seconds later, the triangle was struck, ending the 90 seconds of shooting time. The mountain man set the Springfield's butt on the ground and held the barrel. His heart was pounding and his legs felt weak. "This damn thing was worse than facing the Confederates," he muttered.

The spotter walked by and whispered, "You got yourself a rifle. Make sure they bring you your target."

"Damn," Beau breathed. He hadn't thought about targets being switched around. He kept his eye on the young man who had ran down to get his. A larger boy who had gotten the Whitworth shooter's target seemed to want to compare the hits, but the youngster with his would have none of it. He took off like a shot and arrived at the judges' table first.

Beau walked over and looked at his grouping. It was in the center and tight. The mountain man put a powder-stained finger on the target as he bent over the table. "You can't stay here," one of the judges snapped.

"I understand," Beau replied. "I do apologize. It appears I put a smudge on the target."

The judges turned their backs to everyone as they measured and pondered the three targets. The spotter came back carrying a mug of beer. "Hot work this shooting. Did you get a look at your target?"

"Sure did," Beau said. "I even put my mark on it."

"Well they can't give first place away," he said, smiling. "The judges must be debating who came in second. They had it in mind to give the Spencer to the fellow with the Whitworth. I believe you spoiled that. You know, they put you downwind on purpose."

Finally, the mayor addressed the crowd after some hot discussions with the judges. "I am proud to present this fine Spencer rifle to Beauford Levesque!"

Toby and Mary grabbed on to their poppa, squealing in delight. Richard, Louie, and Lucy looked on joining the crowd, cheering.

* * *

Finally, one evening, everyone but Beau and Louie went to have ice cream. The two men went to a small tavern just up the street from the hotel. After their second drink, Beau started talking about the children.

"I am worried that I won't be able to provide for Mary and Toby," he stated bluntly.

"I don't understand," Louie replied. "From your discussions with Richard, it sounds like you are on your way to a job with the railroad."

Smiling, Beau said, "He had hinted about me working for them, but if I did, where would the children fit in? I couldn't drag them along while following the railroad construction."

Louie stared at his drink for a moment. "Richard had asked me if he thought you would stay in Philadelphia as a consultant. The only time you would be gone was if they needed you west as a troubleshooter."

The thought of a life in Philadelphia flashed through the mountain man's mind. While Beau emitted no sound, his brain was screaming, *No!* Carefully selecting his words, he replied, "Do you think I would fit in here in Philadelphia?"

"Lucy and I are in our 60s and too old to raise the children," Louie said, avoiding Beau's question. "They need someone younger, like you, to bring them up."

Beau motioned for another drink to be brought as he thought for a moment. Then he asked, "Does Lucy feel the same way?"

Snorting, the grizzled old man replied, "I have never seen her happier than after the children came. She thinks they keep her young."

Despite the news of how Lucy felt, Beau's heart sank. He would be putting an unfair burden on his friend Louie now if he spoke with the sister to solve his own problem. Looking at the lined face of his friend, Beau told him, "I will need you and Lucy to bring the children back to Fort Laramie. After you leave, I'll go back to the army and get myself stationed at the fort as a scout, or a soldier if necessary. As soon as I can, I'll build a home for them." Then, laughing, he added, "Maybe I'll find them a mother before I get back to the fort. Lots of widows around after the war."

Louie didn't see the humor in the last statement. He also knew that trouble was growing with the tribes and so was the chance of being killed as a soldier or scout. It appeared both men's problems had been temporarily solved and they had one more drink before heading back to the hotel. Accepting a course of action finally reduced the tension Beau had been feeling. Or maybe it was the drinks he had enjoyed.

CHAPTER SEVENTEEN

Everyone but Richard seemed to be happy with the solution that Beau and Louie had come up with. The cousin had hoped to hire the mountain man. It was a race to build track across the country, and with Beau's wisdom it would have been in his company's favor.

A picnic was planned one afternoon near a tributary to the Schuylkill River. Lucy had the hotel pack them a basket with chicken and other good things. Toby had talked Beau into riding the horses to the picnic while the others took a rented carriage. Mary helped Lucy spread out a blanket to have their meal on while Toby ran down near the water to see if there were any frogs or other things to catch.

The mountain man collected wood to start a fire. Lucy looked at him and said, "The chicken was fried by the hotel. We won't need to cook anything."

"I figured we could use some coffee, and there ain't nothing like a nice fire to make a spot comfortable," Beau told her.

"I agree," Louie said, "and I brought a little something to add to the coffee."

Mary placed her bag onto the blanket. "Do you have something good to eat in that bag?" Beau asked.

Grinning, she replied, "No, I don't." She then pulled out the single shot .45 caliber derringer. "I don't go anywhere without it."

"My goodness," Richard exclaimed. "I don't think you will need a Philadelphia Deringer on a picnic."

She gave him a coy smile. "You never now what kind of trouble a young girl can face." She then placed a book next to the derringer. It was one of Walter Johnston's mountain man books.

"Is that one new?" Beau asked.

"No, but it is my favorite," she said. "It reminds me most of you."

Richard reached over and picked up the book. Beau noticed that Mary's hand casually moved over the small pistol. "I have read this one," he said. "I believe the author lives in the Washington area, and has some kind of ties to Fort Stevens."

Excitement showed on the girl's face as she replied, "I would love to meet the author. Maybe I could get my book signed."

Chuckling, Richard replied, "Maybe I can find out where the author's home is."

Beau had the fire going and the coffee pot filled and warming. He was pleased to get a glimpse of the young girl he'd known on the trail years ago. No man was going to come between her and her gun.

With the coffee on, Beau dug a few things from his saddle bag and rigged up a fishing pole for Toby. Mary gave him a wistful look as he walked past with the pole, and he asked, "Should I make you one?"

Looking down at her skirt and blouse, she shook her head. "I better not," she replied. "Tell Toby if he catches any fish I will cook them for him."

True to her word, when her brother came with three fish, she had Beau cut green sticks and soon had the fish broiling over the fire. They made a nice addition to the picnic meal. The sun was low in the west by the time they packed everything up and headed back for town.

The attachment to the children was growing rapidly in Beau. The awkwardness that they had felt during their first days in Philadelphia was gone. Once again the mountain man was able to see the youth he'd been familiar with on the trail. He no longer regretted the thoughts of not getting back to the mountains. When Toby got old enough, he'd make another trip to the Yellowstone with the boy.

It took Richard a few days to find the address of the book's author. Mary squealed with excitement when he told her. He told her it would require a three-day round trip by train to go to Washington. It took very little pleading to get Louie and Lucy to agree. They decided that they would leave from Washington on their trip back to Fort Laramie.

Richard had business to take care of and wouldn't be able to go. Beau was undecided. While he had once wanted to meet the author, time had dampened the desire. After Bart had told him the author lived in Washington, his vision of the author had changed to someone who spent time around taverns listening to old trappers or hunters who were visiting the capital to get ideas for the books, rather than someone who had been in the West.

Everyone was busy packing the day before they were to head for Washington. Mary had been asking Beau to change his mind, but the mountain man had it in his head that he'd talk with the army and, with luck, be back at Fort Laramie shortly after the children got back. He no longer needed money for winter supplies and could use some of it to ship his horses as far west as the train went. He'd then ride the rest of the way to the fort.

That night, he sat with Mary after their meal. Toby had gone with Louie and Lucy for one last ice cream before leaving Philadelphia. "I can't believe you skipped ice cream to be with an old bugger like me," he kidded her.

"I would rather be with you, poppa, more than anyone else," she said. "I wish we were spending the next few days here so we were together. I would like that more than seeing the author."

"No, you wouldn't," Beau told her. "You will see me all the time at the fort. You may never get back to Washington."

Suddenly, she took his hand and looked at him with tear-filled eyes. "Please come with us to Washington, poppa." Once again that mountain man was looking at the little girl he'd found in the mountains.

He was done. All Beau's determination to see them off tomorrow was gone. "I'll come with you," he whispered.

Beau refused to wear the ditto suit to Washington. He dressed in his army uniform, including the slouch hat. Toby was delighted to see him. "You look like a real army man."

"Right now, I am an out-of-work soldier," the mountain man told the young boy. "When I get to Fort Laramie, I'll be a real soldier."

Mary sat next to him, smiling proudly, having talked her poppa into making the trip. The wheels of the train clacked as they hit the joints in the track. It only took five hours to go from Philadelphia to Washington. By horse it would have taken four to five days.

The station in Washington was busy, with a mix of military and civilians. Many of the soldiers were taking their first leg on the way back home. As they walked through the station, they passed an area with wounded. Many were missing arms or legs, or lying on stretchers with more severe injuries. Their destinations were probably to other army hospitals to relieve the crowding in Washington.

The group would only be spending two nights, so their luggage, including many things purchased in Philadelphia, were left in storage to be put on their scheduled westward train. Louie carried a carpet bag containing things they would need for the short stay. Beau just had his haversack.

The address they had received from Richard was to the northwest of Washington. Louie hired a carriage that was a tight fit for five people and they were off to meet the author. Beau had decided that if the author asked him anything about being a mountain man, he'd be polite but give him little information.

The carriage had a roof, which gave them some protection from the hot midday sun. All around them were batteries with idle cannons and trenches that had been used for the defense of Washington.

Beau had heard that President Lincoln had visited Fort Stevens during the Confederate attack. It had been fought a year ago in July. They passed some burned buildings and foundations of some that had been demolished, no doubt results of the battle. Toby asked Beau an endless stream of questions every time they passed a battery.

The carriage took them north of the fort. The area had been spared from the fighting, which had happened more to the south. They passed several small farms before stopping at a long driveway secured by a gate. Beau could see an impressive white home situated on a hill. It was surrounded by trees and he could also see a barn with a cupola and weathervane to the south of the house.

"I take it the author doesn't want to be visited," Louie said.

The driver got down and checked the gate. It was not locked and he swung it open. Taking the reins, he led the horses through before swinging the gate closed. The driveway was all of a quarter-mile. Mary had taken her book from her bag and clutched it in her hand. The driver stopped the carriage under a spreading oak in front of the house.

"Shall I wait for you?" he asked.

Louie nodded, "I would appreciate that. Our stay might be short."

Mary climbed out of the carriage and asked, "Should I go and knock?"

"That would be alright," Lucy told her. "Once he signs the book, don't waste the writer's time."

Getting down from the carriage, Beau needed to stretch his legs. He looked at the construction of the barn. It was a good design. While it was not large, it could hold a couple of horses and cows. He was betting that there was a small building behind the barn by the sound of chickens.

Half walking and half running, Mary hurried to the door. There was an impressive knocker, which she used. At first, she heard nothing. She was about to knock again when there was the sound of footsteps on a wooden floor. There was the click of the door being unlocked and then it swung open.

"Can I help you?" an elderly woman asked. Her hair was showing some gray and was pulled back into a bun. She was holding a glass of lemonade. Her look was pleasant, so Mary was able to bolster her courage and held up the book. "I was told Walter Johnston lives here and was hoping I could get him to sign my book."

The woman's face broke into a half-smile "Walter Johnston, you say."

She looked up at the carriage filled with people staring back at her and the old man standing off to the side. "Give me the book," she said. "I will take it to Walter."

With the book in hand, the woman disappeared inside and Mary listened as she went a few steps. Soon she was back and handed the book to the young girl. Feeling more confident, Mary asked, "Could I see, Mr. Johnston? My poppa would like to meet him."

Giving the girl a pensive look, the woman touched her cheek with the cool glass. After a brief hesitation, she shook her head. "Mr. Johnston is busy."

"I understand," Mary said, remembering Miss Lucy's caution about wasting his time. Before turning she added, "It's just that my poppa thought he might know him."

Looking at those in the front of the house, she said, "No. I am sure he doesn't."

Convinced that the two should meet, Mary couldn't be dissuaded. "My poppa is the mountain man, Beau Levesque . . ."

Her words were cut short as the woman's glass crashed on the stone landing. "I'm sorry," the young girl apologized as she bent to pick up the pieces of glass.

"Don't. Don't do that," the woman said. "You'll cut yourself."

The woman bent down to pick up the broken glass and whispered to Mary, "Where is Beau?"

Mary pointed, and the woman said, "The old man?"

Dropping the pieces of glass, the woman walked across the yard toward the mountain man. Beau looked up with surprise. "Ruth? Mrs. Stiles?" he asked.

"Ruth Stiles was my mother, I'm Hanna," she said.

At that moment, Beau could have been knocked over with a feather. He was completely defenseless. That explained Walter Johnston knowing so much about him. "You're with Mr. Johnston?"

She shook her head. "My husband James was killed last year by a sniper when they attacked the fort."

Those watching the two had no idea what was going on. All they saw was the woman throw her arms around the mountain man and she was evidently crying. Then she pulled away and quickly turned her back on Beau.

"I'm sorry," Hanna said. "After losing James, I've been alone."

"How about Walter Johnston?" Beau asked.

All of a sudden, Hanna turned to him. The smile he remembered was back. "*I* am Walter Johnston. Or at least that is the name I use when writing."

Beau then knew why the stories in the books sounded so familiar. While on the wagon train he used to tell about his life as a mountain man. Evidently, Hanna had been listening and had used them for her books.

Curious as to what was going on, Louie and Lucy came over. "You're acting as though the two of you know each other," Louie said.

"We do," the mountain man replied, then he called to the others. "Mary, Toby, come over here."

After introductions were made, Hanna invited them into the house. Beau couldn't take his eyes off her. Her brown hair had streaks of gray in it. Hanna's slim girlish figure had filled out a bit but she was still a very attractive woman.

While Hanna was pouring everyone lemonade, Louie got up to let the carriage driver know that they would be here for a little while. Before he was out the door, Hanna asked, "How long are you in town, and where are you staying?"

"It will be two nights," Lucy said. "We've not chose a hotel yet. Could you recommend one?"

Smiling, Hanna replied, "You can stay here. I have plenty of room."

While Lucy objected, not wanting to put her out, Hanna wouldn't hear of their going. It was settled. The carriage was sent away with instructions of when to come back, and the small bags they had with them were brought into the house.

As it turned out, the place was owned by her brother David. When James had been assigned to Fort Stevens, her brother had asked them to stay at the house. He was currently with a division in the South.

Looking forward to having company, Hanna asked Beau to go and kill a couple of chickens for their supper. Toby jumped up and offered to help. For the remainder of the day, Mary followed Hanna like a shadow, asking her about her books. Toby was a great help, cleaning and plucking the chickens. Louie and his sister were most comfortable staying at the house rather than in a hotel.

There was nothing stiff and formal about the family-style meal that was served that evening. Lucy and Hanna provided a tasty meal of chicken and biscuits, mashed potatoes and fresh vegetables from the small garden near the barn.

After enjoying brandy or tea after supper, Louie and Lucy excused themselves, wanting to turn in after a long and tiring day. Hanna had given Mary a copy of her latest book and she was reading it to Toby.

Beau dug into his pocket for a cigar. "I am going to step out and smoke," he told Hanna.

"I think everyone is set for the evening," she said. "I think I will join you and take in some evening air."

There was a glider on the back porch, and Beau sat on one side, facing Hanna. The mountain man was a bundle of nerves. He hoped the cigar would help settle them. His hand shook as he lit the smoke. Beau wanted to shout out, *I love you!* He kept quiet, fearing what her response would be. Hanna had lost her husband of 14 years just a year ago. She would still be in mourning.

The glider moved back and forth in smooth motions. Her voice almost startled him when she asked, "How long were you in the army?"

"I joined in '62," he replied.

"Did you come to fight from the Rockies?" Hanna asked.

Smiling, Beau replied, "I actually had just come down from Alaska and seeing the white bears. When I got to Astoria, Oregon, I read about the war in the paper. I headed east and joined the army."

"You saw white bears?" she asked.

Laughing, he said, "I saw white bears and ate raw blubber."

In the dusk, he could see her smiling eyes. "Yuk. I couldn't eat blubber."

For a while, the two sat in their own thoughts as Beau enjoyed the cigar. Her voice was soft when she said, "James was just coming back from seeing the president when the sniper shot him. They told me he never knew what hit him."

"I'm very sorry for your loss," the mountain man replied.

"Were you ever wounded?" she asked.

"I had a cannon ball explode near me and was laid up for almost six months," he told her.

"Are they your children?" Hanna asked. "They call you poppa."

He told her about finding the children when coming back over the mountains. "Louie and Lucy are going to help take care of them at Fort Laramie."

"So, you are going back west," she said.

"I plan to go back in the army, or be a scout," he told her. "Louie and Lucy have a cousin that offered me a job with the railroad, but I was worried it would take me away from the children too much. I don't want them to be a burden on Lucy."

Again, they were silent. The cigar had lost some of its appeal. He searched his brain for something intelligent to say, but his nervousness just wouldn't allow anything to come. He needed a safe subject that wouldn't make her decide to go inside.

He was thinking so hard that he missed understanding when Hanna said something. "What?"

She leaned forward a bit and repeated, "Would you mind if I sat next to you so we could both watch the sunset?"

Beau moved over quickly, shaking the whole glider. "Please," he said. "Yes, sit next to me."

Hanna got up and sat next to Beau. He could feel her warmth and smelled a hint of perfume. He was overwhelmed. She said, "The sunset is beautiful."

"The what . . ." he asked.

He felt her hand touch his. "Beau. Be honest with me. Did the cannon ball affect your hearing? It's okay if it did."

As if a bubble had burst, his mind was suddenly clear. Beau couldn't help but laugh at his behavior. "My hearing is just fine. I believe being around you has left me flustered. I have been in love with you for so many years. Right now, I am scared that I'll say the wrong thing and once again you will go away."

There was no response from Hanna. *You damn fool. You did it now*, he thought.

They both sat watching the sun disappear below the horizon. His cigar had gone cold in his hand. The silence was tearing Beau up inside. He had admitted what he'd been feeling since riding away from the Mormon ferry 25 years ago. His feeling and timing never seemed to be right.

Hanna's voice was guarded as she finally spoke. "When Jon drowned and I was sitting with my mother at his grave, I told her that if you asked me, I would continue to Oregon with you. She told me it would be wrong, but I did not care. You came to say goodbye and then rode away. Mother said it was for the best, but I was feeling the pain of two men that were lost to me."

After a moment's silence, she continued. "Then you came to Fort Laramie. I was to marry James. He was a good man, but I can't honestly say I loved him. It was more that I needed someone. You seemed okay with my getting married and I accepted that you were lost to me. I'll never know, but I believe had you asked me not to marry James, I would have done so. Over the years, I learned to love James and was glad I didn't have to choose. After mother died, I found myself alone when James was gone. I was spending hours thinking about you, wondering where you were. Being unable to forget you I started writing, telling your stories. It allowed me to stay close to you."

Beau remembered saying that she could stay with the wagon train, but he had never asked her to come with him. "I'm sorry," Beau whispered.

"Don't be," Hanna said. "How could you know? I hid my feelings too well."

Again, they sat in silence. The sun had disappeared over the horizon and the last traces of the red sky were gone. Beau had no idea what to say next, but he sure as heck was not moving from this swing until he came up with the right words to make her his.

Then she asked, "Are we going west?"

Are we? he wondered. Then he whispered, "Yes."

"Will we have the children?"

"Yes."

"Will you tell me the story of the white bears?"

Smiling, Beau replied, "Yes."

"Then I say, yes."

She turned her face up to him and he kissed her. It was the kiss he had dreamt of for 25 years and it did not disappoint.

CHAPTER EIGHTEEN

The two were married in a small, white church near Fort Stevens. Louie's and Lucy's trip back to the fort was delayed by a few days. Toby settled what they would call Hanna when he asked, "Do we call you Miss Hanna or mother?"

"Mother would be nice," she told him.

Hanna had done quite well with the books and talked to Beau about buying a house when they got to Fort Laramie. Wanting to be the man of the house and the provider, Beau told her it wouldn't be right. She explained that every dollar she'd made from the books were because of his stories. The money was more theirs, rather than hers. She got her house.

Beau continued with the plan to rejoin the army and was made a sergeant when he re-enlisted. While on active duty he was pulled away for weeks at a time while Hanna kept busy with the children and writing. The first book she sent east for publishing was about the white bear.

A few years later, Louie and Beau were sitting in front of the Buffalo Hide Saloon enjoying an afternoon cigar, when they saw Mary talking with a young officer. "I think he likes her," the grizzled owner said.

"I have seen him coming around a bit," Beau replied, taking a draw on the cigar.

"You best keep an eye on him to make sure his intentions are honorable," Louie warned him.

Beau smiled, "You see that small bag she is carrying?"

"Is she supposed to hit him with the bag?" the owner asked.

"No. But she has a pretty effective Remington Model 95 derringer in the bag," Beau replied. "I taught her to shoot it, and she hits what she is aiming at."

When Beau left the army, he and Hanna relocated to Casper, which had its origins in Fort Caspar. Mary had married the young officer and had three children of her own. They were stationed in the east, but took every opportunity to ride the train to see her poppa and mother.

Toby had a job with the railroad and looked forward to the annual trips into the mountains with Beau and Hanna. The mountain man seemed to have a story about every beautiful meadow and towering vista that they visited, which kept Hanna busy taking notes.

Beau never made it back to Oregon, and those who may have been looking for him never came east. He did give the children information on their relatives in Westport, Oregon, should they decide to want to look them up.

Their house in Casper had a long porch on the west side, with a glider that they watched the sunsets from. Beau still enjoyed a glass of rye, but had given up the tobacco. The two of them liked the quiet time of the evening, sharing stories of their lives, their children, and grandchildren.

Dressed in buckskins and a flat-brimmed leather hat, Beau would often guide hunters north near the Big Horn Mountains, and they would look up at the inviting peaks. He was once asked by one of the hunters, "Do you ever miss the freedom of living the life of a mountain man?"

The mountain man didn't hesitate and replied, "The freedom of the high peaks could never match the joy a man feels having a home and family."

www.ingramcontent.com/pod-product-compliance
Lightning Source LLC
Chambersburg PA
CBHW051235260626
47162CB00002B/439